Praise for the novels of

DELILAH
MARVELLE

"Marvelle seamlessly weaves two distinct threads
into a sizzling yet tender romance…
satisfying and worthy of a cheer."
—*Publishers Weekly* on *Forever a Lady*

"Marvelle adeptly explores the best and worst of
social class divides in this unforgettable story."
—*Booklist* on *Forever and a Day* (starred review)

"Marvelle not only crafts highly sensual novels, her
innovative ideas and plot twists invigorate the genre."
—*RT Book Reviews*

"Not only is it intriguing and mysterious,
it's highly addictive."
—*Fresh Fiction* on *Forever Mine*

"Showcases Marvelle's ability to heat up the pages
while creating a tender love story that touches the heart."
—*RT Book Reviews* on *Once Upon a Scandal*

"Marvelle's story of Radcliff coming to know himself,
and Justine's faith in him, is a quintessential romance."
—*Booklist* on *Prelude to a Scandal*

Forever a Lord

DELILAH MARVELLE

First Published 2013
First Australian Paperback Edition 2013
ISBN 978 174356073 0

FOREVER A LORD © 2013 by Delilah Marvelle
Philippine Copyright 2013
Australian Copyright 2013
New Zealand Copyright 2013

This is a work of fiction. Names, characters, places, and incidents are either the
product of the author's imagination or are used fictitiously, and any resemblance
to actual persons, living or dead, business establishments, events, or locales is
entirely coincidental.

Published by
Harlequin® Mira®
An imprint of Harlequin Enterprises (Aust) Pty Ltd.
Level 5, 15 Help Street
CHATSWOOD NSW 2067
AUSTRALIA

® and TM are trademarks of Harlequin Enterprises Limited or its corporate
affiliates. Trademarks indicated with ® are registered in Australia, New Zealand,
the United States Patent & Trademark Office and in other countries.

Printed and bound in Australia by Griffin Press

MIX
Paper from
responsible sources
FSC® C009448

ACKNOWLEDGMENTS

Thank you to my husband and children,
who continue to support me through my writing career
at every turn. I love you all.

Thank you to my marvelous editor, Emily Ohanjanians.
Your incredible feedback pushes me to see beyond
my own nose. And boy, do I ever need it. Thank you
to Harlequin HQN for continuing to have faith that
I have stories worth telling and selling. Thank you
to my bow-worthy agent, Donald Maass, who nudged me
away from being too vanilla. Heaven forbid!
And last but certainly not least, thank you to
Maire Claremont, who has cheered me on
through every sentence and every page. I adore you. Always.

To Jessa Slade, my incredible friend
and critique partner, who asked one simple "what if"
that not only blew my mind but made this story possible.
Thank you, thank you, thank you.
I couldn't have pulled this off without you.

PROLOGUE

The cries of "Foul! Foul!" now resounded.

—P. Egan, *Boxiana* (1823)

27th of September, 1800
Somewhere in New York City

A LARGE, WARM hand pressed itself against the closed lids of Nathaniel's eyes, drawing him out of a deep sleep. The lingering, tangy sweetness of a cigar clung to his nostrils as the linen sleeve of a male shirt brushed his cheek.

It was him. Nathaniel didn't dare move.

The hand slowly drew away. "Are you awake?" someone whispered in a heavy accent from beside him on the bed.

Nathaniel swallowed and opened his eyes, candlelight fingering its way through the shadows of the dank cellar. He couldn't breathe. Nausea seized him. "I want to go home," Nathaniel choked out, rocking against the ropes binding his hands to his waist. He didn't care that he sounded pathetic or scared anymore. Being ten, he had every right to be pathetic and scared, didn't he?

The golden glow of a lone candle revealed a young man

with sun-tinted hair sitting on the narrow bed beside him. It was the same man who had lingered outside his family's window all those nights in the shadows.

Amber eyes met Nathaniel's for a somber moment. The man held up a wooden soldier whose military uniform had been painted red. He angled it toward Nathaniel. "For you."

"I don't want it."

"If I untie you, and give this to you, do you promise not to hit me? Do you promise to be good?"

Nathaniel fisted his hands and tried to swing his arms up at that face, but his movement was cut short and burned against the tight ropes that bound each arm against his waist. "Why are you doing this?" he choked out.

"You are his son. Are you not?"

Tears blinded Nathaniel, realizing the man wasn't about to let him go. "Perhaps my father misunderstood. Send him another missive. *Please.*"

The man lowered his gaze to the wooden soldier he held. "He understood. He chose to ignore it."

A sob escaped Nathaniel. "No. He wouldn't. I know he wouldn't!"

"We think we know someone until they betray us. That is…how do you English say?…the *lesson.*"

Nathaniel shook his head and rasped, "Send a missive to my sister. Augustine. She…she will come for me. I know she will. Or my mother. Ask them for whatever you want and they will ensure you get it. I know they will!"

"No." The man fingered the wooden soldier but didn't meet his gaze. "To involve anyone but your father would only see us all hanged."

"I don't understand."

"You will."

Nathaniel swallowed. "Are you going to kill me?"

The man's mouth quirked. "I am a good many things, but I am not a murderer, little friend. In Venezia, even when we are angry, we do things with…honor. Nothing like you British."

Nathaniel swallowed again. What had his father done to this man? He dared not fathom.

Holding out the wooden soldier, the man propped it on Nathaniel's chest. "I bought him for you."

Nathaniel tilted his body just enough to get that soldier off his chest. It thudded onto the mattress between them. "I prefer to go home to my sister and my mother. My father may not love me, but I know they do. They will want me back. I know they will."

"They are no longer your family. I am." Hovering, the man drew in close. So close, Nathaniel could make out the stubble on that youthful face, and the glint of a ruby pin tucked into that meticulously knotted cravat. Sharp, amber eyes intently searched Nathaniel's face as if deciding on something.

Nathaniel pressed himself hard against the linens, digging his entire body into the mattress. Though the man hadn't touched him or hurt him in any way, except to bind him with ropes after Nathaniel repeatedly swung at him, something chanted that, if provoked, this Venetian was capable of more.

The stinging smell of cognac mingling with cigars penetrated Nathaniel's nostrils as the man breathed out, "I have many books in English. What would you like to read?"

Nathaniel stared up at him, inwardly quaking. It was like the man was trying to befriend him. "I'm not telling you anything."

The man tapped Nathaniel hard on the forehead with a scarred finger, then leaned back and rose to his full height of almost six feet. He bent his head to prevent hitting the low timbered ceiling. "Food will be delivered in the morning. Eat."

Head still bent, the man veered out the narrow door with heavy steps that eerily echoed in the small space. The door slammed shut and a loud clink of the key being turned in the rusty lock broke through the silence, signaling Nathaniel had been sentenced to solitude again for not cooperating with the man's request they be friends.

Nathaniel choked out an anguished sob that burned his throat. He tried to sit up, to use his body or his head to move, but couldn't budge in any particular direction. He sobbed again, forced to stare at those dank, shadowed walls that felt inhabited by evil entities about to reach out clawed hands and strangle him.

He couldn't breathe. He couldn't breathe knowing there wasn't even a window in the small cellar to tell him the hour. He glanced frantically toward the lone candle set on the small side table set against the wall. It flickered hauntingly, the dripping wax well below its stub.

"Let me fall asleep first," he whispered to it, not wanting to be left alone in the darkness.

The candle wavered. It then stilled and flicked into a mere glowing dot as the flame dissipated into a stream of curling smoke, leaving him in pulsing darkness and silence.

He squeezed his eyes shut, wailing helplessly until he felt like his body was swaying on a vast ocean set to drown him. His sobs and the darkness eventually lulled not only his body but his mind.

No one was coming for him.

Not his father.

Not his mother.

Not his sister.

No one.

CHAPTER ONE

To those, Sir…who would not mind Pugilism,
if Boxing was not so shockingly *vulgar*—the
following work can have no interest whatever.

—P. Egan, *Boxiana* (1823)

New York City—Gardner's wharf
13th of June 1830, afternoon

OVER THE COURSE of a rough life filled to the brim with gambling, drinking, swearing and boxing, Edward Coleman had taken residence in eleven different parts of the city in an effort to avoid three things: the creditors, his wife and his mother-in-law, who were all determined to bleed him dry.

Not having heard from any of them in too many years to count made him wonder if perhaps he'd mastered the art of the moonlight flit a bit more than he'd wanted. But then again, fate had never liked him all that much. He didn't even know *why* he was astounded at glimpsing his mother-in-law pushing through the dust-ridden male masses just beyond the milling fence at the match.

The woman had aged considerably since he'd last seen

her, but that bundled coif and pert little nose remained the same. A gaggle of young men in grey wool caps, coats and trousers, whom he knew to be Jane's brothers—and my, how they'd grown—strategically wove through the packed boxing crowd behind her.

Mrs. Walsh had only ever sought him out when she needed one of two things: money or money. The United States government could make use of a woman like that.

Coleman swung back toward the fence. "We should go."

His friend, Matthew Joseph Milton, leaned toward him. "Go?" Those dark brows rose a fraction, causing the worn, leather patch over his left eye to shift. "What about your fight? You're up next."

"I know." Coleman knotted his shoulder-length hair back with the twine he'd yanked off his wrist. "But something came up. As such, I can't stay."

"Something came up? Whilst we were standing here?"

"Yes and yes."

Matthew lowered his stubbled chin. "I may have one eye, but that doesn't make me stupid. What is it? Are you in some sort of trouble?"

"No, I—" Blood sprayed from the ring past the fence, covering the front of the only great coat he owned. Coleman hissed out an agitated breath and scanned what remained of the fight. "Amateurs. They can't even keep the blood within the boundaries of the fence anymore."

Matthew snorted. "You never do." Still watching the fight, Matthew froze. "That bastard is going down with my dime!" Matthew hooked a rigid right fist. *"Feck!"*

"I told you not to bet on him."

The well-muscled youth, whose lacerated features had

been disfigured by the unrelenting blows of eighteen rounds, attempted to stagger up off his knees, bloodstained trousers barely clinging to narrow hips. Another bare-knuckled fist bounced off his sweat-soaked head as more blood splattered from that nose and mouth toward the crowd. The youth collapsed onto the wood boards laid out on the flattened sunburned grass.

Several men groaned in disappointment, hitting the fence as the youth was dragged off to the side.

Coleman glanced back again, gauging how much time he had. Mrs. Walsh was still pushing through the crowd and didn't appear to have noticed him. Yet.

He propped up the collar on his great coat to better hide his face and tossed out at Matthew, "I'll see you tomorrow. If Stanley comes looking for me, tell him I broke my hand."

"Broke your—" Matthew caught his arm. "Coleman. We *need* money. Or we're back to robbing shipments at the docks for the next two weeks. Hell, I know our troop is called the Forty Thieves, but do we really have to live up to our name?"

Coleman unhooked his arm from that hold. "If I stay, we'll lose whatever I take from my fight."

"What do you mean? To who?"

A rolled newspaper bounced off the back of Coleman's head. *"Thought you'd up and disappear on me, did you?"* a woman belted out from behind.

Coleman didn't even bother shielding his head. He deserved it for having ever married Jane. "To her," he told Matthew.

Matthew swung toward the aggressor and shoved the rolled newspaper back and away. "Where is your sense of refinement, woman? A paper is meant to be read. Not mangled on the heads of others. Now put it away."

Coleman grudgingly turned and eyed all nine Walsh boys gathered at varying heights behind their elderly mother. Their wool caps were adjusted in every possible direction but the one they were designed for.

Coleman hesitated. Each wore a black band on the arm of their wool coats. His gaze jumped to his mother-in-law, whose plain gown had been stitched of bombazine.

Someone had died. And he knew full well Mrs. Walsh had no living husband or relatives.

His pulse drummed. "Mrs. Walsh. Jane didn't…?"

Tears glazed those dark eyes. "Aye. She did." Drawing thin lips together, she set her aging chin. "Poured too much laudanum into her whiskey barely a week ago. Never woke up. I wasn't there when it happened, but that's what the coroner is sayin'. She was with a—" She wouldn't meet his gaze. "She was with a friend when it happened."

Meaning a man. The very last of several hundred, no doubt. Not that Coleman had been any more loyal. God bless poor Jane. She had her men and he had his women and that was why it had fallen apart. Neither of them were capable of monogamy.

Coleman shifted his jaw and looked away, knowing he should have felt something in that moment. Anything. Remorse. Sadness. Bitterness. But the truth was, he knew it was going to end like this. He had done everything to keep Jane from mixing laudanum into her whiskey. But there were some things a man couldn't box.

Mrs. Walsh hesitated and added, "Someone told me you'd be millin' today. I don't want to be a burden, but we need seven dollars to bury her. I won't have her dropped into a dirt hole."

He swiped his face. He didn't have seven dollars.

Matthew leaned in. "Coleman. What is this? Who is she talking about?"

Coleman's chest tightened. Christ. He had spent years crawling away from a past he didn't want to remember, and now, everyone was about to know his business. Of course, if there was anyone he knew he could trust to know his business, it was Matthew. Though only Matthew. "My wife," he eventually muttered. "She died."

Matthew grabbed his coat. "What? *You're married?*"

"Yes. I am. Or rather…I was." Eyeing his mother-in-law, who had grown quiet, he sighed. "Mrs. Walsh. I can only offer five if I go in and fight. The prize is for ten and I have others depending on me. Will that be enough?"

She half nodded. "We can do without the wreath and flowers. And I can dress her in one of her old gowns." She brought her hands together, fingering the newspaper she held. "There be another matter pertainin' to Jane."

Coleman folded his arms over his chest to keep himself from fidgeting. He had never learned how to say no to a woman. Not even when it came to his damn mother-in-law. It was a curse. "What is it?"

That bundled grey-brown hair, which was sliding out from its pins, bobbed as she unraveled the rolled newspaper. She took apart page after page, tossing it to the ground. "Apparently she contacted these men before she died. I can't read it." She fumbled to fold and refold a page and pointed at what appeared to be an advertisement. "Heaven only knows why, but they came to my door askin' what she knew. I wasn't able to answer. Maybe you can?"

"I doubt it. Jane and I haven't spoken in years." Coleman took the newspaper and read it.

INFORMATION WANTED

A British boy by the name of Nathaniel James Atwood who disappeared in the year 1800 under suspicious circumstance is being sought out by his family. Information pertaining to his disappearance, his whereabouts or his remains shall be well rewarded. Please send all inquiries to His Grace, the Duke of Wentworth, or his son, Lord Yardley, who will both be residing at the Adelphi Hotel on Broadway until further notice.

A pulsing knot seized his throat. He knew he should have never told Jane spit.

Coleman crumpled the paper and tossed it at the ground. "I don't know. Maybe she wanted to dirk them for money. Did you ask her?"

"She was already dead." A strangled sob escaped Mrs. Walsh. She covered her mouth with a trembling hand, those features twisting.

He winced. He shouldn't have said anything.

Every single Walsh boy now stared him down, their youthful faces hardening to an age closer to his own. One of them flicked out a razor and rounded his mother.

Matthew yanked both pistols from his leather belt and pointed each muzzle. "Don't make me go *click,* razor boy."

Mrs. Walsh popped out both arms, to shield her boys, who all scrambled back.

Coleman dragged in a breath. "Put the pistols away, Milton. He's just a boy."

Matthew grunted and shoved them back into his leather belt. "A boy who ought to learn some manners."

The crowd around them dinned.

Coleman heard his name being called.

Knowing his designated fight was set to begin, Coleman flexed his hands and glanced toward the milling fence. A burly dark-haired man stepped into the fenced arena and stripped. Throwing large bare hands into the air, Vincent the Iron Fist, as he was known throughout the ward, yelled at the crowd to cheer as the umpire repainted the fighting line with broken chalk.

It was time to spray blood and earn ten dollars.

Leaning in toward his mother-in-law, he squeezed her arm. "Stay here." Stripping his coat and yanking his linen shirt up over his head, Coleman bundled them and tossed everything toward the only man he'd ever entrust his clothes to: Matthew. "For God's sake, don't let her watch," he said, gesturing to Mrs. Walsh.

Matthew caught his clothes and slung them over his own shoulder. "I'll turn her the other way."

"You do that." Ducking beneath the crudely nailed planks that divided the crowd from the fight, Coleman entered the grass-flattened area.

Hordes of men gathered closer to the fence, making the planks sway.

"Fist the piss out of him, Vincent!" someone hollered. "He's a Brit!"

"Brit or no Brit," another joined in, "I've got fifteen dollars riding on him. You hear that, Coleman? Fifteen dollars. *So don't let me down!*"

It was pathetic knowing his name was only worth fifteen. But then again, it was better than the half-dollar he was worth years ago.

Rising shouts filled the humid summer air as he stalked toward the chalked line, the piercing heat of the sun pulsing from the sky against his bare chest and face.

Massive shoulders and heavily scarred knuckles headed toward the opposing chalked line. Vincent the Iron Fist brought two beefy fists up to his unshaven round chin, widening his stance.

Widening his own stance, Coleman squared his bare shoulders and snapped up both fists. Tightening his thumbs around his knuckles, he waited for the umpire's signal, his chest rising and falling in slow, even pumps.

Cheers and shouts rippled through the air.

The umpire lifted his hand and swung it down. "Set to!"

Vincent darted forward and whipped a fist at his head.

Coleman jumped away, boots skidding, and jumped back in, determined to rip out every last thought of poor Jane. Gritting his teeth, he rammed a shoulder-powered fist beneath those exposed ribs, hitting the expanse of flesh with a crunching sting that jarred the swinging arm.

Coleman knew the son of a bitch was going down.

Staggering against the hit, Vincent stumbled back toward the fence and onto the ground, chest pumping.

"To the line!" The umpire pointed to the chalked marking. "Half a minute to get to the line. One! Two! Three! Four! Five! Six!"

Coleman jogged back over to the line, keeping both fists up. "Come on, Vincent," he called out as the umpire kept counting. "Get up. Give me and the crowd a fight. You're making us both look bad."

Vincent set his jaw, scrambled up and jogged over to the line before the last ten seconds.

The umpire raised a hand between them. "Round two, gents. And...*set to!*"

Vincent darted forward and shot out an unexpected side sweep that cracked into the side of Coleman's head, causing him to stumble against the searing blow. His focus wavered as a blur of hits assaulted his drifting senses. Blood now tinged his mouth and dribbled from his nose as Coleman dodged and blocked only those blows that were necessary in an effort to conserve strength.

The sequence of knuckled fists quickened, cracking down onto and into Coleman's shoulders and arms.

Vincent grunted in an effort to keep the blows steady.

Leveling his breathing, Coleman systematically counted those hard hits as they penetrated his muscle and bone, jarring him with pain. Between ragged, staggering breaths, Coleman counted every swing, until he found the pattern he'd been looking for. Five swings and a pause. Five swings and a pause. The man was a hall clock.

Five brutal punches pummeled Coleman's shoulders again. Darting forward right at the pause, Coleman rammed a fist below that ear. The jarring of his own muscled arm against the side of his opponent's head announced that he'd delivered the perfect hit: a blood vessel shot.

Vincent's eyes bulged. He staggered, his swollen, blood-slathered hands jumping up to shield his head.

Gritting his teeth, Coleman jumped in and hit the now-exposed side until his knuckles were clenchingly numb. Belting out a riled roar he'd been holding, knowing Jane had stupidly lost her last breath to laudanum, he slammed a fist up and deep into Vincent's lower ribs, trying to break them all in half.

Vincent wheeled back and collapsed onto the ground. His gnarled, swollen hands covered his side as he gasped. Bright red blood streamed from his nose and lips as he rocked in anguished panting silence.

"Back!" the umpire called, holding out a hand and ordering Coleman to get back to the chalked line.

Peddling toward the chalk line with both fists still up, Coleman waited, chest heaving and nostrils flaring. He could feel his right eye swelling shut as sweat dripped from his forehead to his nose and down the length of his chin. He swiped at it, smearing blood from his nose, and awaited the verdict.

The crowd counted down in unison.

When Iron Fist didn't rise, he knew he'd won.

The umpire pointed at Coleman. "Here be the champion of this here quarter! The next and last quarter is set to begin with new opponents in fifteen minutes. So place your bets, gents!"

Coleman sometimes felt like he was cattle. No one ever even announced his name when he won. But that was street fighting for you. It was about money and blood. Nothing more.

In a blur of shouts and the waving of hats in the dust-ridden summer heat, Coleman dropped his arms, spit out the acrid blood that had gathered in his mouth and staggered over to the side fence where his earnings waited. Stanley, who always assisted Coleman in coordinating his street fights at fifty cents a piece, tsked, his unkempt whiskers shifting against his round face. "Why the hell do you keep doin' these measly dollar street fights? You're not gettin' any younger, you know. In fact, most boxers your age are not only retired but dead."

"I appreciate the confidence, Stanley."

"You need to cease runnin' out on the investors I bring and take on bigger fights over on Staten Island, is what. Because it's breakin' you. And it's breakin' me. I can't make a livin' at fifty cents a fight."

"If you don't like the money I bring, walk. Because I'm not about to take on an investor. Every one I've met is nothing more than a money-licking asshole looking to own me." Coleman could feel the welts on his body swelling, stretching his pulsing skin. He refocused. "I want my ten. Now."

Stanley grumbled something and held out the tin bucket. A tied sack, filled with coins, waited. "Ten. And I booked another street fight for you in two weeks. You can pay me then."

"Good. I appreciate it." Coleman reached into the bucket and yanked out the muslin sack. Shifting the weight of the coins in his swollen hand, he jogged back toward the fence.

He ducked beneath the planks and rejoined the crowd. Leaning toward Mrs. Walsh, he grabbed her bare hand and set the muslin sack into it. *Goodbye, Jane. I'm sorry it ended like this for you.* "Take all of it. Buy her the wreath and the flowers and a new gown and keep whatever is left for yourself and the boys."

She glanced up. "You loved her. Didn't you?"

Coleman said nothing. He didn't want to lie to her. Because he'd never loved Jane. He'd learned to help women like Jane get out of stupid situations, yes, and enjoyed having sex with said women he got out of stupid situations, yes, but love? He'd never known it or felt it. Nor did he want to. Love was a messy business that not only fucked with a man's head, but made a man do things he shouldn't.

Mrs. Walsh grabbed hold of him and yanked him close. "Come to the funeral."

He flinched against the touch that seared his bruised body. Unlatching her arms, he stepped back and shook his head. "I really don't want to see her in a casket."

"I understand." She patted the small sack of coins. "May God bless." She nodded and moved into the crowd.

The Walsh boys lowered their gazes and disappeared after their mother, one by one.

Coleman blankly stared after them, knowing it would be the last time he'd ever see them now that Jane was gone.

Matthew rounded him and held out his linen shirt. "I've known you for eight years, Coleman. *Eight.* Why the hell didn't you tell me you were married?"

Coleman grabbed the shirt and pulled the cool linen over his sweaty, blood-ridden body, wincing against the movements. "Because it wasn't much of a marriage. It was more like me helping a girl out of a situation and keeping her legally out of other people's hands."

Matthew held out the rest of his clothing, which Coleman also grabbed and put on. "I'm still sorry to hear she passed."

Coleman shrugged. "It was only a matter of time. She was overly wild and consumed laudanum and whiskey like water." He perused the trash-strewn ground. Finding the advertisement he'd earlier tossed, he swiped up the balled newspaper and shoved it into his pocket. For later.

Three hefty men, including a tall, well-muscled negro in a frayed linen shirt and wool trousers, suddenly pressed in on him and Matthew.

Coleman's brows went up, realizing it was Smock, Andrews and Kerner—members of their group, the Forty Thieves. "You missed the fight." Coleman thumbed toward the milling fence and smirked. "Although Vincent's blood is still on the ground. Feel free to look around."

Smock swiped a hand across his black, unshaven face. "We're not here for the fight."

Everyone grew quiet.

Oh, no.

Matthew quickly leaned in. "Jesus. Is someone dead?"

Andrews scrubbed his oily head with a dirt-crusted hand. "Nah. But it ain't good, either."

Kerner's bearded face remained stoic.

Coleman stared them down and bit out, "Does someone want to tell me what the hell is going on? Or are we going to stand here like bricks and play charades?"

Kerner's bushy brows rose to his shaggy hairline. "Apparently, two girls went missing from the local orphanage. There's been grumblings in the ward as to what happened. We're talking prostitution. Sister Catherine called on me this morning and is terrified knowing the rumors are true. These missing girls are barely eight."

Coleman hissed out a breath. The amount of sick bastards in this world taking advantage of children made him want to break rib cages all day long. He was damn well glad he wasn't the only one putting up fists. The sole reason he and Matthew had created the Forty Thieves was to clean up the rancid aspects of the slums they all lived in. The trouble was, there was too much to clean and very little money to clean it with. "I say we get the boys together and decide who can resolve this mess best. Milton? When and where?"

Matthew pointed at Coleman. "Anthony Street. In three hours. The usual place. Someone has to know something. Maybe we can buy a few tongues. Though God knows with what. Informants these days only want money. Kerner, Smock, Andrews, come with me. We need to get our hands on twenty dollars. Coleman? Clean yourself up. Your face and nose need tending." Matthew rounded into the crowd with the boys following suit and disappeared.

A humid wind blew in from the wharf, feathering Coleman's pulsing skin. He made his way back to the milling fence and stood there, amidst the dust and shouts, staring at nothing in particular.

He probably shouldn't have given Mrs. Walsh all ten dollars. Informants were anything but cheap and expected at least a dollar apiece.

Coleman momentarily closed his eyes, knowing what needed to be done. All that mattered was doing right by those girls and the countless others like them, and giving them the chance he never got when he was their age.

Reopening his eyes, Coleman slowly pulled out the crumpled advertisement from his wool coat pocket and stared at the words *well rewarded*. He didn't know who the hell this Duke of Wentworth and Lord Yardley were or why they were looking for Nathaniel after almost thirty fucking years, but he did know one thing. He would swallow what had once been and use these men to get as much money as he could, to set him and the Forty Thieves up to help anyone in a similar predicament to these girls.

Everything in life came at a price. And knowing there were children whose very lives depended on whatever he and Matthew could buy, it was a price he was more than willing to pay.

CHAPTER TWO

Distinction of rank is of little importance when an offense has been given, and in the impulse of the moment, a Prince has forgot his royalty, by turning out to box.

—P. Egan, *Boxiana* (1823)

The Adelphi Hotel
Evening

LEANING AGAINST THE silk embroidered wall of the hotel lobby, Coleman scanned the polished marble floors and rubbed his scabbed hands together.

"Sir?" a hotel footman called out, holding out a white gloved hand. "Could you please not lean against the wall? It's silk and damages easily."

Coleman shifted his jaw and pushed away from the wall. Although he'd scrubbed with soap and shaved around every scab from his last fight, his patched wool clothing lent to a dirtiness no soap could touch. He was used to it, but sometimes, just sometimes, it still agitated the hell out of him when others treated him like some thug. He was a boxer. Not a thug. There was a difference.

Quick, echoing steps drew his attention.

An older, dashing gentleman with silver, tonic-sleeked hair jogged into the foyer of the hotel, dressed in expensive black evening attire from leather boot to broad shoulder, save a white silk waistcoat, snowy linen shirt and a perfectly knotted linen cravat.

Skidding in beside that older gent was a good-looking man of no more than thirty, whose raven hair had also been swept back with tonic. A black band hugged the upper biceps of his well-tailored coat.

Apparently, everyone was in mourning these days.

It was depressing.

They faced him, their brows rising in unison at realizing he was the only person waiting for them in the lobby.

Coleman knew the best and only way to go about this was to make these men believe Nathaniel was dead. Because that part of himself was.

Adjusting his wool great coat, Coleman strode toward them. "I'm here on behalf of Nathaniel. You have two minutes to convince me you're worth trusting."

Both men stared, no doubt weighing his words.

The younger of the two approached. "Two minutes? I suppose we had best talk fast." Grey eyes, that eerily reminded him of someone he once knew, searched his face. "Are you— What happened to your face?"

Agitated by the question, Coleman widened his stance. "The same thing that's about to happen to yours, if you don't tell me who the fuck you are and why you're looking for At-wood."

The man leaned back. "I can see you're exceptionally friendly. Which would explain the face." He cleared his throat, adjusting his evening coat. "The name is Yardley.

Lord Yardley." He gestured with an ungloved hand toward the older gentleman. "That there is my father, His Grace, the Duke of Wentworth. We, sir, are Nathaniel's family. *Close* family. If he is still alive, as you are leading us to believe, we would like to speak to him in person. Not through another person. If you don't mind."

What if these men had been sent to hunt Nathaniel down? To silence him? It was possible. "I never said he was alive. But if you want further information, it's going to cost you."

"How much?"

"A thousand."

"A thousand?"

"Yes. Dollars. Not pennies. Consider it a bargain. You look like you can afford more."

"So you actually *know* something?"

"Yes."

Lord Yardley lowered his shaven chin against his silk cravat. "You wouldn't be the first claiming to know something. The question is, *do you*?"

Coleman wasn't about to trust either of these men to shite. "I need a thousand before I say another word."

Lord Yardley narrowed his gaze. "Keep at this and I will personally ensure you forget your own God-given name. The information comes first. Money last."

The Duke of Wentworth approached. "Yardley. Enough. Calm down."

Swinging away, Yardley threw up both hands. "These people are leeches. Every last one of them. All they want is money. What happened to humanity wanting to help others for the sake of goodwill? I'm going for a walk down Broadway. It's the only thing that ever calms me down."

The duke pointed. "No. No walks. Not now. You will stay

and finish whatever this is." Brown eyes that were surprisingly intelligent, albeit solemn, observed Coleman for a moment. "We have been in New York, sir, for months making endless inquiries. We are beyond exhausted and are hinging a breath of hope on the possibility that you may know something. Do you?"

Coleman shifted away from the duke, trying to distance himself from the eerie reality that the past was tapping on his shoulder. "It depends on what you want with the information."

Those features tightened. "If Atwood still lives, which we hope he does, inform him that his sister's husband and her son are here to collect him. If, however, he is dead, we also wish to know of it. All we want is information that will lead us to resolve this matter and give it peace."

Coleman stared, his plan to claim the money crumbling with every word. This man was married to his sister? It wasn't possible. Trying to keep his voice steady, he confided, "Allow me to speak to his sister first. I will decide then."

The duke swiped his face. "I cannot produce her."

"Why not?" he demanded, unable to remain calm.

"She died." That voice, though well controlled, bespoke a deeply rooted anguish.

Coleman staggered, the marble floor beneath his boots momentarily swaying. For the first time in a very, very long time, tears connected to who he had once been pricked his eyes. Auggie was barely six years older than him. She couldn't be dead. This had to be a trap. "I don't believe you. Auggie isn't dead. You're lying."

The duke's gaze snapped to his. "How did you know her name?"

Lord Yardley watched Coleman. "Glass-blue eyes and

black hair. And his accent. 'Tis anything but American."
He stepped closer, lips parting. "Dearest God. It's him. It's
Atwood. It has to be."

Fuck. He'd stupidly outed himself. Coleman swung away
and stalked toward the entrance of the hotel. He wasn't staying for this. He didn't even want to know what had happened
to Auggie. He didn't.

Booted feet drummed faster down the lobby, after him.

"Nathaniel?" the duke called out. "Nathaniel, stay. For
God's sake, stay! Atwood? *Atwood!"*

Sucking in a breath, Coleman darted toward the entrance
leading out to the street. Grabbing the oversize doors, he tried
to shove them open, but his scab-ridden hands were too dis-
connected from his body to cooperate.

"Atwood!" The duke grabbed his shoulders and yanked
him away from the doors.

Though his fists instinctively popped up to swing, Coleman knew pulverizing his own sister's husband was not what
he owed her. "Atwood doesn't exist anymore," he rasped.

The duke slowly turned him. "I have stared at the painted
miniature of you as a child so many times. No one has eyes
quite like yours. I don't know why I didn't see it. The bruises
on your face were very distracting."

Coleman couldn't breathe.

The duke leaned in. "Your sister devoted everything to
the hope of finding you. And this is how you repay her? By
running from her family when they come to you? Don't you
care to know what happened to her? Or how she died?"

A warm tear trickled its way down the length of Coleman's
cheek. He viciously swiped at it, welcoming the pinching
from grazing the bruise on his face.

The duke held his gaze. "She died in childbirth. Many

years ago. It would have been a girl. Our third. Neither survived. I just lost our eldest son, as well. Typhus took him. Yardley here is all I have left of her."

Coleman stumbled outside that grasp and leaned back against the door, feeling weak. He had been running and running from the past to the point of delusion, and now, it would seem, he had become that delusion. At least he had protected Auggie's good name to the end.

Dearest God. None of this seemed real. "And what of my mother? Is she dead, too?"

The duke shook his head. "No. She is very much alive."

He drew in a ragged breath. "I'm glad to hear it." He nodded. "She was good to me." He swallowed, trying to keep his voice steady. "And my father? The earl?"

"Still alive."

Coleman set his jaw and tapped a rigid fist against his thigh. "Of course he is." He pushed away from the door, knowing his father's face had replaced so many faces in the ring since he took up boxing at twenty. His pent-up hatred for the man was but one of many reasons why he'd never sought his family out. Because he would have smeared his father's blood across every last wall in London. "Is he here in New York?"

Yardley approached. "No. He doesn't know we have been looking for you."

Coleman raked long strands of hair from his face with a trembling hand. "And why doesn't he know?"

The duke sighed. "Augustine always believed he was responsible for your disappearance. And I have seen more than enough to believe her. I therefore opted to never include him in whatever investigations we conducted. Including this one. We feared he would impede."

These men clearly knew his father.

Yardley leaned in. "Come upstairs and have a brandy. Talk to us in the privacy we all deserve. Please."

Coleman half nodded and drifted across the lobby alongside them, submitting to the request. He followed them up, up red-carpeted stairs until he was eventually ushered into a sweeping lavish room graced with windows facing out toward Bowling Green Park.

It was like he was ten again and looking out over New York City for the first time. It was eerie. He awkwardly sat in the leather chair he was guided into.

A glass filled with brandy was placed into his hand. He could barely keep it steady. The amber liquid within the crystal swayed. The last time he had touched crystal of similar quality was when he had smashed a decanter against that cellar wall he was being kept in and screamed until he could feel neither his body nor soul. He felt like a freak then. And he felt like a freak now. For here he was sitting with his long hair and butchered face holding an expensive tonic meant to be sipped by lace-wearing fops. He'd never felt like he truly belonged anywhere. He was neither fop nor street boy. His boxing was the only world that made sense. Fight or fall.

Yardley slowly sat in a chair across from him. "My mother had a dream you were still alive. It induced her to create a map of your whereabouts which I had kept since her death. That is why we are here. Because of her. Her soul was clearly connected to you. She was never able to let you go."

Coleman drew in a ragged breath. He had dreamed of Auggie on occasion, too. She had once appeared in a boxing match beside him, startling him into missing a swing. She never said a word in his dreams. Only smiled. And now, he knew why. She'd been smiling from beyond.

The duke brought his chair closer and sat. Leaning forward, he whispered, "What happened to you the night you disappeared? Can you speak of it at all?"

Coleman stared into his glass of brandy. The boy he once knew insisted he say something. In the name of his sister. "I spent five years confined to a cellar after my father had crossed a man he shouldn't have."

Yardley dropped his hand to his trouser-clad knee. "*Five years?* By God, what was done to you?"

Coleman continued to stare down at his brandy.

The duke leaned in closer. "Were you beaten?"

Bringing the brandy to his lips, Coleman swallowed the burning liquid. "I wish I had been. I take physical pain incredibly well."

Both men fell silent.

Coleman sensed they wanted him to say more. But in his opinion, he'd already said enough.

The duke searched his face. "How did you escape?"

Coleman took another quick swig. "I didn't. One day, my captor opened the cellar door, put a wad of money into my hand and told me to start life anew. So I did. And you're looking at it."

Yardley observed him for a moment. "After holding you hostage for five years the man just let you go? Why?"

Coleman shrugged. "It might seem difficult to believe, but we became incredibly good friends. He knew he had kept me long enough and wasn't interested in taking me to Venice. He was getting married and people in his circle would have started asking questions. They were already asking questions."

"You *befriended* this man? After he— Did you not go to

the marshals after you were released?" the duke demanded. "To press charges?"

Coleman shook his head, his breath almost jagged. "I didn't want what I knew of my father touching my sister or my mother. It would have destroyed their lives if I had re-surfaced."

The duke held his gaze. "How many were involved in your disappearance? Who were they? And when were you smuggled out of New York?"

"There was only one man involved in my disappearance. A Venetian. And I never left New York."

"You never...? All this time, you've been...?" The duke closed his eyes and grabbed his head with both hands. "Jesus Christ." He rocked against his hands for a long moment.

Coleman set aside the brandy on the small table beside him and rose in a half daze. "I appreciate that you shouldered my sister's plight, even after her death. I know if she had been the one missing, I would have fought for her to the end, as well. My only regret is that I didn't get to see her one last time. I would have liked that. She and I didn't part on the best of terms and I—" He swallowed hard, trying not to give in to emotion. With his sister gone, what more was there to return to? Nothing. Their mother had always lived for their father. Who was he to break her delusions of a man she loved? "I should go."

Yardley rose. "Go? No. You can't. We are here to take you home with us. To London. Where you belong."

Coleman walked backward toward the door and swept a more than obvious hand to his beaten face. "Do I look like I belong in a ballroom, gentlemen? Too many years have passed for that."

The duke rose. "Atwood. You can't leave when we've just

now found you. We have yet to know you and genuinely wish to assist you in making the transition back into our circle. It will take time, mind you, but—"

"No." Coleman shook his head. "I abide by my boxing name, not my titled name, and want no other life than the one I have now. People depend on me. I have a purpose other than living with regret."

The duke swung away, placing a hand to the back of his neck. "Yardley, speak to him. Because I am not thinking clearly. And neither is he."

Yardley quickly strode toward Coleman and leaned in, his rugged features tightening. "To take on any other name than the one you were born unto, knowing everything you and my mother have suffered, would be an insult to her *and* you. By God. You have allowed a lifetime to pass. If you cannot face this now, when will you ever?"

The boy didn't understand. This wasn't about being unable to face the past. He'd faced it. He'd lived it. This was about facing the anger he had yet to unleash on the only person he'd ever wanted dead: his father. Not his captor. *His father.*

Coleman widened his stance. "If I return to London, I'll do more than face my father. I'll kill him."

Yardley pointed. "No you won't."

"You don't know me," Coleman said between clamped teeth. "I've beaten people into bloodied pools of unconsciousness for far less."

"Killing him isn't going to change what happened."

"Neither will letting him live."

His nephew touched his arm. "Setting aside all that has come to pass, surely you understand that you owe your mother a breath of peace. A peace my own mother never got in her lifetime."

Coleman released a breath. Yes, he did owe his mother peace. But if the poor woman were to ever know the truth— Christ. What a mess. It was obvious he couldn't walk away and pretend he didn't want to go back. "I need time."

Yardley lowered his shaven chin. "You've been gone for almost thirty years. How much more time do you need?"

Coleman pointed a finger at that mouth that dared mock him. "What you don't understand, *nephew*, is that I have a life separate from the past. I've got people depending on me. Thirty-nine, to be exact. They were there for me when no one else was and I'm not about to pull their teeth out of their skulls by up and leaving. I can't. I need time to make the transition."

Yardley hesitated. "How much time do you need?" he asked more gently.

Coleman shrugged. "I don't know. A few months. I share in a lot of responsibilities. Until I can shuffle off those re-sponsibilities to people I can trust, I suggest you both return to London and let it rest."

Yardley's eyes widened. "We're not about to leave with-out you."

"You have no choice," Coleman bit out. "Because when I walk out of here, you cease to exist until I find my way back to London. Why? Because I can't have anyone in New York, or the United States for that matter, knowing I'm a fuck-ing viscount. I'll lose my credibility on the street and with the ward in half a blink and won't be of use to anyone. It's bad enough walking around this city with a British accent. It doesn't earn you spit. Americans despise us Brits, and I can't readily blame them the way our militia swept into their city and burned down Washington barely sixteen years ago. I was here when it happened and all of New York thought they were next. They were lynching Brits on the streets like they were rabbits."

The duke swiveled toward them. "I respect that you need to protect your current way of life and that you also need time, but you cannot leave us to worry. At the very least, let my valet tend to your face, whilst we also trim off that hair so we can take you to a good tailor and invest in some new clothes and boots for you."

Murder and hellfire. Did he look that pathetic? "Don't talk to me about my face, clothes and shite that doesn't really matter. I have clothes. I have boots. And I like my hair, thank you. I know how to take care of myself, gentlemen. I've been doing it my whole life."

The duke gestured toward Coleman's bruised face. "You call *this* taking care of yourself?"

Coleman sighed. He forgot what it was like having a family. "I'm a pugilist. It's how I earn a living. And it may not look like it, but I'm good at what I do. Hell, politicians and pub keepers alike have been trying to buy me out for bigger mills since I was twenty. And unlike most of these bare-knuckle hoydens, I get better with age because I know how to train. I'm now known in the sixth ward for knocking men out in ten rounds or less."

Yardley's dark brows rose. "Ten rounds or less?" He let out a low whistle. "I would hate to get into a fight with you." He shifted closer. "If boxing is truly your snuff, Uncle, London is the place to be. 'Tis incredibly popular with the masses. *Especially* the aristocracy. Many of the men I went to Oxford with were always betting on the fights. I never cared for the sport myself, per se, but you, as a pugilist, would feel like a horse at the derby."

"Yardley." The duke glared. "You are digressing."

"I am not." Yardley glared back. "I am trying to get this man to London. What are you doing in your attempt? Grouching? Hardly helpful."

It was like listening to two butchers arguing over who had the better cut.

"If he does come to London," the duke continued with a huff, "it will be to take on his duty as lord. Not become the next champion of England by smashing in the faces of others. Whoever heard of such a thing? The aristocracy would faint." The duke muttered something else, strode over to a sideboard and grabbed up a leather pocketbook. "How much money do you need, Atwood, until we see you again? Did you still want that thousand?"

Coleman would have gladly taken a thousand but it felt wrong exploiting his sister's family—his family—that way. "Twenty dollars will do." That would at least buy enough informants to help Matthew hunt down those girls.

"Twenty? Don't be absurd. The cheapest ticket to cross the ocean to get to us will cost you almost ten."

"You asked me how much I wanted and I'm telling you. Twenty. There is no need to insult what I consider to be a lot of money."

The duke paused, pulled out a banknote and tossed the pocketbook onto the sideboard, his silvery hair glinting in the candlelight. Striding over, the duke also retrieved a small silver case from his coat pocket. Pulling out a calling card, he held it out, along with the crisp banknote. "You will find us at this address in London."

"Thank you." Coleman tugged both loose. Shoving the banknote and card into his pocket, he held out a hand, knowing he ought to be civil. "I appreciate knowing I have someone other than my boys to depend on. I haven't been able to say that in years."

His brother-in-law shook his hand and eyed him. "I have something else for you. Before you go." The duke strode toward the four-poster bed on the other side of the room.

Slipping a hand beneath the pillow and linen, the duke withdrew a leather-bound book which had been fastened closed by a red velvet sash. Fingering it for a long moment, the duke drew in a breath, turned and strode back. "It was Augustine's diary. Half of it pertains to you. She ceased writing in it when we married. She tried to move on. Despite her trying, she never could. She never did." The duke blinked back his emotion and held out the diary.

Coleman felt those damn tears assaulting him again. He stared unblinkingly at the leather-bound book.

Although a part of him wanted to refuse it, to keep the past at a distance, he knew that by refusing it, he would be denying himself an opportunity to say goodbye to his sister. He doubted if he'd ever be able to bring himself to read it, but at least he'd be able to hold it until he was ready to go back to London.

Coleman grasped the book, his fingers grazing the soft velvet sash. He stilled, remembering her writing in it. He remembered seeing her dark head intently bent over its pages, writing under a lone candle's light whilst sitting at her desk in New York. He'd once trudged into her room and had asked her why she kept a stupid diary, to which she had looked up and said, *We all have secrets, Nathaniel. I simply happen to write mine down.*

He never had to write his down.

He was his own secret.

And damn it all, he couldn't pretend anymore. He couldn't

pretend he was anything but Viscount Nathaniel James Atwood, the boy who had disappeared at ten. He had spent his
whole life waiting for a sign as to what he should do with
the secret he had carried for almost thirty years. And here,
this, was his sign.

It wasn't meant to be a secret anymore.

CHAPTER THREE

Why should a man, whose blood is warm within,
Sit like his grandsire cut in alabaster?

—P. Egan, *Boxiana* (1823)

London, England, February 1831
The Weston House

LADY IMOGENE ANNE NORWOOD traced a lone finger across the window, staring out into the cold, still night. Despite the darkness and shadows, a full moon illuminated the cobblestone street beyond the carriage gates and eerily outlined the oaks that swayed in the wind.

She glanced toward the French clock beside her bed, dimly lit by a single candle. A quarter after two and still no Henry. She doubted if her brother realized how much she worried about him. He smoked like a stove filled to the grates with ashes and spent most of his time watching men box as if seeing blood spray gave him genuine satisfaction.

He used to be so much more. But poor Henry had invested too much into a venture that had left them with nothing. In a desperate effort to erase what had been done, he had then sold his good name of Marquis to the highest female bidder in the aristocracy to save what remained of their lives. It wasn't as if they had much to begin with.

Imogene couldn't help but feel responsible for his endless quest for more money. Though she was now nineteen, countless doctors and quacks had paraded in and out of the Weston household since she was seven because of her. And they were anything but free. Neither was the sludgy, healing tonic she was forced to drink with a pinched nose every afternoon at four.

She was tired of being a burden to him.

She was tired of being defined by an illness.

Imogene turned back to the window. Her brother was probably avoiding his wife again. Not that she blamed him. Lady Mary Elizabeth Weston was a floating frock whose constant flaunting of her own wealth sent Henry into a fury. And that didn't include the rest of the marriage or the whispers about Mary secretly meeting with Lord Banbury.

It was a good thing Mama and Papa had both long since passed and weren't around to see how miserable Henry was. Each of his poor children had died within the first few months of their lives, and Mary hadn't been with child since. That was about the time Mary had drifted off into the arms of another.

Life had been anything but kind to her poor brother.

The gates clanged open, making Imogene straighten beside the window. A black lacquered carriage with the Weston crest emblazoned on its doors, rolled through and rounded the graveled path toward the entrance.

Shoving her blond braid over her shoulder, she gathered her robe and nightdress and dashed across the room. Flinging open the bedchamber door, she sprinted down the moonlit corridor, rounding corner after corner and bustled down, down, the main stairwell.

She slid to a halt as the entrance door opened.

A cold wind swept through, setting the candles flickering within the sconces as Henry strode in and stripped his top hat, scattering blond hair across his forehead. Closing the door, he jerked to a halt, startled green eyes settling on her. "Gene. Why are you still up? Are you not feeling well? Do you need me to call for Dr. Filbert?"

"No. I'm fine." Imogene hurried into his arms and tugged him close, squeezing out the cold clinging to his evening coat. The heavy scent of cigars clung to his clothing. "I couldn't sleep. Where were you? You reek of cigars."

"I know. I had one too many." He patted her head with gloved hands and pulled away. "There was a boxing exhibition over at Bloomsbury. I stayed to the end."

"Another boxing exhibition?" She sighed. "I keep telling you, 'tis a waste of respectability and time."

"It depends on how you view waste." He leaned in and said in a low, riled tone, "Did you know that the last boxing champion of England made almost a quarter of a million pounds for himself and his patron, Lord Ransford? *A quarter of a million!* If I could get my hands on several thousand of my own money, money I wish to God I had, I'd find myself a boxer capable of taking that title, fist the money from the win and divorce Mary on grounds of adultery. With money like that, no scandal could ever touch us. The problem is I'm worth nothing more than my name and she knows it. In my opinion, she and Banbury deserve each other. I only wish she had the decency to keep it quiet. Everyone knows. Even all of the men at the boxing coves. It's humiliating."

That wretched, wretched woman. It was the first time

Henry had ever dared speak of divorce. Which meant he was well beyond miserable. To even whisper of divorce in London society was to speak of ruin, not only for him but her. Knowing that made *Imogene* want to invest in said quarter of a million just so he could live the way he deserved. In peace.

Imogene paused. A quarter of a million pounds? For a mere boxing title? Bumblebees on high. That would be like meeting God. No, no. That would be like *being* God. It was an obscene amount of money.

She blinked. "How much would it cost to invest in a boxer?"

He eyed her. "About four to five thousand, not including any and all training costs. Why?"

Her heart pounded. Her inheritance from her grandmama, which was set to be released from the estate in the next week now that she was finally of age, was ten thousand. "I have ten thousand that will soon be mine. I want you to invest it for me."

"Invest? In what?"

"In finding us a boxer so we can turn our ten thousand into two hundred and fifty thousand. Will you do it?"

A startled laugh escaped him. "Gene, I wasn't by any means insinuating we—"

"Why not?" She grabbed his arm and whispered, "We could split the profit and neither of us would be dependent on anyone ever again. As you yourself just said, with money like that, your divorce would be but a puff of passing smoke we could avoid by leaving town. After everything you have endured, Henry, and most of it on my behalf, let me do this one thing for you. *Please*."

His amusement faded. "You aren't serious, are you?"

She set her lips and face to show him just how serious she

really was. She was tired of them struggling for their dignity. It was time to invest in said dignity. "Find us the best boxer there is and I will cover the investment up to a full ten thousand."

Glancing toward the stairwell to ensure they were alone, Henry hoarsely whispered, "For God's sake. Aside from the throat slitting my divorce would create, your first Season is set to commence this upcoming April. I cannot and will not gamble with your future by placing myself before your good name. That money is also meant for you and whatever husband you take. You know that."

She swallowed and shook her head. "I have already professed how I feel about taking a husband. I would only be a burden to him. And I don't want to burden anyone anymore. Look at what my illness has done to your life. I have stripped you down to nothing. I have turned you into nothing."

"Gene." He leaned in close and seized her hands, squeezing them hard. "You need to cease blaming yourself. You are *not* a burden. By God, you are the only joy I have left."

She said nothing.

Henry searched her face. "Surely you don't want to live the life of a spinster. You have so much to give in both mind and soul. You will deny yourself children, happiness and a home of your own because of my stupidity? You can't. I won't let you. What is more, everyone in our circle is expecting you to debut."

She shrugged away his hands, knowing he didn't understand. "I will debut, for that is what you want of me, but based upon my health, I am not about to submit. It would be nothing but a hardship for whatever man takes me. I would rather we speculate. Think of what all that money could do for us. We would never be dependent on anyone ever again."

He shook his head. "No, Gene. After having lost everything in a venture I should have never invested in, I know better than to embark upon this. We simply have to accept that neither of us will ever rise above what we have. It is what it is."

Tears pricked her eyes and what felt like her soul. "There has to be more to life than me choking on medicine and you choking on a bad decision. We can't—" Her throat tightened beyond its ability to let her breathe. She jumped toward him and grabbed his hands, causing his top hat to roll to the floor.

Feeling a stutter coming on, she fiercely clamped her teeth together, wishing she had been born with a different life. She wanted so desperately to convey everything within her, but knew it would only tumble forth broken and stupid and worthless.

So instead, she shook his hands and kept shaking and shaking them within her own, letting him know that if they didn't try to change their lives it was *never* going to change. It wasn't right. *It wasn't right!*

"Gene!" Firmly prying his hands from hers, Henry nudged her chin up hard, forcing her to look at him. "Do you need me to send a missive to Dr. Filbert?"

She winced and shook her head, knowing it would only cost them money for the call. Trying desperately to calm herself, she squeezed her eyes shut and focused on what always helped. Envisioning a field. Swallows dipping low. The sun rising, causing hues of pink to smear the sky. And the soft wind caressing her face, sending strands of hair floating.

Shades of her panic lulled and the strain on her throat faded. She opened her eyes and drew in a shaky breath, letting it out in renewed calm. She could breathe. Though, oddly, her limbs felt like they were floating and the room was swaying.

Henry's features tightened in concern. "I will send a missive to Dr. Filbert at once."

She shook her head.

"He can help you. And he has. You know that."

"No," she choked out, forcing her words to obey. Fortunately, the stutter had passed. "I...I have my medicine. I...I'm fine."

"He is genuinely concerned for the state of your health and mind, Gene. As am I. It isn't normal what you keep doing. It isn't normal to keep playing the role of a goddamn mute when you get riled or panic. Are you telling me it is?"

She plastered her hands against her ears, not wanting to listen to him anymore. She hated when he reminded her of what she was. She knew what she was.

Henry flinched. Tugging her close, he smoothed her bundled hair with a comforting hand. "I'm sorry. You know all I ever do is worry. Ever since the incident, you...you've never been the same."

She lowered her hands and nodded against him, fingering his embroidered waistcoat that pressed into her cheek. Sometimes, she wished she had enough money to buy everything. Including the happiness her brother deserved. And maybe, if there was any money left over, she could buy a new life for herself. One where she was in control of *everything* and one word from her and it was done. "Let me do this," she pleaded against him. "For you *and* for me. Please. We won't know until we try."

He drew away, rubbing her shoulders, and slowly released her. Raking both hands through his hair, he let them drop and eyed her. "And what if we lose it all? What then?"

She inwardly cringed. "Then our lives remain the same. We remain under the jurisdiction of your wife. And...*Banbury.*" It was cruel, but the man needed a little push.

Henry shifted from boot to boot, his features tightening. Glancing intently toward the stairwell, he met her gaze again. "If we do this, you can't breathe a word of it to anyone. Especially Mary. Aside from the investment itself, divorce is a messy and barbarous business. Do you understand?"

Her heart skipped, knowing that both of their lives were about to change with this decision. "I won't say a word."

He swiped his face. "I've been watching fights long enough to know exactly which men to invest in. Give me time. The best pugilists are usually hidden between the cracks." He hesitated. "All I ask in turn is that you debut and take on the Season. Not necessarily a husband, but the Season. You never know how things will turn out or who you will meet. Can you agree to that much? For me? Knowing what I'm about to agree to myself?"

Imogene half nodded. "Yes. Of course. I can. I..." She blinked rapidly against the dizziness overtaking her ability to focus or speak. The edges of her vision frayed. Oh, no. It was happening again.

"Gene?" her brother echoed.

She fainted.

On the other side of the ocean

NATHANIEL—AS HE'D become accustomed to calling himself again—could see the boys still waving in the distance as they blurred against the horizon of buildings. It was surreal to be leaving the Forty Thieves and New York behind. It was like abandoning the only family he'd ever known.

But at least Matthew was still at his side.

It would make the transition easier.

It was also the best way to keep the man alive.

The chugging vessel trailed constant veils of sooty smoke from its stacks, strong winds sweeping them out toward cloud-ridden skies and massive waves that relentlessly swayed the packing ship.

Knotting his hair back against the whipping wind, Nathaniel drew in a deep breath of cold, sea air. His sister's words, which he had tucked against the inside of his great coat, weighed in reminder. Although he had undone the journal's sash many a time throughout the months, he only ever tied it back up, unable to read a single word. He still didn't have it in him to swallow the reality that all he had left of his sister was pages.

Matthew leaned in against the iron railing of the boat beside him, still staring out at the coast of New York City that had shrunk to the size of a hand, fading against the sea's vast horizon. "So you're telling me you're an aristo and that your father was an aristo who pissed on another aristo who then pissed on you?"

Nathaniel paused. God bless the son of a bitch for oversimplifying everything. "More or less."

Matthew glanced toward him, his patch shifting against his cheekbone. "So what do you want me to call you? By what name?"

Nathaniel gripped the iron railing hard. "It doesn't matter. I can still be Coleman, if you want. The boxing circles, even in London, won't know me as anything else. So I have no choice but to abide by that name. I just wanted you to know the truth. I've kept it from you long enough."

"I'd say. None of this seems real. How the feck could your own father—"

"I don't want to talk about this anymore." Nathaniel tapped an agitated fist against the railing. "Your mess is what we need to focus on. I suggest you sleep with your pistols in hand until we get to London. God only knows who is on this ship and it only takes one man to slit your throat."

Matthew groaned. "I appreciate your concern, and going through all this trouble of dragging me along to ensure I don't end up dead, but sleeping with pistols in hand is a bit much."

Nathaniel pointed rigidly at Matthew's head. "In my opinion, it isn't enough. Sleep with the goddamn pistols before I up and knock your domino box out of your mouth. I'm not about to let you get lynched by some street boyo who has no understanding of how invaluable you are, not only to me but the ward. The boys need you back alive. Without you there is no them and you know it."

Matthew observed him for a long moment. "You seem to forget that I'm used to all the attention. If you had left me behind, I would have been more than fine. I would have managed. I always do."

"Managed?" Nathaniel echoed. "Seventeen men were planning to take you down. It wasn't something you could have *managed* on your own."

Matthew grunted. "I suppose." He sighed. "So how long am I sentenced to a life abroad anyway?"

"I can't readily say. Marshal Royce said once the city rounds these bastards up and eliminates the threat against your life, he'll notify us. I'll be forwarding him an address when we get into London."

Matthew smiled. "You're a good friend. You know that?"

Nathaniel rolled his eyes. "Don't play the harp. You've saved my ass many a time, you know."

"And I would do it again."

"Which I also appreciate."

Matthew hung over the railing, watching the waves beneath. "So what made you decide to go back to London now? Why didn't you go home with your family when they first came to you all those months ago?"

Nathaniel glanced toward Matthew. "I never run out on people who need me. Not after everything I've endured. And you and the boys needed me."

Matthew reached out and pinched his jaw. "Now, now, don't get prissy on me. That isn't like you."

Nathaniel smirked and shoved his hand away. "Keep those hands to yourself. I'm not interested."

Matthew let out a laugh. "Don't flatter yourself, Mister fecking Viscount." Matthew nudged him. "But ey. At least we'll be living all posh once we get to London what with you being an aristo, right?"

Nathaniel snorted. "If you mean posh as in us moving in with my father, I don't think so. I'd sooner slit his throat. I plan on looking into some milling coves and try to make some money that way before I figure out what happens next." Nathaniel stared at the misty horizon that swayed with the ship, knowing that once in London, bigger things on the horizon awaited him. Like facing a father he wanted dead for reasons he would never be able to share with anyone but Matthew. What if he really killed the bastard? What if he—

Matthew nudged him again. "So where are we going to stay?"

It was like answering a thousand and one questions. Nathaniel shrugged. "I don't know. We'll find a hotel."

"It better be cheap. I've only got six dollars."

"Whilst I only have four."

"Nice, that. It's the dead leading the dead." He paused.

"Ey. I've got an idea. My 'stepmother' is in London. Maybe we can hunt her down. She'd put us up."

"What? Georgia?"

"Yes. Georgia. How many stepmothers do I have?"

"Don't be dragging that poor girl into our mess."

"She ain't poor anymore. She found herself a rich one." Matthew smirked and readjusted his eye patch. "So what about this family of yours? Your sister's husband and son. Can't we stay with them?"

"No. We're not exactly their type of people, Milton. Nor do I plan on announcing myself to anyone until I figure out how to wade through this mess. A man just doesn't show up thirty years later to yell out to the world, 'Here I am, oh, and by the by I'm thinking of killing my own father.'"

Matthew hesitated. "Why do I have this feeling London is going to make a mess of both our lives?"

"Because it probably will. But in your case, it's better than being dead."

"I'll say." Matthew eyed him and pushed away from the railing. "I'm going to settle into our cabin. You coming?"

Nathaniel swallowed, feeling his throat closing up at the thought of those low timbered ceilings and that musty windowless room lit by a lone lantern. He was *not* sleeping below deck. "No. I plan on sleeping out here."

"On deck?" Matthew echoed, dark brows rising. "And what if you roll the wrong way and plunk into the ocean?"

Nathaniel glared. "I know how to swim, Milton. But as you damn well know, I'm not one for small spaces. So take the fucking cabin and leave me to have my deck."

"All right, all right. Do you want me to sleep on deck with you?"

Nathaniel rolled his eyes. "If I ever need a man to help me

sleep, I give you permission to throw me overboard. Now go get some rest. I'll see you in the morning. And sleep with your pistols. Just until we get to London."

"Fine. I'll humor you." Matthew nodded, shoving his hands into his great coat pocket, and strode down the length of the deck toward the cabins below deck.

Blowing out a slow breath, Nathaniel leaned against the railing, letting the cold wind whip at his face. The ocean seemed overwhelmingly endless. It was amazing. There were no walls or ceilings, only vast, endless sky and water.

When night eventually cloaked the ship, Nathaniel settled himself with a lantern below an eve, using his coat for a blanket and bundled ropes for a pillow, which he set under his head.

Fingering the ropes, he stared up at the swaying night sky that had smoothed into clarity and revealed glimmering stars. Though he rarely got lonely, for his head kept him too busy for that, in that moment, with the roaring of the waves that meshed into silence, he would have liked a woman to keep him warm on deck beneath all those stars.

He paused. No. What he really wanted and needed was to get fucked. It had been well over a month, which was the longest he'd ever gone without it. Aside from boxing, sex was the only thing he genuinely enjoyed.

It was a good thing most women found him attractive enough to accept his proclivities, because he sure as hell had nothing to give a woman these days. Certainly not money. But then again, maybe London would change that.

CHAPTER FOUR

The cup, filled with wine, having gone round, the Champion thus briefly addressed his patrons, "Gentlemen, for the honour you have done me in presenting this cup, I most respectfully beg of you to accept my warmest thanks."

—P. Egan, *Boxiana* (1823)

Many, many weeks later—evening
Cardinal's Milling Cove
London, England

THERE HAD TO be a better way to make money.

Nathaniel tugged his frayed linen shirt down and over his sweat-sleeked arms and chest, more than done with teaching others how to better swing. He had only made thirteen shillings that whole night offering a fifteen-year-old boxing lessons. He really needed to stop feeling sorry for people before he himself starved.

He paused.

Sensing he was still being watched by that fop against the timbered wall beyond the spectators, he blew out a ragged breath. Some no-name aristo with a fancy horsehair top hat and a Havana cigar had been coming around and watching him almost every night since he'd been in London.

Given Nathaniel's experience with strange men in top hats and cigars, he didn't appreciate it. Tonight, realizing his money-making plans were progressing slower than he'd hoped, he *really* wasn't in the mood for it. Shoving past several locals who had gathered around him, also asking him for a boxing lesson at thirteen shillings a piece, Nathaniel stalked over to the man.

More than ready to take the bastard on, Nathaniel yelled out, "I don't appreciate being followed or watched by some nameless prick. Are you going to stop? Or do you need me to make you stop?"

Blond brows went up as the cigar was instantly lowered. Pushing away from the wall, and out of the shadows the lanterns didn't illuminate, a rugged-looking blond-haired gent of about thirty with sharp green eyes met Nathaniel's gaze from below the satin-trimmed rim of his top hat.

The dandy angled toward him and wagged the cigar. "You, sir, are without any doubt the best pugilist I have ever had the honor of observing. I was hoping you and I could talk about a potential venture."

Nathaniel rolled his eyes. He should have known. Wealthy boyos like this one didn't hang around milling coves unless they were sniffing for potential investments. "Unless you have five thousand to give, don't fucking bother. I need real money. Not talk."

The man leaned toward him. "I can offer you five thousand on signing *and* give you a swing at the title. Are you interested?"

Nathaniel perused the man's evening coat, embroidered

waistcoat and polished boots. He looked like he could afford everything he was offering. The sort of money he and Matthew desperately needed. They had both been living shilling by shilling. Nathaniel had even been playing cards with what little money they had in an effort to bring them quick money.

Cards weren't his thing. He'd lost every hand. He was incredibly good at betting on fights, though. The problem was one had to have at least ten pounds to get into any of the good bets. Which he didn't have.

Interestingly enough, however, this aristo was offering Nathaniel far more than money. This aristo was offering something other investors never had. A chance at the title. "You're actually offering me a chance for the Champion of England?" he drawled. "A real chance?"

"Yes. I think you have it in you to win based on what I've seen thus far. And unlike other men, I not only have a name, but the means to line up the right trainer and the right fights to make it happen. It's simply a matter of if you want to make it happen." Sticking his cigar between his teeth, the gent stuck out a white gloved hand. "The name is Lord Weston. But I prefer you just call me Weston. You go by the name of Coleman, yes?"

Nathaniel eyed that hand but didn't take it. He wasn't stupid. "What do you want from me, *Weston?*"

"I want your boxing skills in a ring. Because I'm beyond impressed." Weston blew out a cloud of smoke in Nathaniel's direction and pointed with the cigar toward the narrow, lantern-lit entrance. "How about you and I go to a local pub and talk?"

Nathaniel's nostrils flared from the acrid stench of smoke penetrating his throat. He *hated* cigars. They reminded him of his days in the cellar. "Put out the cigar first. It agitates me."

The man paused and pointed at him. "Don't overstep your bounds, boy. I'll smoke if I want to. I'm the one making the offer here, not you."

"Is that so?" Nathaniel snatched the cigar from that gloved hand and dashed it out on his well-calloused knuckles, the burning sting brief but welcome. "There goes your offer." He tossed the cigar at the man, letting it bounce off his waistcoat. "I don't do business with assholes."

Swinging away, Nathaniel muttered to himself about the rudeness of people and strode toward the crate where he kept his great coat whenever he came to train and box.

Weston veered in again and snapped up both gloved hands. "I'll never smoke in your presence again. Just give me a chance to make an offer. I've been meaning to do so for a few days now."

Nathaniel set his shoulders. There was only one way to know if the man was remotely serious. Nathaniel pointed to the floor on the other side of the lantern-lit timbered room, where men were lining up to spar. "Go in and box for me. I'll watch and we'll take it from there."

Weston's brows rose. "What?"

"Do you even know what you're looking to invest in? I want you to show me you know how to box. Go on."

A rumble of a laugh escaped the man. "I know what I'm looking to invest in. I've been part of the local boxing crowd since I was twenty. Ask around. People know who I am. There is no need for you to—"

"I don't care if they know who you are. All I care about is whether you're willing to box in the name of impressing me."

Weston eyed him. "I'm more of what you call a spectator and have only ever boxed over at Jackson's with a few peers of mine. Not—" He waved rigidly toward the unshaven, unbathed, half-dressed local men crowding for a chance at another fight.

Nathaniel widened his stance, determined to make his point. "I'm not asking you to win, Weston boy. I'm asking you to prove that you're willing to take the same hits I am. A man who isn't even willing to put himself into the ring isn't someone I care to trust or go into business with or hand over my boxing career to. You decide what matters most. Your nose or the offer."

This was about when most investors skidded out, which had only ever pleased Nathaniel. Rich investors had no qualms about taking advantage of boxers and Nathaniel knew better than to jump at every offer.

Weston glanced back over at the gruff, well-muscled men lining up. "Apparently, the devil has a sense of humor." Casually removing his top hat, he handed it to Nathaniel. "Here. Hold this for me."

Nathaniel hesitated and took the top hat. This was new. Wealthy men usually weren't keen about getting their own blood on their shirts. At least not the wealthy Americans he was used to dealing with back in New York. He couldn't help but feel a renewed sense of respect for the aristocracy. He didn't realize they took their investments so seriously.

Weston removed his gloves from his hands and undid his cravat, stuffing everything into the top hat Nathaniel still held. Removing his coat, waistcoat and linen shirt, the man revealed a fit frame that bespoke many hours doing some sort of sport.

Weston draped the clothes across Nathaniel's arm and pointed at him. "Don't take off with my clothes, now. I know which hotel you're staying at—*Limmer's*—and I know who you associate with, including your one-eyed, pistol-toting friend, Matthew Joseph Milton."

Nathaniel tightened his hold on the top hat and clothes. "Sniffing isn't a quality I want in an investor."

Weston leaned in, those green eyes sharpening. "Sniffing is the *only* quality you want in an investor. It proves that I can protect not only my investment but yours, by thoroughly investigating everything before I put a boot into it. I've been bilked out of thousands before, so I damn well ensure I always sniff out every last rotting detail. The only thing that worries me about you, Coleman, is that you already have a reputation for taking meals from investors but never following through. Know one thing separates me from other investors—unlike them, I'm not here to own you. But I am here to make a profit. We're talking about a quarter of a million pounds if you take the title. And all I'm asking in return for my investment is half."

Nathaniel stared at the man. It was the first time anyone had ever thought him capable of taking the championship. Winning fights for bets was one thing. Fighting the championship was quite another. Even at half, taking the championship and the money that came with it could do more than change his life. That sort of money could make everyone lick his boots. And after a lifetime of kneeling, it was time to stand. "I'm genuinely intrigued." Nathaniel thumbed toward the direction of the boxing floor. "Finish impressing me and we'll talk more about your offer."

Weston adjusted his trousers on his hips, his features tightening. "It's my first go at bare-knuckle boxing, but in my opinion, you're worth the sacrifice." Staring him down one last time, Weston pushed through the crowd, lining up for the next match.

Nathaniel winced, knowing it was the man's first go at bare-knuckle boxing. A part of him wanted to stop the poor bastard, but the morbid cynic in him, who had been dirked by too many people, had to see if this man was even worth blinking at.

CHAPTER FIVE

And now, Mr. Editor, I crave your attention
to a few words more, which I trust,
will quench the thirst of...(?)

—P. Egan, *Boxiana* (1823)

5:07 a.m.
The Weston House

IMOGENE LINGERED BY the rain-slathered window of her bed-chamber and stared unblinkingly at the carriage gates that were blurred by the weather and darkness. She glanced toward the French clock. According to her lady's maid, who had woken her barely minutes ago, the valet was beyond worried. Henry had not yet returned from the milling cove. Although the valet had also roused her sister-in-law, Imogene doubted the woman had even rolled over in concern.

Mother of heaven. Setting a shaky hand to her mouth, she wondered if she should call for Scotland Yard.

The gates unexpectedly clanged open, making her whoosh out a startled breath. A black lacquered carriage rolled through and rounded the graveled path. Henry!

Gathering her robe and nightdress from around slippered feet, she dashed across the room. Flinging open the bedchamber door, she sprinted down the darkened corridor, rounding corner after corner, and pounded down the main stairwell, heading for the entrance door.

Breathing hard against the pounding of her heart, she unbolted the entrance door, flung it open and waited.

The carriage stopped. When the door opened and the steps were unfolded, but no one stepped out, she panicked. Sensing her brother needed her, she dashed out into the rain. Ice-cold, whipping sheets of water stung her face and soaked her robe and nightdress as she hurried toward the stopped carriage that was dimly illuminated by lanterns swinging beside the driver's seat.

Shoving her way past the footman toward the open door, she skidded against the wet gravel and angled herself closer to see inside the carriage. "Henry?"

Her brother, who was rising from his seat, yanked his coat over his head, burying himself in it before she could see him. "Jesus Christ, Gene! What—" Stumbling into the darkness of the upholstered seat, he roared, "Get back inside! You aren't even damn well dressed!"

"Weston, *sit*," someone gruffly commanded in a low baritone from within the shadows of the carriage seat. "And cease yelling at her. How is that helpful?"

Henry leaned toward that voice, still keeping himself buried within the coat. "I can't have her seeing my face!"

"I understand," that low baritone offered. "Cease yelling about it and let me get her inside for you, all right?"

Her throat tightened as she edged back. Who was in there with him? And what was going on? She swiped away the beading rain from her face in an effort to try to see.

A well-framed man with shoulder-length silvering black hair that fell around a chiseled face in wet waves loomed in the carriage doorway. Those broad shoulders barely fit against the opening as he hovered above her, setting one edge-whitened leather boot on the first stair, whilst keeping the other on the main landing of the carriage.

Her eyes widened, noting his frayed coat had been torn at the curve of that muscled shoulder. Dearest God. What sort of company was her brother keeping these days? A yellowing linen shirt, open indecently at his masculine throat without a cravat or a waistcoat, had been sloppily tucked into a pair of wool trousers.

Astoundingly pale eyes that reminded her of the clearest skies of a winter morning held her gaze from above for a thundering moment. The wavering light from the lanterns flickered shadows across his rugged face, accentuating high cheekbones and a fine nose that was a touch crooked. He lingered in the opening of that carriage as if to ensure she was aware of him.

Which she most certainly was.

Those dominating ice-blue eyes momentarily erased everything, including every last drop of cold rain. She blinked, realizing that the rain had, in fact, stopped. It was as if the heavens had cleared in the name of this man.

He leaned down toward her, holding on to the side of the open door with a large, scarred hand. "Weston had his first go at real boxing earlier tonight and lost. Miserably. You don't want to see how miserably. Just know he and I are now good friends because of it. We actually spent most of the night talking and cleaning him up. Or at least trying to." His voice was smooth, deep, and bore a surprisingly sophisticated accent given his rough appearance. "You really don't want to see him in his current state. I suggest you retire, tea cake."

Tea cake? Her lips parted and she honestly couldn't decide what horrified her more. Knowing her brother had allowed himself to be pummeled due to his own stupidity or knowing that she'd been called a tea cake by some vagrant whilst standing in a rain-drenched robe and nightdress.

"Can you step back?" he asked. "I'd like to get down. I'm not overly fond of carriages."

She stepped away from the carriage entrance, trying not to stumble on the wet gravel. *That* was why he'd lingered. Not because of her, but because she'd been blocking his ability to move.

She really *was* a tea cake.

The man jumped down with a thud onto the gravel, his great coat billowing around his large, muscled body as his riding boots splashed into the puddle. "Are you going in? Or do I have to carry you in?"

Her heart skittered. Something about this man made her world pulse. And she couldn't decide if it was a good thing or a bad thing.

He paused. "You're putting on quite the show." Raking his gaze over her breasts, he swiped the corners of his mouth with the tips of his fingers. "Not that I mind—they're incredibly lovely, but you may want to go inside."

Her eyes widened as she slapped her hands over the front of her robe. She wasn't wearing a corset. Cupping her hands harder against her breasts, she felt her puckered nipples well-outlined against the wet material sticking to her palms. Her heated face pricked against the cold wind.

He lowered his stubbled chin as if to get a better look at her face and extended a bare, scarred hand toward the entrance. "Are you going in or not?" He spaced out his words as if she were mentally incapable of understanding. "Because I can still see everything. Even with your hands in place."

She gasped, completely mortified, turned and dashed past the portico and back in through the open door of the house, her slippers clicking and sliding across the marble. Skidding out of sight, she scrambled into the darkest corner of the foyer, setting herself against the farthest wall where no one could see her.

In a daze, she flopped against the wall, breathing hard. He'd seen everything.

She stared up at the mahogany stairwell that led up to an open landing above. After a blurring week of every aristocratic socialite fawning over the way she walked and danced and breathed, this was simply too much.

Male voices and heavy steps drifted into the foyer.

She froze, holding her breath.

"Remind me to never bring you home with me again," Henry said in a riled tone, hidden just beyond sight. "Did you really have to comment on her breasts? In my circle, we don't talk to women that way."

"I got her inside for you, didn't I?" that baritone casually provided. "Consider it a compliment I thought your wife's breasts attractive enough to even comment on."

She almost choked.

"That wasn't my wife!" Henry staggered toward the stairwell, the coat still pulled over his head. "That was my sister, Coleman. *My goddamn sister!*"

"Consider it an even bigger compliment."

"Weston?" A female voice bloomed throughout the foyer like a horn. "Who is…whatever are you— Why are you hiding under a coat?"

About time you noticed something amiss, Imogene thought. Her gaze jumped up to her sister-in-law standing at the top of the staircase, which was barely in view from the dark corner Imogene was tucked in.

Wrapped from shoulder to toe in a clinging, gold silk robe whose train splayed down part of the stair, Lady Mary Elizabeth Weston reminded Imogene of a Roman princess lounging about a palace. All the woman needed were the grapes. Sour grapes.

"*That* is my wife," Henry grumbled almost inaudibly from within the coat. "And though she and I aren't on the best of terms, I will mind you not to comment on her breasts, either."

"No worry in that," came the stage-whispered response. "They're not as impressive."

Imogene stifled a disbelieving laugh against her pressed hand. Now *that* was funny.

The tall, broad back belonging to this "Coleman" appeared in view at the bottom of the staircase. "Let me help you up." Taking Henry's arm and draping it over his midsection, he guided him up the stairs. "Go slow."

Imogene could practically hear her brother wincing as he staggered up each step.

Mary bustled down the stairs, trying to grab Henry's other arm. "I am *never* letting you go to another boxing exhibition again. 'Tis a waste of whatever is left of your face. A true gentleman would never watch such filth, let alone participate in it."

Henry yanked his arm away from hers. "Yes, you know all about real gentlemen, don't you, Mary?"

She sputtered, following Henry up the remaining stairs. "How can you treat me like this?" She waved toward Coleman. "Bringing in some vagrant from off the street to see me in my robe!"

"He isn't a vagrant. And unlike Banbury, he isn't here to see you," Henry coolly obliged. "He was assisting me home, given my condition."

When they had reached the landing, Henry grabbed Coleman's shoulder, the coat swaying lopsided over his head. "My driver will take you wherever you need to go."

"Uh...no," Coleman provided. "The ride over was daunting enough. I'll walk. Now go. Get some rest. And call in a doctor, will you? You may have to get that eye lanced."

Imogene's lips parted. *Lanced?*

Henry pointed at him. "My offer still stands. Think about it until I see you at Cardinal's next week."

"I'll let you know by the end of the week."

"Good. See you then."

Cardinal's? That was one of the milling coves Henry frequented in the hopes of finding— Her eyes widened. Her brother had found a boxer. Upon her soul. This was their boxer! The man who was going to change their lives.

When Henry and his wife's frantic, pitchy voice disappeared farther into the house and silence drummed, Imogene intently watched as this Coleman jogged down the remaining stairs.

His long-legged stride echoed as he strode through the foyer. To her astonishment, he didn't head for the entrance door. But toward...*her.*

Her damp robe still clung to every inch of her skin, making her feel like a seal at the menagerie about to get its first visitor.

He veered toward the space of the darkened corner she was tucked into.

She must have been breathing too hard.

He paused before her in the fuzzy darkness. "I couldn't leave without saying goodbye." The crisp scent of fresh air tinged with the smell of leather drifted toward her, the faint outline of those broad shoulders lingering close. Long, wet hair framed his shadowed face. "How are you?"

Her mouth went dry. She'd never heard a male voice dip like that before. Not in a way that made her stomach dip along with it. It was like he wanted something from her.

"Is there a reason you're standing in the darkness alone?" he inquired. "Were you waiting for me?"

It sounded like he was hoping she was.

Imogene stared up in the direction of that deep voice and tried to decide if he intimidated her or not. His voice was incredibly debonair and didn't match his gruff appearance.

He hesitated. "I can hardly hear you breathing. Is everything all right?"

She trembled against the increasing cold that pinched her skin and knew it was time to go before she made an idiot out of herself. Quickly rounding the man, she leaned away to ensure she didn't brush up against him and only hoped he wouldn't follow her up to her room.

He sidestepped and blocked her from leaving. "Wait." He removed his great coat from long, muscled arms, exposing the frayed linen shirt beneath. "Come here."

Her breath hitched as she scrambled back and bumped into the wall behind her. "What are you—"

"You're soaked and you're cold. Now come here." He yanked her forward with a firm hand.

She froze.

He draped his coat around her. "There." Large calloused

fingers bumped her throat as he positioned and adjusted the coat into place around her. "Warm up."

The soothing warmth of his coat, which his body had heated well, sank into her moist skin. The rough wool nestled around her body smelled like musty leather and smoky wood from a blazing fire that mingled with the scent of coal and the ocean. She had no doubt it smelled of all the places he had been to and seen.

Large hands stilled at the collar of the coat he had been adjusting around her throat. His hold tightened on the wool and he leaned in. "You smell good."

Her pulse danced against his fingertips, which still clung to the coat. She probably did smell good. She had stupidly spilled perfume on her robe earlier that night.

"Do you have a name?" His tone was patient. "Weston called you Gene. Is that your name?"

Her breaths now came in jagged takes. Why did everything about this man make her panic *and* melt at the same time? It wasn't right.

His hands fell away. "How is a man supposed to get anywhere with a woman who doesn't talk?" He shifted toward her. "Do I scare you?"

She lowered her gaze to her hands. "No. Though I…I was a bit unnerved by what you said to me outside. It was uncalled-for."

He paused, his voice unexpectedly softening. "I'm afraid I'm a bit rough when it comes to women. I'm not accustomed to small talk. And if I'm ever feeling amorous I usually tie them up."

She glanced up, astounded, and met his shadowed gaze. It was like he said everything that was in his head. She had never met a man who did that before. "You…tie women up?" she rasped in disbelief. "What do you mean by that?"

He stiffly stepped back. "I've clearly said too much." He sounded agitated. "I should go."

He probably thought she was judging him. And she couldn't have that. Not when he was about to change her life *and* Henry's.

She grabbed his biceps, yanking him back and held him in place. "No. Stay. We probably should get to know each other."

He stilled, the muscle beneath his clothing hardening beneath her fingers. "Know each other?" His chest rose and fell in deep takes as he intently held her gaze in the soft shadows. "You mean you want to take this upstairs, to bed?" A slow smile spread across his lips. "Did my talk of tying you up intrigue you?"

She quickly retrieved her hand, fully aware of his pulsing warmth and gawked up at him. "Uh…no, that wasn't what I was… I…I was merely…" She winced and tried not to panic lest it bring her stutter on. In truth, she was surprised it hadn't reared its head yet, being in the vicinity of this daunting man. "Are you a boxer?"

He paused. "I am. Yes." He appeared incredibly surprised by the question. "Why do you ask?"

It was like meeting one of those shirtless men inside Mr. P. Egan's book, which Henry kept in the study. The boxing book she had been reading ever since Henry had commenced looking for a pugilist for them to invest in. Her heart pounded knowing that gritty world of swinging fists, which was only permitted to men by men, was standing before her. "Are you any good at it?"

He smirked. "I'm not one to brag."

She tightened his coat around her shoulders. "So you *are* good at it?"

"As I said, I'm not one to brag. So don't make me."

Imogene bit back a smile. She rather liked him. She felt like whatever he said, he meant. "Do you still have all of your teeth?"

A cough of a laugh escaped him. "Yes. Though I have come close to losing them many a time."

"Ah." She tried to come up with another question. Boxing. Something to do with boxing. "And do you...box often?" Oh, now, her brain was turning into wine jelly.

"Not as often as I'd like. I give lessons over at Cardinal's and have even taken a few matches since coming into London, but nothing worth my time. It barely pays anything. I'd need a patron for that, and though your brother has offered, I'm still not particularly fond of being owned."

"Owned? Oh, no, no. Henry isn't like that. He would never—"

"There is no need to defend him. 'Tis how boxing investments are conducted."

"Oh." The particulars of the investment itself were something she and Henry had never fully discussed. "So...how would an investment be conducted if...well...my brother were to invest?" She didn't want to scare him off by saying *she* was the investor.

He hesitated. "You seem incredibly interested in boxing. For a woman."

"I am. But it has nothing to do with me being a woman." Gad. That sounded moronic. "I just want to know. What do you mean by being owned?"

He eyed her. "Your brother would basically control every aspect of my life both in and out of the boxing ring until the championship. Everything from who I associate with to who I fight and what I eat and how I train."

She blinked. She would get to control this man like that? *Completely?* How utterly fascinating. Henry never told her any of that. "I didn't realize it was so involved."

"Everything involving the title for the Champion of England is. Aside from the prestige, we're talking millions of pounds in bets placed throughout the land. Of which, of course, I would only see a fraction. But a fraction of millions is still staggering and beyond impressive."

"It most certainly is." She dug her fingers into the palm of her hand. Still feeling awkward, knowing that she was actually talking to the man who was going to change everything, she randomly blurted, "You have a most unusual accent. British, yet not. Were you born in London?"

"No. I was born and raised in Surrey."

"Surrey. So where are you from now?"

"New York."

"America? How exciting. Is it nice there?"

"When you close your eyes."

"It doesn't seem like you cared for it."

"It was a place to live. Nothing more."

"I see. And do you plan on going back?"

"Does it sound like I plan on going back?"

Her brows came together. This man certainly didn't elaborate much. She asked, he answered. That was all. It was as if he was a wall tolerating their conversation. He was clearly bored. Not that she blamed him. Everything about her life was as mundane as staring at her medicine. Her investment scheme with Henry was the only exciting thing to have *ever* happened to her. Which was pathetic.

She stripped his great coat from her shoulders and held it out. "I shouldn't keep you."

"You aren't keeping me." He took the coat and shrugged himself into it, adjusting it around his large frame. "I always have time to entertain a beautiful woman."

An odd giddiness poked at her knowing he thought she was beautiful. *Her.* She pressed her fingers nervously into her thighs, shifting the wet material of her robe. Maybe she should say something more. "Fortunately it stopped raining. So your walk home ought to be pleasant."

"Is that your way of telling me to go?"

"No. I…I'm trying to make conversation."

"Are you?" Amusement tinged his voice. "Might I point out, you're not very good at it."

She cringed and shifted against the wall. "I know."

He shifted closer, the heat of his body drawing unnervingly close. "How old are you?"

She pressed herself harder against the wall, until she felt the plaster beneath the silk embroidered paper. "Old enough. Why?"

One hand and then another pressed against the wall beside her head, caging her in with his muscled frame. "Old enough for what?"

Her breathing shallowed. "For anything."

Another slow smile teased his lips. "If I tied your hands behind your back or above your head, would you be amenable to it?"

A strange fluttering overtook her stomach as he hovered above her in dominating silence. "Am I supposed to answer that?"

He cocked his head, still watching her. "Let me give you some advice based on what I'm seeing here. Never let a man you don't know this close to you again. There are a lot of ass-holes that prey on women like you. Consider yourself fortu-nate I'm not one of them."

Assholes? She blinked.

His voice grew husky. "Are you warm yet? I can take off my coat again. In fact, I can take off whatever you want me to. All you have to do is ask."

She felt the foyer sway and locked her knees together to keep herself from sliding down the wall. Something about the way he had said it made her want to drape herself against him.

His right hand left the wall and trailed to her shoulder. He gently curved his palm in and brushed past her throat, mak-ing her suck in a sharp breath.

Rough padded fingers nudged her face up toward the fuzzy outline of his own face. "You're very pretty. Do you know that?"

Why did she sense this man was going to change *more* than her finances? She swallowed, feeling his lips hover-ing above hers. Should she let him kiss her? It wouldn't be a sin, would it?

The heat of his breath tickled her mouth.

She grew faint. Very, very faint.

He released her and pushed away from the wall. "I have to go." Turning, he stalked toward the entrance, his boots thud-ding against the marble with what appeared to be a determi-nation to not only leave but never be seen again.

A long breath escaped her. He was leaving? After all of that talk of him doing whatever she asked and his strange quest to bind her hands? What happened? Did she suddenly cease being pretty?

Stumbling away from the wall, she glanced up at the stairwell, thankful it was empty, and hurried after him. "Mr. Cole-man?" she whispered so no one would hear.

His large frame paused, still holding the entrance door open as he kept his back to her. "Coleman is my boxing name. It's not my real name."

"Oh. I beg your pardon. What is your real name?"

"Just call me Nathaniel. Now what do you want?"

Imogene brought her hands together in an effort to re-main calm. Unlike all the blurred aristocratic faces she'd met this past week in countless ballrooms that had sent her into a cringing, stuttering panic, he had brought everything into focus and made her realize what had been missing all her life: a genuine strength to be more than her illness. "You didn't say goodbye."

He glanced over his shoulder, those striking clear blue eyes capturing hers in the candlelight of the foyer. "Are you asking me to kiss you?"

She gawked. "I… No. *No.* Why would I— All I was point-ing out, and very respectably, mind you, was that you walked away without bidding me farewell."

He slowly closed the door and faced her again. "I walked away for a reason."

Her brow creased. "I hope I didn't offend you in any way."

Shifting his jaw, he strode back toward her, his coat bil-lowing menacingly around his solid movements as if he were about to take flight and land on top of her.

Though she wanted to throw up her hands and dash up the stairs to find Henry, she knew that would only make her look the ninny that she was.

He paused half an arm away, blocking her view of the foyer. That crisp scent of leather, wood and coal drifted toward her again. He lowered his gaze to hers. "You didn't offend."

Everything about him was a bit *too* exciting. She almost couldn't think. "I didn't?"

"No." He held her gaze. "My mind simply isn't where it should be and I'm not one to take advantage of a clearly virginal woman."

Her eyes widened. "What do you mean by that?"

"Oh, now, you can't be *that* naive. What do you think goes on between men and women when no one is looking? They don't sit and play cards."

She fisted her trembling hands, which had gone from damp cold to damp hot, realizing *exactly* what he meant. She knew about kissing. She also knew that when bedchamber doors closed at night, something happened that resulted in children. So did he mean to say he wanted both? "Are you offering on my hand?"

His mouth quirked. "Not in the way you think." He edged in tauntingly. "This is probably where you should turn and run, tea cake. Before all this pent-up self-restraint you see... *flies.* Because I'm not known for restraint when it comes to women."

She swallowed. He was teasing her. "If you doubted your self-restraint, you wouldn't have told me."

He eyed her. "I'm not always this nice to women."

"If I felt in any way threatened by you or this situation," she confided, "I would have screamed by now. I can scream, you know. I try not to, given Dr. Filbert insists I never strain my throat, but I can. I'm not as frail as everyone thinks I am."

He hesitated. "Doctor? Is something wrong with you?"

She shrugged. "I have fainting spells and issues with my throat. There was an incident when I was younger. I could barely swallow without being in pain and lost almost a quarter of my body weight when I was seven."

He stared, his features darkening. "I'm sorry to hear it."

She shrugged. "I was rather fortunate. I could have died. Everyone was surprised I didn't."

He said nothing.

"My name is Imogene, by the by. *Lady* Imogene. But you can call me Gene."

He stared at her in a way that resembled a panther gazing upon its prey. Then, suddenly, he edged back. "I really have to go."

She tried not to panic. What if he didn't take the offer? What if she had scared him away with all her stupid talk of doctors and death? "We should take tea sometime. Here at the house. Next week in the afternoon? Yes?"

He kept staring. "I'm not looking to be domesticated."

"Oh. I… Well…tea is very informal. As long as I have a chaperone it would be very respectable. You and I can get to know each other and be friends."

"Friends?" His gaze traced her eyes to her lips and back to her eyes again. "You're a woman."

Her cheeks grew hot. "Men and women can be friends."

"Men and women aren't meant to be friends. Trust me in this. Good night…*Imogene*." He turned and strode for the entrance door and opened it. Glancing back at her one last time, he stepped into the darkness beyond, closing the door behind him with a thud.

Imogene hurried to the closed door and lingered, wishing he would come back. Everything about him was so beautifully raw and real. She didn't realize a man could make a woman's toes curl in her own slippers.

It was divine. *He* was divine.

Setting both hands on the door, she pretended for a breath it was him. Her pulse thrummed against the carved wood as she traced her fingertips against it. She smiled dreamily. Together, they would take that quarter of a million and rule the world.

She paused. Wait. She had just let him walk out the door without *any* guarantee. Scrambling to open the door, she threw it back and ran out into the night after the man she knew was going to change her life.

CHAPTER SIX

When Greek meets Greek, then's the tug of war.

—P. Egan, *Boxiana* (1823)

NATHANIEL PRAYED FOR inner strength. He'd never met a woman who had actually made him want to do more than rip clothes off. Attraction to a woman was one thing. He'd had plenty of those since he was sixteen. But this fierce need to dig his two hands into each and every breath she took was beyond anything he'd ever known or touched.

Raking back his rain-dampened hair in disbelief, he trudged down the gravel path. How he had managed to escape her and that house without giving in to what he *really* wanted to do was beyond his own understanding.

The darting steps of slippers urgently running after him in the darkness made Nathaniel turn. His breath hitched as Imogene's curvaceous figure, draped in that hand-bitingly clinging wet fabric, bustled toward him.

Despite the darkness, the row of glass lanterns hanging off the iron railing lit just enough to illuminate the seductive bounce of those well-outlined breasts as she jogged toward him.

He stiffened—everywhere. The woman clearly didn't realize how much he *could* see.

She alighted before him, primly threw her long blond braid over her slim shoulder and glanced up, that quiet, oval face, flushed cheeks and those stunning bright hazel eyes meeting his gaze. "I couldn't let you go quite yet. Not until you promise me you will take my brother's offer."

He fisted both hands, fighting the two opposing voices raging in his head. One told him to go. And the other one told him to rake his hands down every inch of her wet robe before stripping it off. He couldn't decide which voice he should listen to and had been mindlessly arguing with both ever since he first saw her. "Not to disappoint you, tea cake, but I'm going to need a few days to think about the offer. I've got people to talk to." Mainly Matthew. He hadn't been informing the poor bastard of much these days.

Her blond brows flickered as her voice dipped in concern. "Do you need a better offer?" She leaned in closer, bringing that lavish, crisp scent of lilies. "Was the money not generous enough?"

He drew in a ragged breath, wishing she wouldn't lean in so damn close. Because all he could think about was the same thing he'd been thinking about when he had her up against the wall in her house. How he wanted to take those wrists into each hand, pull them up over her head and knot them into place with her own silk stockings. That way, he could have free rein over that luscious body and do whatever he wanted. "The sort of offer I'm thinking about, Imogene, probably isn't going to suit you *or* your brother." He was all about being honest.

She searched his face amongst the shadows. "I will make it suit us. What were you thinking?"

A gruff laugh escaped him. If she were any more naive, he'd have to pinch her adorable ass. "You really don't want to know what I'm thinking."

"But I do. I really do. I genuinely want to assure you that—" She blinked rapidly, her features momentarily blanking.

He hesitated, sensing something was wrong. "What is it?"

She staggered and then to his heart-pounding astonishment, swooned.

Jumping toward her, he grabbed hold of her slim body before she hit the gravel, the wet fabric of her robe and nightdress shifting against his bare hands. "Jesus."

What the hell just happened?

Quickly sliding his hands beneath her and with a single toss, he effortlessly hefted her up and into both arms, rolling her body toward his chest, and glanced down at her.

Her head rolled back, exposing the length of her throat and her full lips unconsciously parted in the shifting light and shadows of the lanterns.

He quickly leaned in toward her mouth, setting his ear against those lips. Relief trickled in at realizing she was still breathing.

Get her to Weston. That way, it's off your hands and it's not your fault. Tightening his hold on her, he jogged his way back toward the entrance and veered in through the entrance door she had left open.

Her small hands jumped up to the lapels on his great coat, tightening their hold.

He jerked to a halt and glanced down at her in the dim candlelight of the foyer, his pulse roaring in his ears. "What happened? Are you all right?"

She stared up at him, her hazel eyes unfocused. She momentarily closed her eyes before reopening them and half nodded. "Yes. I...I fainted, didn't I?"

"Yes," he breathed out.

She winced. "I do that."

Not good. "Do you want me to call for your brother?"

"No. He...he would only call upon the doctor."

He eyed her. "Don't you want him to call the doctor?"

She slowly shook her head. "No. Dr. Filbert always puts me on bed rest. Then I'm not allowed to do anything for days. Not even read. I hate it." She tightened her hold on the lapels of his coat and peered up at him. "Can you take me up to my room instead? Please?"

It was the softest and sweetest of pleas he had ever had the pleasure of hearing. It actually made his throat tighten. He searched that pretty, rain-dampened face. "Is that what you want?"

She half nodded and leaned her blond head against him as if she completely trusted him, which she must, considering she was asking him to take her up into her bedchamber. "'Tis up the stairs on the right. Keep to the right and turn two corners." She sounded weak, her voice faint. "It will be the eighth door down. And please don't tell Henry. He always makes a fuss whenever I faint. Promise me you won't tell him."

He couldn't help but instinctively cradle her closer in response to that plea. "I promise."

He made his way up the main stairwell. Once he was on the landing, he carried her, her slippered feet dangling, toward the direction she had given him, turning two corners. It was eerie wandering about such a lavish home. It had been thirty years since he'd found himself in an abode bigger than the peeling walls of a lone room he had leased from an ironmonger back in New York. Nathaniel eventually found the eighth door on the right in the vast corridor.

"Is this it?" he whispered down at her, so no one could hear him.

"Yes," she whispered back.

The door was wide-open, candlelight glowing from within. He strode into a very feminine-looking bedchamber, with pale pink walls. On the right was a dressing table covered with a white lace runner and various crystal perfume bottles, painted pink tins and jewelry boxes. On the other side, against the far wall, was a large four-poster bed covered with white linens and an array of plush pillows.

The room personified her. Tranquil and pretty.

Striding over to the bed, he gently lowered her onto the linens, slipping his bare hands out from beneath her. He tried not to linger on the feel of those curves.

Holding his gaze from where she lay against the pillows, she smiled weakly. "Thank you."

The way she looked up at him, so trustingly, made him lean down and gently kiss her smooth forehead. "You're welcome," he murmured against her skin. Something about that quiet, oval face and those stunning bright hazel eyes that had clearly seen so little of the world had made him want to swallow her whole and remember a time when all that mattered was skipping a stone across water.

He'd never kissed a woman on the forehead before. He'd licked it, and nipped it, but never kissed it for the sake of kissing it.

Even worse…he didn't stop there. Nor could he. He gently kissed the side of her temple, then trailed his lips to her soft cheek and kissed that, and then trailed his lips to her chin and kissed that. She smelled like fresh rain and lilies. It reminded him of the dew-ridden fields outside of New York where he'd lie in the grass for hours whenever he wanted to escape the bustle of the city.

Though she drew in a notable breath that made her breasts rise up toward him, she didn't move.

Nathaniel did everything he could to keep himself from burying himself into her and that scent. His chest tightened with the awareness he was overstepping his bounds given her innocence. He straightened and stepped away from the bed.

She stared, her cheeks flushed. With both hands still flat against the linens, she whispered up at him, "Why did you do that?"

He shifted his jaw, feeling like he had disrupted her peace. The peace he'd been trying to absorb, he realized. "It doesn't matter." He stepped back again. "I suggest you get out of those wet clothes." He paused and added, "After I leave."

He turned and strode out of the room, closing the door behind himself to ensure he didn't look back. His pulse raced as he tried not to think about what he had just done, though it was rather tame given his nature and what he usually inflicted upon a woman. Nathaniel was infinitely relieved when he finally made it outside, closing the entrance door behind him.

CHAPTER SEVEN

I could have done a great deal better, Sir,
but I was afraid I might hit you
too hard and you should be affronted.

—P. Egan, *Boxiana* (1823)

NATHANIEL GLANCED TOWARD the sky that was lightening at
the edges of the darkness that had once been. He could hear
the chirping of birds against the pulsing silence.

It was like the dawning of a new life.

He felt so oddly empowered after having kissed Imogene.
Like he could face anything and do anything.

He set his jaw. Waiting be damned.

Now that he had had a chance to kiss heaven, it was as
good a time as any to finally kiss hell. He was done waiting.
Like Matthew kept telling him, he wouldn't be able to move
forward in his head or in his life until he did this.

Jogging down the wide stairs, he made his way down the
gravel carriage path and out past the gates. He walked and
walked and walked in jaw-tightening silence until—

Recognizing the square up ahead enclosed by wide, pris-
tine roads and tall, stone houses, he slowed. It was exactly

where Weston said it would be when he had asked if he knew where the Sumners held their residence.

Nathaniel crossed the cobblestone, splashing up water that reflected the morning sky brightening to yellow-pink against the rising sun.

The Sumner House.

His pulse roared. The brass lion knocker on the door was still there. The same brass lion he used to jump up and tap before walking through the door. The iron fence that quartered off the cobblestone road was still there, with the Sumner crest that he used to drag his father's cane across. Thirty years had changed nothing, except for the size of the trees.

He lingered on the path, still staring at the door. Memories flooded his soul as the ghostly figure of his sister in a silk pleated bonnet and a pale pink gown bent toward the ghostly figure of himself as a boy. Trunks were being carried out of the Sumner house by footmen and strapped onto the large coach set to take them to Liverpool, where they would board a ship to New York. His father planned to invest in land for the purpose of leasing and making a profit, given funds were short. His mother insisted that they go as a family. Auggie had promised him that the trip would bring their family together.

How wrong she had been.

He slowly made his way up the set of stairs leading to the vast terrace home. Though he hesitated, he reached out and forced himself to twist the iron bell on the side of the entrance.

It was done. There was no going back.

Moments edged past, and with it the occasional clattering of coach wheels and clumping of horses' hooves from the cobblestone street behind. Leaning back, he eyed the vast windows, noting all of the curtains were open. His gut turned and he wondered if he should leave. Before he did something stupid. Before he—

A click vibrated the large entrance door and it swung open. A thin, grey-haired man in blue livery peered out.

Nathaniel's throat tightened. By God. It was Wilkinson. He'd gotten old.

Wilkinson squinted. "What business have you to be calling this early?"

The man was as crusty as ever. It was surreal seeing him again. "Wilkinson. Is that you?"

"Do I know you, sir?"

Maybe he ought to ease into this. "Uh…we met. A long time ago."

Wilkinson narrowed his gaze. "We did?"

Nathaniel tried to remain calm, even though he felt overwhelmed. It was like *seeing* all thirty years flit in a blink. "I'm…I'm actually here to speak to Lord Sumner." He could do this. He could face his father, couldn't he?

"At this hour, sir? Clearly the time means nothing to you. His lordship still sleeps."

How was his father capable of ever closing his eyes? "His sleep just ended. I ask that you bid the man to rise. Tell him he has a visitor."

The butler pulled in his wobbling chin. "I highly doubt, sir, that you have any business of such great import that would require—"

"Inform his lordship that his son is here to see him. I'm certain that will get him up."

"His—" Wilkinson's eyes widened. "Dearest God. I thought you looked eerily familiar but I— Master Atwood?

Is it truly you? Have your own two feet finally brought you home?"

Sensing the man had, indeed, recognized him, a shaky breath escaped him. "Yes. Though I'm not much to look at anymore, am I?"

The butler stared, his thin shoulders deflating. His gaze traveled from Nathaniel's hair to his boots and settled on his face. He stepped back. "I will admit your eyes are very much his. But how is it possible? After so many countless years of nothing surfacing how have you come to be?"

Knowing the man needed more assurance, Nathaniel eventually offered, "From what I remember, you'd take a rose from my mother's garden every Friday afternoon during the summer and deliver it to a young woman at the market. Miss…Folding? No. Miss…Golding I believe was her name. Wasn't it? Whatever became of that?"

Wilkinson's eyes dewed. "She married someone else." He sounded haunted. "'Tis truly you, then. 'Tis truly you." A trembling hand clamped over his mouth.

Nathaniel leaned in and said in a low tone, "It is. And sadly, I have nothing but memories to prove who I am. Now that we have been reacquainted, I am asking you give me an audience with my father. I have waited thirty years for it."

The old man blinked rapidly, lowering his hand. Glancing toward the street, he pulled the door wider. "Yes. Of course. Please. Do. Come in. I… Come in, come in."

"Thank you." Nathaniel stepped into the large foyer.

The door closed, darkening the hallway. Several lit candles illuminated the honey-colored silk-brocaded walls that clothed the expanse of the dim foyer. He remembered this entrance. Not even the paper on the wall had changed.

To his astonishment, Wilkinson grabbed him and yanked

him close. "This house hasn't been the same without you, my lord," Wilkinson choked out. "Perpetual sadness has haunted us all."

Nathaniel stiffened against that unexpected hold but gave way to patting the old man. The man who used to sneak him strawberry-covered crumpets out of the kitchen. "I appreciate the warm welcome, Wilkinson. I honestly didn't expect you to even recognize me."

"You were the boy I never had, my lord. How does a man forget the son he always wanted?" Wilkinson drew away with a hard sniff and gestured toward a room whose curtains had yet to be drawn. "I will ensure his lordship sees you at once. I cannot even imagine what he will... I am beside myself. Absolutely beside myself." Wilkinson eyed him one last time and hurried up the stairs as best his aged body would allow.

Slowly walking into the dimly lit receiving room, filled with furnishings and large portraits and mirrors, Nathaniel wandered toward a French writing desk. The same desk his mother used to sit at and accept or decline invitations and write letters. Back in the day, he clung to the edges of that desk, asking her countless questions about everything she did before the governess tugged him out of the room. Eerily, even the inkwell was still sitting in the same place. His mother had always been one for perfected routine. He remembered that much about her.

A single invitation that had been set out atop a pile of parchment paper made him lean toward it. Recognizing the name of the host, he plucked it up.

Imagine that. His brother-in-law, the Duke of Wentworth, was hosting an event. He set the invitation back on the desk, positioning it exactly where it had lain.

Finding nothing else of interest, Nathaniel strode toward

the middle of the room and, easing out a shaky breath, faced the open doorway. Setting both hands behind his back, he dug his fingers into the skin of his wrist below the cuff of his coat and locked it hard against his back.

He could hear the clock on the mantelpiece behind him click another hand into place. It had been thirty years since he took his father's pistol, loaded it and used the panel in the wall to sneak outside the house under the moonlight and face the man with the cigar who had been intimidating his family—the man whose ties to his father he couldn't have imagined. Unbeknownst to him, the pistol's hammer was broken and unable to fire when he needed it to.

He had spent thirty years regretting it, and took up boxing to ensure he'd never be without weapons again.

Steady footsteps echoed down the corridor, making him fist both hands. His jaw tightened.

A stout, white-haired man in a Turkish robe and slippers appeared and stood motionless in the doorway. Grey, inquisitive eyes settled upon him, that sagging, round face no longer resembling the dashing, rugged face of the Earl of Sumner.

This was his father?

Jesus fucking Christ.

It was anticlimactic.

This was but an old man he could easily snap between two knuckles and flick away like dust. And he wanted to do just that. "You've aged, Father. And not very well, at that."

Those lips parted. The earl entered the room, his movements staggered and uneven, as if age had made his limbs brittle. "Who are you?" he rasped.

How Nathaniel had managed to even breathe knowing he was standing within a swing of his father was beyond his own understanding. "I think you know who I am."

"Who are you?" the earl demanded, his voice now returning with more strength.

Nathaniel tried to keep his voice calm lest he give in to riling himself too much. "Your son. Your heir. Your blood. Your kin. Do you need a full name and a birthplace to go with it?"

His father's grey eyes widened as he scanned his appearance. "You look nothing like him."

Nathaniel set his jaw. "What did you expect given I spent most of my life on the streets of New York where you abandoned me?"

The earl grew quiet.

"Do you require proof?" Nathaniel pressed. "I can answer any question you want. About you. About Mother. About poor Auggie, who is no longer with us. We can even take out portraits of me as a child and hold them to my face. Eyes don't change."

"There aren't any…any portraits of him left. I removed them when he— I couldn't bear to look at him."

"I bet you couldn't." Nathaniel chanted for the strength not to send a fist through his father's skull. If he gave in to raising his voice, his control would be lost. That much he knew. "How is your reputation these days? The same as it was back in New York?"

A trembling, vein-ridden hand pointed to the doorway. "Leave. Leave, before I—"

"Before you what? I would think twice before issuing threats, old man. All it takes is these two hands—" Nathaniel held them up "—and the snap of your neck and it's done. You wouldn't even have time to scream."

The earl stared, his aged face paling to paste.

More than ready to deliver the message from the boy whose life had been murdered between four dank walls and a bolted wooden door, Nathaniel dropped his hands and his voice to lethal. "I could have easily forgiven what Casacalenda did to me. After all, I was the one who stupidly left the house and put a pistol to the man's face demanding he never intimidate us again. How was I to know there was a much bigger story? I was astounded to no end he treated me as well as he did given what you did to him and his life. He never touched me. He never beat me. He gave me everything I wanted, except my freedom, for years. He even dined with me every night in the cellar when he wasn't traveling and taught me how to paint and sketch. He was a good man. A very broken man, but a good man. I've long since forgiven him. I had to, given his misery and his own loss. But how am I to forgive *you?* How do I forgive what you did to not only him but me?"

The earl shook his head ever so slowly from side to side and whispered, "You speak of things I know nothing of."

Nathaniel narrowed his gaze. "Lie to the world and to God who is watching and waiting to judge you when your time has come, but not to me. Casacalenda told me everything. And I do mean everything. Every one of your secrets and every one of your lies. There isn't a thing I don't know and the only reason I never came back was to protect mother's and Auggie's name from rotting before all of society."

The earl blinked rapidly, his lips tightening. "I refuse to stand here and submit to this vile form of intimidation." The earl swiveled toward the doorway. *"Carter! Dixon!* Come at once. At once!"

"It's going to take more than two men to get me out of the house." Nathaniel widened his stance and set his shoulders, trying to exude a level of calm he didn't feel. "I want to see my mother. *Now.*"

The earl's face had bloomed red to the roots of his white hair, his body trembling as if he were about to burst. "What do you mean to do? The doctors say any undue stress might end whatever is left of her life. Is that what you want? To kill her? The poor woman has suffered enough. Leave her in peace. Leave us both in peace. Whoever the devil you really are."

Nathaniel stared, sensing that the man was in earnest. Was his mother truly that ill? "What is wrong with her?"

Two well-built footmen rushed into the room. "My lord?"

The earl snapped a hand toward him. "Get this bastard out. *Get him out!* And don't *ever* allow him entrance into this house again lest Lady Sumner's very heart stops. Is that understood?"

"Yes, my lord!"

The two footmen darted toward Nathaniel and grabbed an arm each, shoving and muscling him hard in the direction of the foyer.

Nathaniel couldn't breathe, knowing his father had betrayed him. *Again.* In a whipping blur, Nathaniel viciously snapped out a fist at the face closest to him and crunched into a set of teeth with the bridge of his knuckles. A choked cry filled the room as blood sprayed and he shoved the man hard. Jumping forward again, he delivered the same rigid blow to the other, snapping that head to the side.

Both footmen fell away like stone pillars, one collapsing onto a walnut table that smashed a vase into powdery shards, the other tumbling down into a dazed heap against a chair that flipped right along with him.

His chest still heaving, Nathaniel jumped toward his father and grabbed him hard by the neck with a hand.

The earl gagged, those eyes wide.

Tightening his rigid hold on that weathered neck he wanted to annihilate, Nathaniel seethed out through bared teeth, "I will spare my mother from seeing me until I am presentable in both my appearance and in my life. Because heaven forbid she see what you have reduced me to. I will also spare her from knowing the truth I have carried with me these thirty years. Because I don't want her last moments spent in hateful regret. She deserves peace. But you? Oh, no. If you think I plan on forgiving you for what you did to me and my life in an effort to protect *your* fucking name and *your* fucking life, that is where you're wrong. I will haunt you until you beg for forgiveness upon both knees or are dead. Whatever the hell comes first."

The earl's veined hand reached up and attempted to touch his face. "No one needs to know," he whispered hoarsely, those panicked eyes acknowledging the truth. "Let me die first. Then the world can know."

It was like the man wanted to die. Releasing his father with a shove, before he himself submitted to something insane, Nathaniel swung away and stumbled out of the room and the house.

Through a pinching haze that barely allowed him a steady gasping of breaths, Nathaniel wandered down endless London streets he didn't know, trying to make sense of what had just happened.

When he eventually found his way into his hotel room at Limmer's, he walked past the crowded entrance and shoved any men who wouldn't move toward the walls. They scrambled back and stared as if he were mad. In that moment, he was.

Nathaniel quickly made his way through the trash-strewn lobby and hauled himself up the steep, wooden staircase. He needed to talk to Matthew and straighten out his thoughts. Before he did something stupid.

He tried Matthew's door only to find it locked. He knocked. "Milton?" he called out. "Milton, I need to talk to you. Are you there?"

No movement came.

Nathaniel dug trembling fingers into the side of his head, trying to remain calm. A few weeks ago, Matthew had met some aristo widow on the riding path, and ever since it was as if the man had no intention of going back to his real life. Even though the swipe on his life was over and the boys were waiting for his return. God. If Matthew didn't go back to New York, it would end more than the Forty Thieves. It would end what little virtue remained within the Five Points.

Nathaniel was to blame for all of this. He had brought Matthew here and had made a mess of not only the man's life but his own. And for what? To face a father, who was waiting to die? To face his mother and his sister's son and husband, who would only suffer if the truth about why he disappeared ever got out? All he wanted was for his father to admit his guilt and he could let it go. The past, after all, was done. Over. But how could he let go of a past that refused to be acknowledged?

Nathaniel unbolted his own leased room and whipped the door shut. Stripping his great coat and shirt, he dropped to the floor, planting both hands flat apart. Gritting his teeth, he commenced pushing his entire body up and down, trying to huff out the tension in his muscles.

He eventually lost count of body lifts at one hundred and eighty. His bare, sweat-sleeked shoulders, chest and arms burned in protest as he pushed on. When he could no longer lift his body in even takes, he rose to his feet and hissed out a harsh breath.

Swiping up his shirt, he buried his drenched face in it. Whipping it over his shoulder, he veered to the corner of the room and squatted, digging his fingers between loose floorboards. Prying one up, he reached into the narrow space beneath and carefully pulled out his sister's diary. He had learned to depend upon holding it and touching it whenever he desperately needed to remind himself that someone had once thought him worthy of being in existence.

Smoothing a hand over the leather and sash, he veered back to the other side of the room and collapsed onto the sunken straw tick on the floor, his entire world swimming.

Digging his fingers hard into the leather of the diary he wished to God he had the strength to read, he tucked it beside him and whipped off the linen shirt from his shoulder.

He could still see his father's veined hand reaching up, attempting to touch his face. He could still hear those hoarse, broken words. *"No one needs to know. Let me die first. Then the world can know."*

Nathaniel lay there, staring unblinkingly at nothing, unable to push out the reality that his father had indeed knowingly left him in that cellar to rot.

Dazed, Nathaniel drifted into a deep sleep he hadn't known in years. When he eventually awoke, he found himself staring at a cracked, mud-smeared window. The light of the day filtering through that window was fading and edges of impending darkness fingered their way across the dank room.

The cellar.

Nathaniel gasped, his chest too tight to let in any air, as perspiration beaded his upper lip and forehead. He almost screamed in riled disbelief until he realized there was a window. Not just walls and a door. There was a window.

He drew air into his lungs, trying to steady himself and his mind. Jesus Christ. Rolling onto his back, he blankly stared up at the ceiling, knowing his father and all of London would be at the event the duke was hosting.

Nothing would ever be able to make him forget his days and years spent in that cellar. Not whilst he lived. And not whilst his father lived.

A large roach crawled in tick-tick-ticks across the uneven planked floor, taunting him into joining the lower species. Picking up Auggie's diary, Nathaniel rose onto booted feet. Striding over to the wooden crate where he kept his leather belt, pistol and dagger, he knew what needed to be done.

CHAPTER EIGHT

What Devil could have provoked him to exhibit his
wonderful stock of honour, virtue, and benevolence in
so public a manner, I am at a loss to divine.

—P. Egan, *Boxiana* (1823)

The following night

AS IF ON CUE, eight well-muscled footmen in powdered white
wigs scrambled into a firm shoulder-to-shoulder body wall,
preventing Nathaniel's entry to the vast ballroom beyond
the foyer.

He stared toward that glittering world majestically showcased by shimmering crystal chandeliers and oversize gilded
mirrors that reflected rows and rows of candlelight and silk
and color. Refined music from violins and flutes mingled
with the thrumming gaiety of countless cultured voices that
drifted out toward him into the corridor.

It was the life he had been born into.

Once upon a fucking time.

He tightened his gloved hold on the hilt of his dagger
sheathed within the scabbard belted to his hip and knew the

only way he was going to get in was by announcing himself. "Inform His Grace that Viscount Atwood has at long last arrived in London and wishes to see him."

One of the footmen squinted, clearly doubting his intentions based on not only the dagger but his appearance.

He knew he should have brushed his hair. "His Grace is expecting me."

The footman hesitated.

"The duke married my sister," he added with hardened authority. "That makes me his brother-in-law. Now take your fancy prick of a wig and get him before I put your liver into your hand and make you swallow it through your nostrils."

"Stay here," the man ordered, jogging down the corridor and disappearing into the ballroom.

The line of footmen rigidly held their place but didn't meet his gaze.

He obliged them by doing the same.

Hurried steps eventually made him glance toward the direction of the ballroom. The Duke of Wentworth darted out of the masses, followed by the footman.

Dressed in full evening attire that made the man look strong and debonair, the duke waved aside the line of footmen. "Stand back. All of you." He reached out and squeezed his arm, his aged face and dark eyes brightening. "By God. Atwood. You do us great honor."

"I wish I had come in better spirits." Nathaniel set his shoulders and stepped outside of the duke's reach, trying to stay focused. "Is my mother here?" He wanted to make sure she wasn't.

"No. She left a short while ago. She wasn't feeling particularly well."

Nathaniel swiped his face. "Is she very ill? How serious is it?"

"The doctors aren't certain as to what happened, but one side of her face collapsed. The poor woman hasn't the means to even smile and suffers from severe headaches."

Nathaniel's shock yielded to fury. "Jesus Christ. And you're letting her attend events?"

The duke held up a hand. "She insists on attending them and is physically very able to do so. It brings her joy. Aside from mingling with guests, she wanders about the house and looks through Augustine's belongings. I'm not going to keep her from visiting with whatever is left of her own daughter."

Glancing up at the ceiling to keep himself from submitting to emotion, Nathaniel asked tersely, "And my father? Is he still here?"

"Yes." The duke hesitated. "Don't think the worst of me, Atwood. Your mother insists I include him in everything I do. She and your father have become exceptionally close since Augustine's passing."

Anger spiked through him. His father was not going to live the lie. Not anymore. "Tell your footmen to let me pass."

The duke's brows shot up. "Pass? To do what?" He wagged a hand toward him. "You are not about to intrude upon my guests looking like that."

"Why not? I bathed and I shaved."

"Atwood." The duke grabbed his arm. "You cannot expect your father or people to accept you all in one night *and* dressed as you are. We have to slowly reintroduce you into society and allow word of your return to blow in. Now come with me. And heed that it is *not* a suggestion."

"Given you graciously insist." Nathaniel followed the man

down the corridor toward another section of a very impressive house that led into what appeared to be a study.

The duke pointed to a leather chair. "Sit."

"No."

The duke shifted from boot to boot in what appeared to be agitation. "Might I at least inquire where you are staying?"

"Limmer's."

The duke blanched. "Oh, no. No, no, no. I wouldn't even send the French militia there for a night. No family of mine is going to be living like a pauper. I have plenty of rooms. I will have a footman collect your belongings within the hour."

Nathaniel leaned toward him. "Just because we are bound through my sister's memory doesn't mean we are also bound to live in the same goddamn house. Don't insist on something that isn't going to happen or you and I won't be getting along. Wherever I do live, it will be paid for by me for me. Is that understood?"

The duke eyed him and eventually shook his head. "Pride runs a bit too strong in this family. You and I will revisit this another time. Agreed?"

"Revisit all you like. It's not going to change a thing. Now what else did you fucking want?"

The duke pointed a curt finger at his mouth. "Enough with the tongue. Show your family the respect it deserves. Would you have spoken to your sister like that?"

Nathaniel tightened his jaw, knowing the duke was right. "No, Your Grace. Forgive me."

The duke raked his hands through his hair. "Do you still have her diary?"

"Of course I do. What a thing to ask."

"Have you read it?"

"No. I haven't."

The duke dropped his hands and stared. "Almost a year has passed since you approached us back in New York and we have not heard so much as a word as to whether you would even be coming. And now this? They are her words, damn you. Words she had breathed life into, and half of them were dedicated to you. If you cannot find the strength to read them, you are unworthy of ever knowing them and I demand you give it back. I don't know what she ever meant to you, but I do know what she meant to me."

Nathaniel swallowed. It was with awe he had the honor to witness how his sister had touched this man's life. She had found something he never thought possible. Real love. "I'm not ready to read it quite yet. It's been difficult enough for me to face knowing I missed any opportunity of seeing her again. You have had years to adjust to her death, whilst I have barely had a year. So let me keep it." *Let me keep it until I no longer have a need for it.*

The duke huffed out an exasperated breath and pointed to the leather chair again. "Sit. And whatever you do, don't wander about dressed as you are. I didn't invite people here tonight to meet a disheveled phantom everyone thinks is dead. There are ways to go about this. Now stay here. I need to find Yardley. He up and disappeared on me. *Again.*"

"I'm not in the mood for a family gathering."

"It's important he see you." The duke grabbed his arm. "He suffered a very serious accident back in New York, not long after that night you came to us at the hotel. He was hit by an omni and his mind was rendered entirely blank. Though he has regained most of his memory, he hasn't been the same since."

Rendered his mind blank? Nathaniel's brows rose, remembering Matthew telling him about the man Georgia had brought into her tenement back on Orange Street. A man who had lost all memory of who he was. A man who Georgia had followed to London. Georgia. London. And his nephew was in…London. Blood on high. It couldn't be. "Did he go by the name of Robinson, per chance?"

The duke's eyes widened. He released his arm. "Yes. How did you know?"

Nathaniel scrubbed his chin with the back of his hand in disbelief. Matthew wasn't going to believe this but apparently Georgia, that freckled street rat who only ever gave them both trouble, was set to marry his nephew. "I heard about it back in New York. From yam sellers to the boys alike. Is he all right?"

"He has long since regained most of his memory, but for some reason, much of his trip to New York—anything before the accident—doesn't exist. He doesn't remember meeting you."

"Christ." It would seem everyone's mind was unstable these days. Knowing he might as well get to the point, he muttered, "I should probably admit that I've actually been in town for some time."

"What do you mean? Why haven't you—"

"Because I needed time to wade through this mess on my own whilst I also earned some money. At first, I was intent on leaving London and going straight to Venice to retrieve the man who held me hostage to prove my claim. I decided against it, however, because in doing so, it would have created another set of ungodly complications for you, Yardley and my mother. So I decided to approach my father on my own and take it from there. And I did. Yesterday. As expected, it didn't go well. He denies everything, and with him denying who I am, and there being no painted likeness of me in existence, I can't readily prove to anyone I'm really Atwood, can I?"

The duke set a fisted hand against his mouth. After a long moment, his hand fell away. "But I can prove it. And I will. First, I need to find Yardley. You two can talk whilst I run about and tend to guests before people commence wondering what is going on. Stay here." The duke stepped out, sliding the study doors closed behind himself.

Nathaniel sighed and scanned the study lined from floor to ceiling with shelves of old, leather-bound books. He stilled, his gaze falling on the only painting to grace the room. He made his way toward it and lingered before it in a half daze, completely submerged in disbelief.

He stared up at a pretty, dark-haired woman whose gloved hand was propped against a tree just beyond a rose garden. She was dressed in a flowing pink gown, which barely allowed the tips of her white slippers to peer out.

Though the woman didn't smile, those large grey eyes stared out at him with a strong, shining presence that choked him into remembering the only person who had ever mattered. His sister. His mother had been far too occupied in trying to convince his father she was worthy of his love.

He remembered a girl of sixteen. Not…not this. He fisted both hands. So many years erased. And he would never get them back. All he had left of Auggie now was a crypt. A crypt he had yet to visit and doubted he would ever be able to visit, given he hadn't even been able to read her diary.

His father had taken everything away from him. Everything.

And for it, he would die. Tonight.

The doors of the study slid open, announcing someone

had entered the room. The doors slid closed again and the floorboards creaked.

Nathaniel sensed someone lingering behind him.

"No portrait did her justice," a male voice humbly offered.

Nathaniel turned and faced his nephew.

The yellowing glow of the study's candles illuminated a shaven, lean face and grey eyes.

Nathaniel gripped the hilt of a dagger that was attached to the leather belt on his hip, wishing he had been part of this family Auggie had created for herself.

"I'm your nephew." Yardley eyed the dagger. "Yardley."

"I know who you are. We met. Back in New York."

Yardley hesitated, then blurted, "Forgive me for not being able to remember. I had an incident that—"

"I know. You needn't worry. I'm not all that memorable, anyway." *And I'll be dead for what I plan to do.* "Allow me to get to the point of my visit tonight, nephew of mine. One I have yet to convey to your father. After a less than constructive meeting with my father yesterday morning, who refused to let my mother see me, I have decided to kill him. Tonight, actually. After he leaves this house and heads into his carriage. And I intend to have all of London witness it. Why am I telling you this? Because when you are brought before the jury, I don't want there to be any doubt as to what my motives were. Tell them it wasn't revenge but a savage need for peace."

Yardley stared, his features tightening. "Don't do this. Killing him will only see you hanged."

"Exactly. Peace."

His nephew edged toward him. "Killing him and then getting yourself hanged will change *nothing*."

Nathaniel flexed his leather gloved hands. "I know."

"Uncle. If you do this, you will not only destroy yourself, but you will ruin my father, and me, as well. You'll also be destroying the wife I hope to take and the children I hope to have. All we would ever know and hear and see would be the blood you rashly spilled and the mess you leave for us to mop up."

Waking up thinking he was still in a cellar was the real mess Nathaniel had to live with for the rest of his days. He pointed to his own head. "I am *not* going to live inside this head a breath more."

"No one understands you more than I. Believe me. Living within a head you would rather step out of is a curse of the worst sort, but there are ways to allay the misery. But not like this. You will find it through the support and love of your family."

As if his father knew spit about support or love. "The Sumners are not my family."

"Right you are in that. The Sumners are not. But we are. I am. My father is. My father loves you, given all that you represent. He loves you enough to unearth his own wife's remains, which I know will kill him, considering what she meant to him. Despite that, you mean to dirk him? You mean to dirk the last person who remains standing in your corner in order to entertain some morbid urge for revenge?"

Nathaniel's heart pounded in disbelief. "He means to disturb my sister's grave? I won't have it."

"'Tis the only means we have of proving your legitimacy. My father told me about my grandfather denying your legitimacy, but *this* would prove it. 'Tis the only known portrait of you in existence with a label of your name and it lies buried with my mother."

Nathaniel closed his eyes, feeling the world sway. "She was buried with my portrait?"

"That she was. She carried you upon her lips and within her heart until her last breath was taken and spent her entire life wanting to find you. If you don't mean to honor the living, Uncle, I ask that you at least honor the dead. My mother deserved as much."

Nathaniel squeezed his eyes tighter and swung away. Poor Auggie. Poor, poor Auggie had suffered as much as he had. A soul-wrenching clarity descended, almost making him stagger. He was damned either way. Whether his father lived or died, the truth would have to stay buried or it would ruin them all.

He had to be stronger in this. He couldn't submit to revenge and destroy what little remained of his sister's family. He had to protect them and was therefore going to have to settle on crushing his father another way. The only way he knew how. By taking back his name before all of London.

After a long moment of silence, he turned back and unfastened the leather belt from around his hips. He folded the belt around the sheath of his dagger and held it out. "Take it before I use it."

Yardley grabbed hold of the belt and dagger and shook his head. "You need to find peace."

Nathaniel set his shoulders and rounded on him. "I hear death is a nice long sleep. Sounds peaceful enough to me."

Yardley let out a breath. "Take back the life that was so maliciously taken from you and create something worthier. Surround yourself with people who will love you and support you whilst taking your place back in our circle where you belong. That is how you will find and know peace. Give yourself a chance to know it. Consider starting a family and commencing anew."

A gargled laugh escaped him. "Taking an aristo for a wife, who'd never understand the chaos within me, would only beget children whose bedtime stories would involve my nightmares. I don't think so."

Turning toward him, Yardley offered in a sympathetic tone, "You underestimate a woman's worth and her ability to redefine a man. A woman can give you hope in a world that has none. She can fight for you when you have ceased fighting for yourself and everything you believe in."

Nathaniel glanced toward him, rather intrigued. "Smitten, are you?"

"Beyond. You should be so lucky."

Nathaniel smirked. Oh, to be stupid again. And to think that the poor bastard was set to marry Georgia. He refused to believe it. "Distract me. What's her name?" Because he still refused to believe it.

"Her real one? Or the one she is parading under? For I will confess I am about to marry two women for the price of one. She is divine intervention. I have never known anyone or anything so exquisite."

Georgia, Georgia, Georgia. She was going to make a mess out of his nephew's life. He was going to have to do something about that. "I could use a little divine intervention." Nathaniel strode back toward him and leaned in, looking to rattle the boy who knew nothing about him or the fact that he knew Georgia. "Would you be willing to share her with your uncle from time to time? When I'm feeling particularly lonely? Or are you the territorial sort?"

Yardley tossed aside the leather belt and blade with a resounding clatter and stared him down. "Do I look amused?"

Nathaniel snorted and patted his cheek. "Now, now, you aristos are so easily ruffled. I was joking."

"Were you?" Yardley reached out and gripped his shoulder hard, digging the tips of his fingers into the flesh beneath. "Don't cross the only family you have left, Atwood. Don't even *joke* about it."

Nathaniel liked this boy. He was fierce and loyal and honest. Few men were. "You needn't worry, nephew. I only cross those that cross me. And you haven't crossed me...*yet*."

Flinging his nephew's hand away, he walked backward toward the entrance of the study, knowing he had a name to resurrect. And he was going to do it by not only letting everyone know who he was, but by taking the championship so he had money to support his new identity—the aristocratic boxer. "I think I'm going to like London. There are just so many civilized people crawling around my boots looking to lick them clean." Like Weston. "Now if you'll excuse me...I intend to find myself a dance partner and scare the shite out of people."

The duke was going to love this.

Swinging away, Nathaniel slid open the doors with a sweep of his arms and strode down the corridor toward the ballroom. The best revenge without spraying a drop of blood would be to take back his name.

And he was doing it. Now.

CHAPTER NINE

Woman, the fountain of all human frailty!
What mighty ills have not been done by woman?
Who betrayed the Capitol? A woman.
Who lost Mark Antony the world? A woman.
Who was the cause of a long ten year war,
And laid at last Old Troy in ashes? Woman!

—P. Egan, *Boxiana* (1823)

KNOTTING BACK HIS hair with the twine he always kept on his wrist, Nathaniel adjusted his great coat and entered the massive expanse of the ballroom. Gold-and-ivory-accented walls and vast, sweeping ceilings trimmed with carvings loomed before him with a splendor he hadn't known in ages.

He scanned bodies of satin, silk and lace weaving about before him and strode past an assembled group of older gentlemen with crystal flutes in their white-gloved hands. Their grey bushy brows rose in unison as they lowered champagne glasses and scanned his appearance.

Though he wanted to punch those round faces in, one by one, like tankards off a bar, based on their expressions alone, Nathaniel opted to coolly incline his head, instead. He had a name to resurrect and maiming old people of nobility was *not* the way to go about doing it. "The name is Atwood, gentlemen. Lord Atwood. How are you?"

They gaped.

"Lord Atwood?" one of the men asked in a startled tone. "Such blasphemy. Lord Sumner's son is dead."

Nathaniel leaned in to the old man, his voice turning to steel. "And how do you know that? Did you attend my funeral? Was there ever one?"

All four gentlemen continued to gape.

Still staring them down, Nathaniel added, "Rumor has it I'm very much alive." With that, he strode past them and into the masses, leaving them to come to their own conclusion.

As Nathaniel moved deeper into the crowd countless men and women whisked forward and back across the dance floor beyond, advertising extravagant coifs and lavish ensembles drenched with emeralds and diamonds and rubies.

The boys back in New York would have coughed their brains out in an effort to rip off jewels from so many female necks.

Setting mud-stained leather-gloved hands behind his back, he glanced toward the nearest wall. Overly coiffed young women and their terse chaperones pressed themselves and their full gowns against the wall upon seeing him, their ostrich fans stilling against both chins and bosoms.

Their astounded rouged faces reminded him of the Venetian carnival masks Casacalenda would wear to entertain him in the cellar by recreating Italian theatrical parodies for him whenever he got bored.

The world was full of loons.

His worn leather boots thudded to a halt at seeing his father barely a few feet away.

The earl startled at glimpsing him.

Flexing his hands, Nathaniel taunted the earl with his presence by drawing closer. One of them would eventually break. And it wasn't going to be Nathaniel.

A man who had been conversing with his father stared and quickly approached Nathaniel. "Sir?" The gentleman hesitated, glanced up and cleared his throat awkwardly, as if just realizing he stood a whole head shorter. He swept a snowy-white gloved hand toward the entrance of the ballroom behind them. "If you please."

What a prick. Who ever knew rudeness could be delivered with such austere refinement? Nathaniel widened his stance. "Are you telling me to leave?"

The man eyed him. "Yes, sir. I am."

"Well, I won't. I'm a guest."

"A guest?" the man echoed. "Sir, you are clearly—"

"I am clearly *Lord* Atwood. And our host is none other than my brother-in-law. So lick it."

The man blinked.

Another gent quickly approached.

And then another.

Three aristocratic men now stared him down.

No matter where he went, no matter which part of the world he was in, people always wanted to fight him. "I take it you boys enjoy pain, to be coming up to me this way?"

Pale yellow skirts assembled indecently close to him. A familiar, delicate waft of lilies poked at his nose as a pretty female face inquisitively leaned in to look up at him, thick blond curls swaying against her gathered coif.

He turned abruptly to the woman peering in on him and froze, clamping his mouth shut in disbelief.

Arched brows and large hazel eyes that had mesmerized

him all but a night ago, stared up at him in equal astonishment.

It was Imogene. And by God, did she look incredible.

Her pale throat dripped with emeralds and the delicate white lace neckline of her silk evening gown was low enough for him to see that provocative and decadent plunge between her powdered breasts. He remembered those. When she had been all wet. Damn. She made his imagination trot wild with images of taming her. On the floor. Against a wall. On a field. In a lake. It didn't matter, so long as she was bound and at his mercy.

Her smooth face faintly tinged with a hint of pink. She lowered her voice as if she were afraid the world might hear. "I thought it was you. What are you doing here?"

He removed his mud-stained gloves, feeling suddenly aware that they were far too dirty to be in the presence of such a beautiful woman. When they were off, he offered matter-of-factly, "I'm socializing with a few friends. And you?"

She pulled in her chin and glanced toward the four men. She lowered her voice again. "They don't look happy to see you."

"Welcome to my life. No one ever is. I'm used to it." Shoving his gloves into his great coat, he heatedly perused her gown and the way it clung to her luscious figure. "You look incredible," he confided. "It makes me wish we were alone again. Only this time, I'd personally see to it something actually happened."

Her eyes widened. She edged away and glanced toward several aristocratic women who leaned toward each other, whispering.

He'd forgotten the rules these aristos played by. Men weren't supposed to be honest in public.

"Sir!" The same huffy brunette he'd briefly met at Weston's house lunged between him and Imogene, wagging her peacock fan up at his face as if it were a stiletto. "You aren't even appropriately dressed to be acknowledging her. Now leave before I have every man in this room carry you out and deposit you into the rubbish bin where you belong."

Knowing this stiff fluff was Weston's wife, Nathaniel bit down on his tongue to keep himself from saying something he'd regret. He usually didn't give a damn for what others thought or said. He'd been through far too much to care, but knowing Imogene was quietly watching and judging this and him made him want to put a fist through every wall in the room. She probably now saw what everyone else did: absolutely nothing.

Nathaniel shoved his way through those who had gathered and stalked through blurring faces. If he took the championship and the money, he would be more than nothing. He would be his own man again. He would be—

"Nathaniel!" a female voice suddenly called out, skirts bustling after him.

He swung around in jarred astonishment. Imogene remembered his name.

Gasping whispers of *"Who is he?"* frilled the stuffy room, edging through the music still playing.

Imogene hurried through the crowds toward him, her pale yellow skirts a-swaying from side to side. She alighted before him, grabbed up a card and a pencil hanging by a velvet string around her gloved wrist and breathlessly announced, "The waltz is set to begin." She glanced up, her cheeks flushed and her bright, hazel eyes genuine. "Shall I write your name in for it?"

He couldn't help but be savagely pleased, knowing she

saw more than a patched coat and unbrushed hair. She saw him for what he was: a man.

Knowing Lady Weston would be bustling her way through the crowds after her at any moment, he lifted a brow. "I take it you're out to hang yourself this fine evening?"

"Are you? Coming in here dressed like that?" She glanced around and said in a bargaining tone, "I can show you what clothes to wear and how to conduct yourself in public. For you clearly need advice. Have tea with me. As my dear mama used to say, anyone who can learn to hold a teacup properly can learn to do anything properly."

He snorted. "I'm not looking to be *that* popular." Although he was rather impressed by her boldness to engage him before all of London, he knew he had to save her from her own stupidity. "Here is a bit of advice—I'm the sort of man who will not only ruin your reputation but your life."

She was quiet for a moment. "I wouldn't go as far as to say you would ruin my life."

Something was wrong with her. He almost tapped her on the forehead. "I'm trying to save your pretty ass from getting spanked."

Her brow creased. "You shouldn't use words like that. Or tea is out of the question."

He rolled his eyes. "Unless tea involves you fully naked with your arms tied behind your back, I'm not interested."

She gasped. "No waltz for you, either."

"Good. It's not like I ever learned how to dance. Now are we done with all these etiquette lessons? Or do you plan on teaching me how to play the harp, too?"

She shook her head and stepped back and back. "You aren't the same man I met two nights ago. He respected me. Whilst you clearly don't."

His throat tightened, seeing the betrayal in her eyes. Why was he playing his defenses against this woman? And what was it about her that made him want to kneel every single time? "No one was watching us that night. Here, we have a full audience. I am trying to dissuade you from being seen with me. Now go." He stepped back and turned away, trying to veer around a staring couple.

Imogene jumped toward him and grabbed his arm the same way she had that night, which startled him into realizing just how much he wanted to be touched by her.

He froze and glanced down at her. "What are you doing?"

She angled him toward herself, then held the pencil against the blank space of her dancing card. "I misunderstood your intentions. For which I apologize. I am genuinely touched by your attempt to protect my reputation. But I don't need protection, given I have no interest in taking a husband. That said...I would be more than happy to lead, seeing you don't dance. Shall I write you in?"

Every muscle in his body felt ablaze, fully aware of not only her but that everyone was watching them. "Why are you doing this?"

She fingered her dance card, but wouldn't meet his gaze. "Because something tells me you would do the same for me if you saw people banding around me and trying to push me out the door." She glanced up. "Or wouldn't you?"

God. How he wanted to grab that beautiful face, lean down and tongue the breath out of her for what she just said. "For you, I would. Yes."

She half smiled. "I told you men and women could be friends." She leaned in. "Now. Play the game I always do when there are too many people around and the panic sets in. They are but birds on the trees and their words are but whistles that matter only to the wind."

She couldn't be real. Because her way of thinking certainly wasn't. "Do we have to dodge their droppings, too?"

She grinned, both cheeks dimpling. "I do it all the time."

He sighed, sensing that saying no to her would be like saying no to the moon and the stars. "You've already damned yourself, so we might as well finish this. Go ahead. Write me in for that waltz. Hopefully your brother won't slap me with a duel for accepting."

"My brother is too much of a gentleman for that. Though he is not above yelling." She sidled closer and adjusted her dance card, propping it against her gloved hand. "You never gave me your full name. What shall I write down?"

"The name is Atwood. A-T-W-O-O-D with a Lord in front of it."

She glanced up and burst into laughter before clapping a hand over her mouth, looking more startled than he.

It was obvious she was laughing *at* him. "What?"

She lowered her voice. "You were being funny."

"No. I was giving you my name. Why is that funny?"

"Your name? You mean you're a peer of the realm?"

"Yes. As a matter of fact, I am."

"But I thought—" She stilled, arresting her merriment and glanced toward Lady Weston, who came to a rigid halt beside them after she had finally made it through the crowds.

"Lady Imogene," the woman said in a lethal, boarding-school tone. "You wouldn't entertain Lord Seton or Lord Danford or any of the respectable men in the room who graced you with their presence tonight, and yet you dare entertain this—this—" She stopped trying to find a word.

"We are going home. And you will explain your monstrous behavior to your brother. Is that understood?"

Imogene bit her lip, then primly lowered her gaze back to her dance card and scribed his name in the empty space as if she were signing the United States Constitution. "I wrote you in for the waltz, Lord Atwood. Though I'm afraid it will involve quite a bit of physical contact. I hope you don't mind."

A gruff laugh escaped him. He could learn to like this one. A lot. "I don't mind physical contact. I'm a boxer."

Lady Weston narrowed her gaze and grabbed Imogene's arm, hurrying them past.

Nathaniel could tell by the way Imogene had winced the woman had grabbed her a bit too savagely.

He sidestepped in front of Weston's wife, bumping the woman hard with his own frame. "Let her go."

The woman's startled dark eyes flicked up from his chest to his face, her face flushing.

Gently taking Imogene's arm, he drew her back toward himself, prying her free. "Don't *ever* touch her like that again. Now step the hell away."

The woman scrambled back.

"Atwood!" The Duke of Wentworth skidded in beside them, eyes wide and frantic. "I asked you to stay out of sight. *This isn't out of sight!*"

"Not to rile you, Your Grace," Nathaniel casually explained, "but I owe this here lady a dance. Now excuse us."

Taking the soft warmth of Imogene's gloved hand, he protectively led her toward the direction of the crowded dance floor. "You said you'd lead. It's not common that I allow someone else to be in control, but in this case I'm holding you to that. Because I have no idea what I'm getting myself into."

Imogene glanced up at him. "I do believe my sister-in-law and His Grace are as speechless as I am."

"Just don't make me look stupid. What am I supposed to do?"

"Oh...well...first, we position ourselves. Stand right here."

He halted. "Here?"

"Yes. Only turn to me. Full shoulders."

He did. Full shoulders.

As she turned to face him, that delicate scent of lilies sensually teased his nostrils again, making him not only pause but breathe in. Everything about her made him want to breathe in. Deep.

Lowering his gaze to hers, a rush of pride punched him knowing *this* woman wanted to dance with *him*. Before all of London and whilst his father watched. It was like touching honor wrapped with silk.

Other couples hurried past them with ruffled looks and left the floor.

It was amusing. All of this was, actually.

Imogene daintily took his hands, arranging one on her corseted waist and gripping the other with one of hers, then sweeping their clutched hands out to the side and into the air.

He tightened his hold on that delicate hand.

Setting her free hand on his shoulder, she primly brought the heat of her body closer to his own. "There. Now wait for the music to commence."

Fully aware that her full skirts were brushing up against his boots, trousers and thighs, and that her breasts were tucked right there before him, he dug his fingers into the smooth, soft silk of her gown. It was like sex. With clothes on. He hissed out a breath. "Are we supposed to be this close?"

Without meeting his gaze, she shyly offered, "Why else

do you think I wrote you in for the waltz? If I am going to suffer a scandal, I might as well make it worth our time."

He crushed her fingers against his hand and refrained from leaning in and licking her mouth with the tip of his tongue. "Careful. I'm beginning to think you like me in the clothes-off sort of way."

A flush overtook her smooth cheeks.

He slowly grinned. "You blush so easily."

"I'm not blushing."

"You most certainly are."

The music commenced.

"To the left," she announced in a harried tone, whisking them both across the waxed floor. She set her chin and held a rigid stance. "Follow my boxed steps, then turn and do it again. Can you keep up?"

"Watch me." Though he missed a few steps and even skidded, somehow he managed not only to keep up, but ensure his boots didn't rip her gown off. He was, after all, a boxer who understood footwork. One had not only to move fast, but learn fast. "We're too close to make this look pretty. You do realize that, yes?"

As they swept across the dance floor she eyed him and offered, "Are you not enjoying yourself?"

"You're letting me touch you. What is not to enjoy?"

In between steps and turns, her hand tightened on his shoulder and hand, making him all the more aware of not only her touch, but just how much he wanted to rip her clothes off. It had been far too long since he had allowed himself to play this game. Far too long.

After a turn and another, she asked, "Are you really a peer of the realm?"

"Yes."

"And how is it I never heard of you before and that you are parading as a boxer by the name of Coleman?"

He avoided her gaze and focused on steps. "It's a lot more involved than I care to admit."

"But you are, in fact, a boxer?"

"Yes."

"An incredibly good one?"

"I like to think so."

"One capable of winning the title of champion if given the chance?"

"If I answer that, I may come across conceited."

She tightened her hold on his hand and his shoulder. "Henry mentioned that you are known for skipping out on investors. Is that true?"

"I'm not one for commitment. No matter what it is."

"That seems to be the dilemma." Her face betrayed a sudden seriousness as she seemed to think something through. "But you and I will resolve that."

He couldn't help but smirk. "I prefer keeping things unresolved."

Her steps suddenly faltered. She swayed against him and staggered. "I…I must take leave of the floor." She leaned heavily into him, drawing him to a halt with both hands. "Before I faint."

Faint? Oh, Christ, no. Not that again. Jerking her tightly by the waist against his side to ensure she didn't tip, he quickly escorted them off the floor, ignoring all of the blurring faces.

He glanced around. There were no chairs. Nothing but walls and people standing in a crush. Hell. "Lean against the wall. Until it passes." Ushering her to the nearest wall, he gently draped her against it. Removing her fan from her gloved wrist, he scrambled to open it. "I'll ensure you get some air. Just breathe." For some reason, the damn thing wouldn't unlatch. He tugged on it harder.

Her hand jumped out, stilling his hands.

He glanced up.

"Not like that," she murmured, lowering her gaze to the fan. Her gloved fingers effortlessly unlatched the peg at the end, freeing the fan into unfolding. "There."

It was obvious he wasn't used to dealing with female aristos and their little fans. Angling toward her, Nathaniel waved it at her flushed face and throat, trying to ignore the fact that half of London was watching him play servant. "Whatever you do, tea cake, don't faint on me. Because I already look ridiculous enough fanning you."

She leaned back her head, momentarily closing her eyes, and smiled. "I doubt you're worried about looking ridiculous," she murmured. She paused and added, "I feel better. It passed."

Thank God. "I'm glad to hear it." His fanning slowed with each wave as he found himself staring at that incredibly seductive pose she held against the wall. Her head was tilted far back, throat fully exposed, her blond curls grazing those flushed cheeks. It was like she was waiting to be stripped.

He paused, realizing he had stopped fanning. "Did you need me to keep fanning?"

She shook her head and reopened her eyes. "No. Thank you." Leaning toward him, she took the fan. "I appreciate you tending to me." She scanned a few passing individuals who were trying to listen in on their conversation. "Will you take tea with me this Thursday? At four. So we can talk in the privacy we deserve?"

He stared. Privacy? "What do you want to talk about?"

"'Tis a very personal matter that would involve commitment on both our parts."

Was she was trying to get them married? Already? Shit. This is what happened when a man started publicly fanning a woman. "Uh…just so you know, I'm not looking to get married again."

Her startled gaze met his. *"Again?"*

"Long story. She died. And I'm not keen on playing that role ever again."

Pushing away from the wall, she straightened and brought both hands together. "How sad. I'm very sorry to hear it." She hesitated, those large hazel eyes intently searching his face. "She was incredibly fortunate to have you as a husband. You are endearingly protective and attentive toward the needs of a woman."

Jesus Christ. This—*she*—was beginning to be a problem. She seemed to think he was a nice man. Oh, he had glimmers of being nice, yes, but not nearly enough to do a woman like her justice. He cleared his throat. "Uh…how are you feeling?"

She smiled. "Better. Thank you."

"Good. I'm glad to hear it." Glancing toward Weston's wife, who was lingering a few feet away, he turned and wagged a finger toward the woman. "You. Lady Huff. Come here. Given she almost fainted, I want you to take her out of this heat. Take her home."

Lady Weston momentarily froze but quickly hurried forward upon command. Rounding him, she sidled toward Imogene and took her arm.

Imogene stared. "Will you call on me? So we can talk?"

Edging away, Nathaniel met her gaze. This was quite the dilemma. But he knew what needed to be said. He instinctively softened his tone. He didn't even know why. Looking at her made him do that. "You are too good of a girl to be having tea with me. Remember that when I don't call. Good night." Turning, he quickly strode toward the direction he knew was the front door.

He could sense she was watching him walk away.

And his chest tightened knowing it.

Turning into the vast quiet corridor that had been cleared of all footmen, he chanted to himself not to look back to see if she was still watching him. Because if he did, he knew he'd yank her up off that floor and carry her back to Limmer's and show her everything she needed to know about him as a man. From the scars on his hands, to the ones on his arms and shoulders and chest, to the way he preferred taking a woman: *bound.*

The unexpected rustling of skirts and steps made him glance toward the staircase. His eyes widened as none other than Georgia Emily Milton, Irish washerwoman from the Five Points, flounced her way down the large staircase, her pinned strawberry curls bouncing along with the rest of her.

What the—

Gone were the dragging, calico skirts and apron. They had been replaced by an elegant off-the-shoulder evening gown and teardrop diamonds that tauntingly hung from her ears and throat, gleaming and shimmering against the vast candlelight.

He'd actually seen her at Rotten Row—the day Matthew had met his lady of the moment, but he still couldn't believe it. The woman who thought herself better than him and the entire sixth ward in New York City and had a tongue the size of Manhattan to match, had managed to squeeze into a world where she didn't belong.

And the woman actually looked half-decent.

She jerked to a halt on the last step upon seeing him. Her green eyes widened. *"Coleman?"* She glanced around frantically to ensure they were alone. "What under heaven and above hell are you doing here? Robbing the guests?"

He snorted. She would think that of him, of course. Georgia's animosity toward him, Matthew and the rest of the Forty Thieves was no secret. "It's good to see you, too, freckle face."

"How did you know I was here?" She lowered her voice. "Did you and Matthew follow me and Lady Burton out of the park when we crossed paths all too coincidentally?"

"Don't flatter yourself."

She glanced around again. "Where is Matthew anyway?"

"Hell if I know. But if I had to guess, he is probably with your lady friend. That woman is all he ever talks about." He paused in response to the glint of her diamonds and let out a low whistle. He pointed at the necklace draping her throat, wondering how much it was worth. Probably a good hundred. If not more. "That looks expensive."

She eyed him. "It is."

Matthew desperately needed money. And so did Nathaniel. Not that he was about to ask the woman if she had money to spare. He cleared his throat. "It was good seeing you. So to speak."

She kept eyeing him. "Do you and Matthew need money? Be honest."

A part of him wanted to say yes but he was too proud to submit to that. "I have to go." He turned but Georgia caught him by the back of his coat.

"Coleman." Her voice hardened.

He grudgingly turned. "What?"

She released her hold. "I left Matthew a rather sizable

amount of money when I took off to become a respectable lady. What did he do with it?"

Nathaniel tried not to feel awkward. "What he always does whenever he gets money. He gave it away. The sixth ward orphanage got most of it."

She sighed not once but twice. "Him and his mercy plights." Lifting her hands to the back of her neck, she unclasped the diamonds and grudgingly held them out. "Here. Pawn it. And tell Matthew to lay off stealing any more horses. This isn't New York."

Nathaniel shook his head. "No. I can't take it."

She rolled her eyes. "Forget about your pride and think of Matthew. I don't want him getting into more trouble."

Matthew sure as hell did need it. And it would keep him out of trouble. Nathaniel half nodded and carefully took the diamonds, tucking them into his coat pocket. He cleared his throat and managed, "I will pay you back when I can."

"Don't bother. I have plenty more." She watched him. "Dare I ask why you're even here?"

He shrugged. "I was visiting."

"With who?"

"With my so-called father, the duke and your Yardley."

She stared. "Your father?"

"It's complicated." Knowing she was going to love his response, he smirked. "It looks like you and I are going to be family, freckle face."

She kept staring. "How so?"

"Didn't you know? Yardley is my nephew."

She gasped and scrambled back. "He is?"

"Try not to faint on me. I'll be fine with it if you're fine with it." He pointed. "Tell the duke I'm taking off to invest in my boxing career, but that I'll be in touch. All right?"

She glanced toward the corridor one last time to ensure they were still alone and quickly said, "I'll be sure to tell him."

"I appreciate it."

"Is everything as it should be with you?" She sounded concerned.

He shrugged. "Nothing ever is as it should be. I'm used to it." He patted his pocket. "Thanks for the diamonds. Matthew really needs money to get to New York." Nathaniel edged back, oddly touched by Georgia's concern for not only Matthew but himself. It would seem this new role of playing a lady suited Georgia. It had...softened her. Imagine that.

CHAPTER TEN

At length, grown desperate, he broke several panes, and, inserting his head through the fracture, bore down all opposition by the following witticism: 'Gentlemen, I have taken some *panes* to gain admission, pray let me in, for I see *through* my error.'

—P. Egan, *Boxiana* (1823)

Later that night
The Weston House

"WHAT THE DEVIL were you thinking?" her brother roared through the flapping towel still hanging over his head, which covered not only his face but the expanse of his robed shoulders. He swung a rigid fist down against the bed he was confined to. "Aside from your ailing health, have you no goddamn respect for your reputation?"

Awkwardly lingering beside the bed, Imogene eventually offered, "'Tis very difficult for me to take you seriously when all I see is a flapping towel. I suggest you take it off."

"I am *not* letting you see my face. And you are *not* changing the subject. Respectable women *don't* associate with

nameless men, much less boxers. Whether you are investing money in him or not!"

She sat on the edge of his bed, trying to pretend she was
more occupied with arranging her gown than listening to
him. "If it makes you feel any better, he isn't all that nameless. His name is actually Atwood. *Lord* Atwood."

"What? Gene. He is *not* a peer of the realm."

"Oh, yes he is. He not only told me so, but—"

"Forget whatever lies the man smothered your poor brain
with. Have you seen him? His hair is reminiscent of 1772 and
his clothing appears to have been worn for equally as long.
He has no money—*none*—and is staying at Limmer's with
a one-eyed man who carries two pistols and a razor because
one pistol doesn't appear to be enough. Where do you see
nobility *or* civility sitting with all this? *Where?*"

She glared. "There is no need to insult him *or* his friends."

"I refuse to believe you are actually defending him. Him!
Did he put you up to this? Is he threatening you to say these
things? Gene. Talk to me. Remember what happened when
you let Mrs. Fink convince you she would burn down the
house if you told anyone about the way she was treating you?
You almost died. Did you learn nothing from that?"

She narrowed her gaze at the towel. "Don't you dare com-
pare him to Mrs. Fink. That woman was a monster. And this
man is anything but. I like him."

"Like him?" he echoed. "What is there to like beyond his
two fists? Men at the coves are scared out of their wits to even
ask him how to spar and you just walked up to him and…?"

She couldn't help but smile. "Despite his gruff nature, he
is incredibly protective of me. You should have seen the verbal lashing he gave your wife tonight before all of London.
You would have enjoyed it."

"I'm not that vindictive," he grouched through the towel. "Thanks to you, however, Mary has started asking all sorts of questions."

"About what?"

"About him. About you. About what our interest seems to be. What am I supposed to tell her? That I'm using your inheritance to invest in a boxer for a chance at a divorce?"

She winced. "I'm sorry. I wasn't trying to—"

"Setting all that aside, I'm concerned not only for your reputation but for you. How involved are you with the man, given the dance you gave him? Be honest."

She heaved out an exasperated breath. "Not as involved as I would like to be."

"What does that mean?"

"I invited him to tea to discuss certain ideas I have about investing in him and he refused."

"Tea?" He snorted. "Men like him aren't porcelain dolls you can set in a chair and talk to about sunlight. Men like him need cages."

She shoved at his knee. "If you had permitted me to associate with more men throughout the years, maybe I wouldn't be so naive. Because clearly, real men are nothing like you."

"I'm not about to deign that with a— Gene. Listen to me. Regardless of whether we invest in him or not, you cannot publicly fawn over him and—and…dance with him. You can't."

She clamped her hands together. "Giving him that dance was the right thing to do. I gave him back the dignity everyone else in that ballroom sought to rip away. You should have seen how they treated him. And how your wife treated him. It was unforgivable. You think she treats you abominably? She treated him the same."

Henry was quiet.

Imogene traced a finger across the thigh of her silk gown, still mesmerized by the image of those ice-blue eyes and that rugged face that had clearly seen so much of the world. Unlike her. If there was a future, she saw it in those haunting eyes that sought to seize the world as much as she did.

She couldn't explain it, but a part of her *knew* he had the fire to become a boxing champion. Of course…if he was known for running out on investors, which the man himself had admitted to, there was only one way to go about securing their investment. She'd realized it as they'd danced together. Now she simply had to convince him of it. And convince Henry, as well.

She sighed. "I think the best way to ensure our investment doesn't flit out on us, is for him and I to wed. I don't mind. And once he wins the championship, he and I can annul the marriage and go our separate ways."

Henry rigidly sat up, the towel shifting on his head. "*Good God!* Have you lost the last of your rational mind? What are you— You barely know him!"

She set a hand onto his knee, trying to calm him. "Unless I marry him, Henry, I won't be allowed to associate with him. And how am I to invest ten thousand pounds into a man I'm not allowed to even associate with? Especially a man known to skip out on investors? If we are to play patron, we do this right. He needs more than our money if we are to ensure his success. He needs guidance through the ditches of a society you and I know all too well."

He paused. "You intend to marry him for the sake of this investment?"

She rolled her eyes. "People marry for the sake of investments all the time. How is this different?" Imogene tapped at his knee. "Here are the terms. We give him a full seven thousand he gets to pocket for himself. I cover all of his training costs and living expenses out of whatever money I have left, and in return, he has to marry me under the proviso that I control his boxing career, like any patron would, and that when he wins the championship, we split all profits in half and go our separate ways. That will guarantee he doesn't stray until we get our money."

"Gene," he rasped, leaning toward her, sending the towel swaying around his face. "For God's sake. I can't imagine handing you over to a man like that. I can't. Not even for half a breath, let alone four months."

She sighed. "You have no choice. I need a guarantee and you owe me a boxer."

"I don't owe you— Jesus Christ. You're beginning to sound bloody deranged!"

"Cease yelling at me."

"I have every right to damn well be yelling, given what appears to be stupidity overtaking all rational thought!"

She narrowed her gaze. "I'm asking you to cease behaving like some...some...asshole."

He froze. "Where the devil did you hear that word?"

She probably shouldn't confide that she heard it from Nathaniel and had asked one of the footmen what it meant. "It doesn't matter. I'm more than old enough to use it. I'm not a child anymore, Henry. I have a right to make decisions on not only what words I use but how I invest my money."

He leaned toward her, bringing the towel closer to her face. So close she could feel the heat from his skin beneath. "You mean to actually marry this man and subject yourself to his advances? Advances he would have every right to make if he were legally your husband? For what? A measly quarter of a million pounds?"

She lifted a brow. "Advances aside, since when did a quarter of a million pounds become measly?"

He leaned back. "I feel ill."

"Henry. I understand your concerns. But I can assure you, there is far more to the man then even he lets on."

He paused. "What do you mean?"

She sighed. "According to gossip tonight, and there was quite a bit of it after he walked out, our pugilist went about the room claiming to be the son of Lord Sumner. He even introduced himself to me as such. I didn't know much about the name, but from what your wife huffed on and on about in the carriage on the way over, he couldn't be who he says he is. According to London gossip, Lord Sumner's lone heir disappeared as a child whilst the Sumners were in New York City—*kidnapped by American loyalists, mind you*—and the boy was never seen again. Not even a body was found. That was back in 1800. Which got me wondering. Given no body was ever found, 'tis possible it's because that body is still walking around. Did you know that prior to any of this coming out, our pugilist told me he came from New York? The same New York where the boy disappeared? He also claimed to have been born in Surrey. And according to your well-informed wife, Surrey is where the Sumner family held their country estate before they sold it in 1820. I asked. *Highly* coincidental."

"You and your imaginings. It isn't all that difficult to masquerade as a person who was never found."

"I disagree. I think he really is this heir. There is a genuine conviction he exudes that I cannot deny. Regardless of whether he is or isn't this heir—and I think he is—you will be negotiating all of my terms and getting him to agree to them. So he doesn't run out on us."

"You actually expect me to—" Henry whipped off the towel, exposing a savagely swollen blue-black and blood-crusted nose, eye, mouth and cheek that made him look like he was dead and deranged.

She choked, slapping an astounded hand against her mouth. "Oh, Henry," she choked out through her hand in complete disbelief. "I... Oh. Look at you."

He glared as best he could through a disfigured, swollen, bloodshot eye. "Yes. Look at me, Gene. Look at me. *This* is the world he is coming from. *This* is all the man knows and loves. And you wish to marry him? To secure your so-called bloody investment?"

"He did this to you?" She refused to believe it.

"No. I was paired with another man. Thank bloody God. Or I wouldn't have *any* eyes left in my head!" He leaned closer toward her, which only made Imogene lean back, given the state of his face.

She didn't want to be near it.

He pointed to himself. "I've gotten to know the bastard rather well, talking to him and watching him over at the milling coves almost every night. He knows how to better hit, how to better move and is showing off skills that I'm telling you, I have never seen in a man. I actually saw him take on a fellow weighing thirteen stone, which he knocked over like a pillow without so much as getting touched. He isn't human. Be he of the realm or not, we're talking about a savage you could never rein in for a day, much less four months, which is how long we have until the championship. And you want to bargain with him? Fool that you are, young and daft that you are, *ill* that you are, you think you can sweep him into your life and sweep him back out again? Is that what you think? And what if he doesn't win the championship, Gene? Have you thought about that? What then? You may never be rid of him is what then."

She lowered her hand. "You and I both know he isn't looking for anything permanent. Believe me when I say getting him to stay will be hard. Getting him to leave will be easy. Which is why matrimony is a good idea. To ensure he stays long enough for us to get our money. Do you think you could even get him to agree?"

Snapping up the towel with the flick of his wrist, he arranged it grudgingly back over his head, burying himself in it. "You and your proverbial ideas."

She leaned in close. "Henry. Can you imagine the fame it would bring him if he is in fact this missing heir? Newspapers well across more than London will be writing about it. And if he were to fight for this title of Champion for us, men would come in droves merely to see *'The Missing Heir'* in person. I know if I were a man, I would. For what would a man who has endured so much in his life fight like? I imagine it would be well worth seeing. *And* paying for. Even if he doesn't win the championship, if we make him popular enough, we can earn us all enough money to create an incredible new life for each of us."

Henry shifted, adjusting and readjusting the linens around his frame. "You and your imaginings sometimes surprise the living blazes out of me. Do you know that? Because you're right. The moment these papers pick up the gossip of him being the missing heir *and* a boxer, it would more than make him popular. Men from every level of society would barter to invest in him, be he this heir or not. And we can't have that. Because he is going to take that title, Gene. I have seen more than enough boxers in my lifetime to know it."

He leaned back against his piled pillows and settled into them. "I will look into who he is before the papers get ahold of this. Which will be soon, after the flurry you and he made tonight. People are going to want to know who he is and I have to find out before they do."

"And what if he is this heir?" she pressed.

He sighed. "I really wish I wasn't as desperate as you." He paused. "But I am," he muttered. He sighed again. "Why is it when you say things, they sound rational, even when they aren't?"

"Henry."

"All right, all right. If he turns out to be a peer of the realm, we will make an offer based on whatever terms you set, given you are of age and it is your money."

Imogene sat up excitedly. "Yes. And as his investor and patron," she pointed out, "he will have to do everything I tell him to. *Everything.*"

"That doesn't mean he will abide by the rules, Gene."

"Oh, he will. I know he will. He isn't quite as rough as he lets on. I think he likes me."

"I'm certain he does. Though not in the way you think. The man knows absolutely nothing about women."

Henry was wrong in that. Nathaniel knew a lot more about women than he let on. She felt it the moment he and she had danced, and he held her so boldly and protectively in his muscled arms. She could still feel his large hands intently touching her, his heat and his pulse molding against hers. It was like the music of that waltz had floated into her very veins and wanted to stay there for the rest of her life. Something told her that having faith in Nathaniel was going to reward her. She just had to convince Henry *and* Nathaniel of it.

Henry rubbed an agitated hand against his arm. "The idea of touching greatness overtakes us all at least once in our lifetime. Most of us simply know when it has meandered into insanity. And let me warn you, you just meandered into insanity."

"I'm not investing ten thousand pounds unless I have some sort of a guarantee. And this is the only way to guarantee it. A husband cannot physically or financially elude his wife without legal ramifications. Or am I wrong in assuming that?"

"No. You aren't." He shifted. "I will do my best to ensure this doesn't turn into a mess."

She smiled. "I adore you for always having faith in me." She leaned over and kissed him through the towel.

"Ow!"

She winced and leaned back. "I'm sorry."

He sighed and fell back against the pillows. "God love you, Gene. God love you."

CHAPTER ELEVEN

In concluding this sketch, we cannot omit
stating of our hero that he is intelligent,
communicative and well behaved.

—P. Egan, *Boxiana* (1823)

Later that same night

UPON ARRIVING AT Limmer's with Georgia's diamond necklace in his pocket, which he knew was going to put a big smile
on Matthew's face, Nathaniel was astounded to discover that
the door to Matthew's leased room had been left wide-open.

Odd.

Jogging toward it, Nathaniel gripped the frame of the door
and leaned in. The straw tick appeared untouched, its linen
neatly folded over, smoothed and laid out across the mattress,
as Matthew always prided himself on doing every morning
after rising. It was like the man never even laid his head on
his own bed. The cracked lantern beside the bed was eerily
still lit and the lone crate which had once held all of Matthew's belongings had been emptied.

Something was wrong. Matthew wouldn't have left Limmer's *or* London without telling him.

Shite.

Nathaniel sprinted down the narrow corridor and skidded down the stairs. Grabbing a man rounding the corner, whom he recognized as one of the men who emptied all of the hotel's piss pots, he shook him. "Have you seen Milton? Room 18? You know, the man with the eye patch?"

The man shrugged.

Shoving the man away, Nathaniel darted out into the street. Last he knew, Milton was trying to raise money for them to make up for what little his boxing brought in.

After roaming not only the docks where Milton worked, but what felt like half the city, and still finding nothing, a squeezing sense of panic overtook Nathaniel.

A half hour later, he burst back into Limmer's, wondering if he had overlooked something in the room.

"Coleman!" The head clerk pointed at him with a gnarled finger from the top of the narrow stairwell. "Richard told me you were looking for Milton. I hate to say it, but Scotland Yard up and nabbed him just a few streets from here. The poor soaplock never even saw the pillow. Several constables came by not even an hour ago to collect whatever he had in the crate. Apparently he did something."

Nathaniel choked. "What the hell did he do?"

The clerk shrugged. "That I don't know. If I asked those bastards about the charges every time they nabbed one of my tenants, I'd never get anything done."

Leave it to Matthew to get arrested.

Morning

"HEAVENS ABOVE, ARE you bricked?" the agitated voice of a woman called out to him within the haze of his sleep. "Half my cognac is gone."

Snapping open his eyes, Nathaniel sat up. The decanter

sitting on his thigh slipped from his hand and though he fumbled to catch it, it crashed onto the wooden floor with a shattering that sprayed amber liquid and crystal alike, slathering his boots with cognac. He jumped onto booted feet, kicking away what was left of the decanter, and shook off the liquid. "Son of a bitch." He had fallen asleep.

After running around well into the morning hours trying to help Matthew, he'd ended up having to dart to Matthew's aristo lover, who had damn well kept him waiting for over two hours whilst she "dressed."

Lady Burton tartly stared him down, now dressed from throat to boot in an ominous black gown, looking like death and vengeance. Her black leather gloved hand tightened around a black bonnet that was bundled with a long black lace veil.

Nathaniel lifted a brow and gestured toward her austere attire. "The objective is not to harm the man but to get him out of jail."

She brought her gloved hands before her, a beaded reticule swinging from her wrist. "That is your opinion, not mine."

It was fairly obvious Matthew had already crossed the woman. But then again, she should have assumed that outcome from the start. "Don't play pious with me. You knew full well what you were getting into the moment you handed that boy your fancy little calling card out on Rotten Row."

She set her chin. "That was before he strapped me with a set of leather belts against my will and left me bound for half the night. Merely because I tried to reason with him after he robbed the vault of a former lover of mine."

Milton, Milton, Milton. Old habits died hard, it would seem. "That wasn't very nice of him, was it?"

She puckered her lips, clearly not amused. "Is he even worth saving?"

"Would I have stumbled in here half-asleep and drunk half of your cognac demanding you assist a man I'd rather see hang? Of course he's worth saving. I also can't have these goddamn barristers digging into *my* life and putting this into the papers."

"Your life. I see." She casually placed the bonnet on her head, tossing back the veil from her face and tied the ribbon beneath her chin. "Georgia told me quite a bit about you. She and I are friends, you know."

Leave it to Georgia to talk. "Most of it is probably true. So don't hold it against her *or* me."

"I take it you find yourself amusing." She yanked the black veil over her head, her face disappearing beneath the lace. "How much money do you think it will take to get Matthew out of my life?"

Ouch. Matthew wasn't going to swallow any of this, given how smitten he was with this woman. "You're not going to actually toss the poor bastard merely because he got jealous and raided one of your lover's vaults, are you?"

"Leave, *my lord.* I will oversee Matthew's release on my own. And if he ever comes near me again, tell him I will do more than let Scotland Yard hang him by the throat. I will ensure they hang him by the cock so he never uses it again."

This love affair between her and Matthew was clearly over. He'd probably have to play martyr and ease the blow for the man by convincing Matthew that it wasn't all his fault. At least there was an upside to this. The boys would finally be getting Milton back. Amen.

Days later
On the corner of Maiden Lane

"I'M GLAD SHE was able to get you out. I only wish things could have worked out between you and her." Oddly, given it was Matthew, Nathaniel actually meant it. He knew the man had always wanted a family and children. And before his most recent interaction with Lady Burton, it had appeared she had been as interested in him as he was in her.

Trying not to think of missing the bastard too much, Nathaniel thumped Matthew heartily on the back. "Stay away from doing any more heists. All right?"

"I will. And give back those diamonds to Georgia, will you? The last thing I want is to owe her a diamond necklace."

"It goes back to the woman tomorrow."

"Good." Matthew hesitated. "So what about you? Any news from that investor of yours?"

Nathaniel leaned toward him and bit back a grin. "As a matter of fact, yes. I received a missive from Weston this morning."

Matthew angled his good eye toward him. "And?"

"He wants me to meet him at Jackson's tomorrow afternoon. It's a boxing academy for the nobility and gentry. Rather serious invitation. And listen to this. His offer includes not five, but a bloody *seven thousand* pounds with all expenses paid at a chance for the championship. I would be stupid not to take it."

"Good for you. You've earned it." Matthew elbowed him. "I'll look for your win in the papers. New York always prints English jargon."

Nathaniel playfully shoved Matthew away. "You won't

even have to read about it. You'll hear the roar well across the ocean, my man."

Matthew smirked. "I have no doubt I will."

"Take care of yourself and the boys. All right? Now go. Before you lose your seat."

Matthew's features sagged. "I've already lost everything else," he muttered. "What's a seat?" Glancing toward the waiting stagecoach, Matthew swung up the wool sack with his clothes onto his shoulder.

Nathaniel held up a hand. "May our paths cross again."

"I have no doubt they will." Matthew held up his hand, in turn, and jogged over to the curb, hopping onto the crowded stagecoach.

When the coach rolled away and disappeared on the horizon of the narrow, cobblestone street, Nathaniel sighed and felt as if he'd waved goodbye to the only person who ever understood what it was like to be a pariah.

CHAPTER TWELVE

It is an opinion strongly entertained in the Army,
that it is much easier to make a good dragoon out
of a *man* who never mounted a horse in his life,
than a post-*boy* who has been riding all of his days.

—P. Egan, *Boxiana* (1823)

Jackson's
13 Bond Street

UNLATCHING THE ENTRANCE, Nathaniel stepped in and closed
the door. The acrid smell of leather and perspiration wafted
toward him as grunts, thuds, commands and shouts filled
the air.

Scanning the vast, high-ceilinged room which was rela-
tively crowded with well-dressed men at different marked
stations, Nathaniel rounded toward a wall of hooks. Boxing
gloves neatly hung by their strings, most of them appearing
unscuffed and so new the leather still had a shine to it. Post-
ers of prizefights from all over England, city and country-
side alike, were tacked and framed on all of the blue-grey
walls serving as decor.

The space and cleanliness was beyond impressive. He was used to dingy, cramped rooms with spit, blood, cigar ash, mounds of sweat-slathered clothes and piss from overturned chamber pots all over the training floors. But here…the entire expanse of the wooden floors had been swept so meticulously he could see the scrapes in the floor.

It was boxing at its finest. A sense of excitement drummed through him. One he hadn't known since he'd first gotten into boxing. This opportunity was a real chance at becoming something.

A tall, stocky, grey-haired gentleman strode decisively toward him, dressed in a flowing linen shirt tucked in tan knee britches, blindingly white silk stockings that outlined well-muscled calves and black leather slippers that barely covered his heel and toes.

Nathaniel hoped to God he didn't have to dress like that. He cleared his throat. "I have an appointment with Lord Weston."

"Ah. So *you* are the infamous missing heir." The gentleman scanned him, before issuing a civil incline of the head. "The name is Gentleman John Jackson. I look forward to personally training with you over these next few weeks. I ask that you please remove your coat so we may weigh you in and put it on the saloon record before you join Weston."

Nathaniel blinked, wondering if he was being mistaken for someone else, because he had never received such a gracious reception. He certainly hadn't expected to be greeted by *the* Gentleman John Jackson who won the title of Champion of England in 1795.

It was unbelievable. He was going to actually train with a legend. "'Tis an honor, sir. A great, great honor. I have read so much about you in all the New York papers. Your incredible ten-minute set with Mendoza is something I aspire to achieve."

Jackson held out a hand. "Your coat, my lord?"

Right. Stripping his great coat from his shoulders, Nathaniel hurriedly bundled it, aware of its sorry state. He handed it to the man.

Jackson turned and let out a whistle.

A young boy in a velvet pea-green morning coat and brown trousers darted over. Standing at marching attention, the boy snapped both heels of his polished black leather boots together. "Yes, sir?"

Jackson held out the coat. "Throw it away."

"Yes, sir." The boy grabbed the bundled coat and darted off.

Nathaniel was too stunned to even object.

Jackson swiveled back to him. "Try to remember that whenever you step into my academy, you represent far more than yourself. You represent me. Training is different from the ring." Jackson pointed toward the windows. "You see that? Those there are windows that face out to the street. Any respectable soul, including women, can see you. You will therefore invest in appropriate boxing attire that will include a waistcoat. Is that understood, my lord?"

The man was gruff but intelligent. Which was rare for the boxing crowd. They were usually gruff but never intelligent. "Yes, sir."

"Good. You will also shear off most of your hair. Otherwise, I am not letting you box with me or anyone else in London."

Nathaniel lowered his chin. "I prefer my hair at its current length. I can knot it and it stays out of my face when I fight."

"This isn't New York." Black button eyes remained affixed

on him. "Few people know what I am about to tell you. I took Mendoza down in a mere ten minutes not because I was a better pugilist than he, but because he had enough hair for me to grab hold of, which I then used to keep him in place whilst I bloodied his flesh into full submission and ended his career. I don't know what the rules are in New York, but there are no rules here in England against holding your opponent's hair. So let me ask you this—do you want what happened to Mendoza to happen to you?"

Nathaniel shifted his jaw. "No."

"Good. Shear it. Short. 'Tis fashionable anyway." Stepping toward him, the man grabbed Nathaniel's shoulders hard. With marked strength, Jackson's hands worked through the frayed linen of Nathaniel's shirt, fingers digging into and feeling the expanse of every muscle on his upper torso. The man thumped his way down Nathaniel's arms and then stepped back, his features brightening. "Incredible muscle tone. Weston certainly has an eye. You are, as he said, impressively fit."

"I should think so. The Five Points is the best training ground there is."

"It shows." Jackson eyed him. "Was the Five Points the sporting club you attended? I know I never heard of it. Was it exclusive?"

Nathaniel lifted a brow and decided against explaining to the man that the Five Points was no gentleman's sporting club. There were sports, yes, and there were men, yes, but no gentlemen. Only pimps, whores and thieves. "Oh, yes. It was very exclusive. I could barely afford it." He tried to keep his tone serious.

Jackson leaned in. "Permit me to confide the deep respect I have for the story that surrounds you. Most of your peers have *no* understanding of why a man boxes. They think it valiant, masculine and designed to keep a man fit. And yes, of course, it does, but what they don't realize is that life forces some of us into putting our fists up long before we even knew it was a sport. *That* is a true boxer."

He liked this man. "Well said, sir."

"I say a lot of things well, but for some damn reason my fists get all the glory." Jackson smirked. "Come with me." Wagging a hand, Jackson made his way past a group of young aristocratic-looking men who had ceased training to acknowledge him.

"Good afternoon, Mr. Jackson!" the young men called out almost in unison.

"Good afternoon, my lords."

The group of men eyed Nathaniel and then Jackson. "By God, is that him?" one of the five asked, pointing to Nathaniel. "Is that *the* missing heir who is setting aside his title for a boxing title? Do we get to fight him?"

Nathaniel smirked. He already felt famous.

"Yes, yes," Jackson called out. "You will all get a chance to spar with him later. Now get back to swinging."

"Yes, sir!"

There was no doubt Jackson, who, according to sporting papers had once worked as a mere corn porter before rising to fame, had earned an impressive and high place in respectable society among aristos and gentry alike. Being the Champion of England earned that for a man.

Nathaniel could only imagine what the title was going to earn for him.

Jackson tapped at a tall, wooden tripod bearing a large scale with iron weights on one side and a wooden seat hanging by ropes on the other. "Sit. And lift your feet until I'm done."

With a swift turn, Nathaniel lowered himself onto the wooden seat. Grabbing the ropes to steady himself, he lifted both booted feet into the air, causing the seat to sway.

Jackson added an iron weight to the set of weights already on the scale and glanced at the bar above the tripod to see if it was level. He added another weight, then another and another before finally stepping back.

Jackson sniffed, looking at Nathaniel's weight on the scale. "It could be more given your height." Pulling out a small pencil from the pocket of his britches, he grabbed up a ledger from beside the scale, flipped it open and wrote something in it. Setting both aside, Jackson asked, "What do you usually eat?"

Nathaniel shrugged. "Stew, mutton, yams. Whatever I can afford."

"You will need to learn to focus on eating better. I will ensure you get a list of what you should be eating. Focus on not only eating well, but eating often. Except during days of combat, that is. Get off the scale."

Nathaniel jumped off, leaving it swinging, and adjusted his linen shirt. "What next?"

Jackson pointed to a door beyond the scale. "In there. Weston is waiting to negotiate the terms."

Nathaniel blew out a breath and strode around the scale, opening the door beyond it. Despite getting to work with Jackson, he felt nervous about handing over his boxing life like this. But it was his best and his only chance at crawling out of the dirt hole he was living in without having to rely on Auggie's family, and he absolutely refused to be a burden.

Stepping in, Nathaniel closed the door with the heel

of his boot and turned toward a cluttered room lit with several lamps.

Behind a mahogany writing desk piled with books, papers and ledgers was none other than Weston, casually leaning back in a chair with an open newspaper held chin-high before him. Weston's dark blond hair was meticulously brushed back in its usual sleek fashion. A grey pin-striped morning coat and matching wool trousers made him look like the well-to-do dandy that he was.

For some reason, the man ignored him and kept reading.

Nathaniel couldn't help but feel irked. "Don't tell me the paper is more interesting than my career."

Sharp green eyes lifted and met Nathaniel's. The paper slowly came down, revealing a smatter of yellow-blue and black bruises across Weston's cheekbone and entire square jaw. "Sit. *Now.*"

Nathaniel didn't like the tone *or* that stare. What the hell was this? "Addressing me like a dog isn't wise on your part. You might end up with a few more bruises."

Weston tossed the paper to the floor with the flick of his wrist and rose to his height of almost six feet, adjusting his morning coat around his broad frame.

Veering around the desk and heading toward him, Weston rigidly pointed. "You—*Atwood*—are an asshole. A real asshole. And I am tossing the word *asshole* at you not because it's a word I frequently use, for I consider myself to be a gentleman, but because you had the bloody gall to use that vile word in the presence of my sister. My nineteen-year-old untainted—*until now!*—sister. What the devil do you have to say for your lack of refinement and crude conduct?"

Nathaniel leaned back. Although he might have said it the first night she and he met, he honestly couldn't remember.

He'd said a lot of things to her that night, which all blurred together into his head because he spent half their conversation trying not to...touch her. "I'm sorry if I did. In all honesty, I don't remember."

"Oh, but you did. How do I know? Because she up and called *me* an asshole. *Me*. Her own brother."

Nathaniel rumbled out a startled laugh. "Now, now, I doubt that little bird even knows what it means."

"Let me assure you, that little bird used it in the context in which it was supposed to be used, *asshole*."

Nathaniel rumbled out another laugh. "Are you certain she didn't hear it from you? Because you seem to be using the word quite a bit."

Weston narrowed his gaze. "Listen here and listen well. I spent the last week and a half taking coaches from one side of town to the other and back again, digging tirelessly into who the hell you really are. And I will say, I have *never* come across anything more bewildering and muddled than the story of your so-called life. American Loyalists, panels in a wall leading to hidden tunnels, countless investigators, including that of the Crown's, baffled at having no evidence, and a calling card with the words *Death to the British* given to the Duke of Wentworth, years after the boy's disappearance, by a nameless man who was never seen again."

Nathaniel widened his stance in agitation. "If you know everything there is to know about my so-called life, why talk to me about it?"

Weston angled toward him. "Because I'm far from done. The Duke of Wentworth, whom I greatly admire and respect, vouches that you are indeed this missing heir. I am inclined to believe him for he is a man of worth and honor. But then there is your father. Another man of worth and honor. I visited him to discuss these same details. After he ushered his wife out of the room, who was intently asking me questions about the man who claims to be her son, he then locked us away in the farthest part of the house as if we were about to discuss the origin of human nature with God himself."

Weston grabbed Nathaniel's shoulder and squeezed it hard. "Not only does Lord Sumner deny your claim, but when I asked him to see a portrait or a sketch of what you might have looked like as a child, to assist me in seeing any resemblance and coming to my own conclusion, he had none to show. None. He *destroyed* them out of grief. Now, whilst I am no longer a father, for sadly, every child I have ever tried to conceive never survived beyond their first few months of life, I do know one thing. Grief doesn't make a father destroy his own child's likeness. I have a lock of every one of my children's hair I keep in a drawer and look at to bring me closer to what might have been. And had they lived long enough, I would have had their likenesses painted and kept all of those, too. So why would a father do such a thing?"

Nathaniel felt a part of himself crumble, the way it had many, many years ago in his youth, but otherwise said nothing. Because he knew all too well why his father had annihilated all evidence. Because he, Nathaniel, represented everything his father had tried to bury. Everything his father had hoped would never resurface. The old man was no doubt panicking but was too much of a coward to do anything about it.

Weston sighed. "I didn't know what to think. I still don't. I even went back to the duke to present him the baffling exchange I had with Lord Sumner, only to be astounded again. The duke informed me that there is still one portrait in existence should anyone challenge the claim of you being Sumner's missing heir. Only…said portrait lies buried with his beloved wife in the family crypt. I insisted he not disturb the grave of his wife. 'Tis crude and senseless. That said, despite the duke's unwavering faith in who you are, I still need assurance and I mean to get it."

Weston crossed his arms over his chest. "If you are indeed this missing heir, tell me what happened. Piece together this mess of calling cards, hidden panels and American Loyalists. Because I'm not about to invest a goddamn farthing into your boxing career until you tell me what the devil you are about and from whence you came. Those are the terms."

Nathaniel's throat pulsed, knowing he had to give just enough to get Weston to calm down. Lest he lose this offer and he was back into the dirt hole. "I can tell you a few things. But I can't tell you everything."

"I need to know more than a few things, Atwood. Ten thousand pounds isn't a flick of lint I'm ready to toss."

Nathaniel's expression stilled. "I'm not about to hang what little remains of my family for your goddamn morbid sense of curiosity. My life isn't a theatrical you can pay admission for."

Weston was quiet for a moment. "What can you tell me? So I may trust what you are saying?"

Flexing his hand, Nathaniel cracked every knuckle. "It wasn't a group of American Loyalists. It was a lone Venetian man who printed up cards with a set of words to create an illusion of being more than he really was. He wanted everyone to think that my disappearance was a nationalist motive against the crown. When, in fact, it wasn't."

Nathaniel drew in a breath in an attempt to keep his countenance calm. "And yes, there was a hidden panel. I knew about it long before I disappeared. It accidentally unlatched itself when I was using the wall for a target with my slingshot. I would use it to play Revolution and never told anyone, lest it be nailed shut. No one came into the house the night I disappeared. I left the house, using the panel, thinking, as any stupid ten-year-old boy with a pistol would, that I could face anything. Only to find myself in a situation I wasn't able to get out of. The rest of the story, *asshole,* you will have to accept never knowing or I find myself another patron. You decide. Do you want a boxer? Or do you want a story? Because you can have the boxer but you damn well won't ever get the story."

Weston's green eyes intently sought his, that bruised face and jaw tightening. After a pulsing moment, he half nodded. "I know conviction when I see it. And I see it. I respect whatever you have suffered and ask that you forgive me for intruding upon what you have every right to hold against your soul." Weston stuck out a hand. "I wish to bestow unto you my firm belief, based upon the Duke of Wentworth's faith in you, that you are indeed the missing heir. It is an honor to welcome you into my circle."

Nathaniel gripped his hand. Hard. "And I wish to bestow unto you my firm belief that *nothing* will impede upon my ability to perform in the ring."

"Excellent. That is exactly what I wanted to hear." Weston hooked his thumbs into the trim of his pockets. "Here is the offer. A full seven thousand for you to cradle when the ink dries, all of your living expenses fully paid and Mr. Jackson himself as your right hand. The terms, which will be stipulated in a contract that will be witnessed by my lawyer when you sign, is that you get to keep half the winnings of every fight, including the championship. Together, we stand to make about a quarter of a million. If not more."

Nathaniel didn't even have to blink. "Done."

Weston adjusted the sleeves of his morning coat. "No. We aren't done quite yet. For although, yes, I will be profiting from your wins, I am not, nor will I be, your investor."

Nathaniel's brows came together. "Who is?"

"My sister. Gene."

His palms felt annoyingly moist. "Your sister? I... What do you mean?"

"What I mean is that I don't have any money to invest. My wife is my money and I'm not one to dig into the pockets of others. Even this has been hard for me to do. I'm here merely to negotiate the terms of the contract for my sister. She will actually be the one investing money in you. And not just any money, mind you. Her inheritance. Which is all the money she has. I thought you might want to know that."

This couldn't be happening.

Weston scratched at his jaw and then winced, realizing all too late that he was engaging a bruise. "There isn't a thing I would deny that girl. I have spent years upon years of my life guilt-stricken, knowing I was unforgivably stupid in my younger years. I tried to save what little money my mother and Gene and I had by hiring the cheapest governess I could. As a result, Gene suffered for *weeks,* because, even at the age of seven, she was damned determined to protect her family from a crazed woman who threatened to burn down the house if she lost her position. A woman whose method of assisting Gene with her stutter was to force her to hold lye in her mouth to 'loosen' her tongue. *Lye.* After Gene almost died from gaping sores that had become infected due to repeated exposure to that lye, I swore to not only give her everything but to protect her from everything. Even if it meant kneeling myself. And I have. Everything I do is for that girl, Atwood. Everything. You need to know that."

Nathaniel's chest tightened in riled angst, *loathing* what Imogene had endured. Yet, unlike him, she had somehow remained...*soft*. It was humbling. He tried to appear indifferent even though he was anything but. "Why are you telling me this?"

"Because even though I initially resisted her and this whole idea, she needs this far more than I need a divorce. She always thinks of herself as a burden to everyone and I want her to realize she is not only of worth but can change the lives of others. And you, and this, may be her chance." Weston slowly shook his head. "Though she would cringe to no end if she knew I was telling you any of this, aside from her fainting spells, Gene also stutters. Whilst she has taught herself to speak incredibly well, when it does overtake her ability to speak, she lapses into forms of silence that are damn deadly. There could be a fire and you wouldn't be able to get her to scream. She withdraws when overly riled or panicked. Mind you, I have always kept her from experiencing those situations for the sake of her mind and health. She suffers from severe ailments and oddities that make her incredibly vulnerable."

Weston pointed rigidly at him, his green eyes sharpening. "You had better treat her with every respect she deserves for however long this ruse lasts. If I hear of anything remotely displeasing—*anything*—you will regret ever meeting me. Do you understand?"

Nathaniel stared. "I'm confused here. What are you saying? What are you asking me to do?"

Weston widened his stance. "I'm tasked to inform you, Atwood, that she won't offer you the contract unless you agree to marry her. Call it collateral for the ten thousand she is investing. We know of your reputation for skipping out on investors, and we will be damned if we are left flailing in the wake of your flight. She also wishes to be personally involved in every aspect of your career until the championship and knows that isn't possible given she is a woman. Unless, of course, she becomes your wife. Four months from now, once the championship has been won or lost, then you and she will split all profits, whatever they may be, and go your separate ways. That is the agreement."

Nathaniel almost choked on the astounded breath he sucked in through his nostrils. "Are you bloody serious?"

Weston was quiet for a moment. "I am."

"She expects me to marry her *and* hand over my entire boxing career?"

"As your patron and investor, she has the right to set the terms of the contract."

"And what the devil does she know about boxing?"

"Absolutely nothing aside from a few pages she has read from a book. Jackson is the one who will actually be guiding you and your boxing. Which Gene will also be graciously paying for. Jackson's skills are anything but cheap. My sister will be focusing on developing your popularity with the masses and insists on attending all of your training sessions and boxing events to ensure her investment remains intact."

He gaped. "What the hell are you talking about? Since when do women attend training sessions? *Or* boxing events?"

"Since Gene fancied it. It won't last, Atwood. Once she sees real blood spray, you won't have to worry about her insisting."

"And what does she get out of this arrangement?"

"Half your winnings and a sense of security that you won't take off with the money. Despite her submitting to being your wife for four months, she would still be your patron and as such, would expect you to follow whatever rules she sets until you go your separate ways. That would include keeping your hands to yourself during all four months of the marriage."

Nathaniel snorted. "No one owns me like that. I own me. You be sure to fucking tell her that."

Weston slowly smoothed his cravat. "I'm afraid I won't be playing messenger. Gene expects you to call on her with your response in the next few days. As you well know, we only have four months to get you into the championship. That doesn't leave us much time."

Nathaniel swiped his face in exasperation. If he went to see her, he could very well find himself in a situation he couldn't get out of. Because he'd find it difficult to say no to her. He'd always had trouble denying women what they needed most, and with a woman like her it would be doubly challenging. He just couldn't say yes to the idea of a woman controlling every aspect of his life for four months. He couldn't give up control—it defined him.

Weston eyed him. "I will give you an entire afternoon to settle all of the details with her."

Nathaniel jerked toward Weston. "What do you mean? Alone with her?"

Weston hooked his thumbs on the lapel of his coat. "No. You won't be *completely* alone. Do I look stupid enough to trust you with a pretty girl for an entire afternoon with no chaperone? No. Your afternoon will be in a controlled environment. I will be just down the corridor from your conversation that will occur in *my* parlor." Weston's features stilled. "And if you make her cry or use words like *fuck* in her presence, God save you, you and I meet with pistols. Don't think you can dodge a bullet. You aren't *that* good. But guess what? I am. I haven't missed a shot since I was ten."

Jesus Christ. "Weston—"

"I have nothing more to say. The rest is between you and Gene. Just remember, you aren't the only one gambling with your life here. We *all* are. And Gene more than the rest of us. So give her the respect she deserves and call on her."

Nathaniel plastered a hand across his mouth in disbelief and eyed Weston before saying through clamped fingers, "I'll call on her with my decision."

"Good." Stepping toward him, Weston tugged on Nathaniel's linen shirt. "Gene asks I make you presentable and insists on paying for it. I know an excellent tailor on Regent Street who can stitch together an incredible outfit in three days. The man can make anyone look good. Even you."

Nathaniel seriously thought about ripping out Weston's beating heart and eating it. "In my opinion, you're both sick. And you're trying to make me sick."

"Atwood. You have the ability to change all of our lives. Gene gets to cradle independence, I get to cradle a divorce and you get to cradle whatever the hell you need to cradle when we all get that quarter of a million. So the question is, do you want to change all of our lives? Or would you rather go back to being Coleman?"

A thin chill seized Nathaniel's breath at the thought.

Why did he have the vexing feeling he was going to do this?

CHAPTER THIRTEEN

We now turn aside from the qualifications of the hero, to view his pretensions as a man of taste; and in this, as in several other instances which we have portrayed, it will be found that all pugilists are not so completely absorbed by *fighting,* as to prove indifferent to the softer attractions of life.

—P. Egan, *Boxiana* (1823)

Five days later
The Weston House

WITH A CALMING breath, Imogene carefully arranged all of the gold-rimmed porcelain plates stacked with small cakes and candied fruit onto the tea table, rearranging what the servants had laid out in an effort to make it look pretty. She dragged her mother's heirloom vase filled with pink roses more toward the center of the table. Tucking a poem she had written beside it, she pressed a forefinger to her lips, kissing it, and then pressed that same finger to the center of the poem, wishing her words luck.

Plucking up a candied fruit from the top tier, she poked it

into her mouth to remove the lingering taste of medicine and quickly chewed the sticky sweetness. Swallowing the last of the candied fruit, she slid her tongue across her teeth to ensure nothing embarrassing remained. Clean.

She stepped back, easing out a shaky breath, and glanced toward the open doors of the receiving room, knowing he would arrive at any moment. After getting Mary out of the house by having her take an invitation on the other side of town, Henry had informed her that he would be in the study and that she had two hours to get him to agree. Two hours before Mary got back.

The calling bell rang, causing her heart to pop.

She scrambled toward the cane chair set beside the tea table opposite the one set for him and sank into it. Smoothing her lavender muslin gown around her thighs, she primly placed both ungloved hands onto her lap and waited.

The butler appeared in the doorway. "Lord Atwood has come to call, my lady."

Her stomach flipped. "Thank you, Dobson. You may send him in. Inform my brother that Lord Atwood has arrived. He wishes to know of it."

"Yes, of course, my lady." Dobson inclined his head and turned to retrieve her visitor from the foyer.

She pressed her hands together harder, chanting to herself to remain calm. Dizziness swirled itself in. She swallowed hard, trying to push it away.

Within moments, steady footfalls approached.

She swiped her moist hands against her gown. What if he didn't take the offer? What if he didn't—

A large, broad-shouldered man loomed in the doorway.

Her eyes widened and she almost grabbed the sides of her chair to keep herself from sliding out of it.

It was Nathaniel. Only...it wasn't.

His long hair had been completely sheared off, exposing a debonair silvering of hair at his temples. The rest of his short black hair fell in even waves across his forehead and barely touched his collar, opening the stunning features of a closely shaven rugged face. He was also exquisitely dressed in an embroidered smoke-blue waistcoat with a silk cravat and a soft black morning coat paired with matching wool trousers that attractively showcased a broad, muscled frame, which his billowing, patched great coat had hidden.

He wasn't dashing anymore.

He was downright virile.

Ice-blue eyes pierced the distance between them in a breathtakingly intimate manner.

Her pulse skittered and although she tried to look away, she felt powerless to do so. "You may close the doors."

He made his way toward her with a long-legged stride. "I would rather we not complicate the afternoon."

Searing heat crept up the length of her thighs and chest. She rose from her seat to greet him, swaying momentarily against what felt like the swinging of the room and only hoped her poor limbs would be able to hold her up.

Everything seemed to drum and hum as he drew steadily closer. The light from the window behind him accentuated the outline of his large body in a soft glow.

He now lingered before her, shrinking the entire parlor into a pinprick with his presence. The crisp scent of soap, hair tonic and shaving cream drifted toward her.

Gone was the man who smelled of leather and smoky wood from a blazing fire that mingled with the scent of cigars, coal and the ocean.

Henry had cleaned him up a bit *too* much.

It was very impressive.

She swept out her hand for him to take in greeting. "My lord."

"I prefer Nathaniel." He glanced toward her hand and coolly met her gaze. "And according to your brother I'm not supposed to touch you."

She blinked and lowered her hand, her cheeks heating. Her brother was taking this a bit too far. She swept a quick hand toward the table beside them. "Will you sit?"

"Standing will be satisfactory, thank you."

She hesitated. "You plan on standing the whole time?"

"Yes. My clothes aren't all that accommodating and are a bit more fitted than what I'm used to. Comfort apparently doesn't exist in the realm of high fashion." He shifted from boot to polished boot and then tugged his morning coat. Tugging again, only more forcefully, he blurted, "Do I look like an idiot in this attire? Because I certainly feel like one. Silk isn't something a man ought to be wearing."

She burst into laughter, all her nervousness gone.

He groaned. "I do look like an idiot. Don't I?"

Tempering her laughter, for she didn't want him thinking that she was laughing at him, she offered, "No. You look—"

"Ridiculous. Like I drank too much champagne." He wagged his cravat at her and then poked at buttons on his waistcoat. "And I have you to blame for this. Weston wouldn't let me call on you otherwise."

She giggled. "You look incredibly handsome. Very much so. I mean it."

He set his shoulders and eyed her. "Handsome I can manage. I suppose."

She smiled. If only she could convince this man to agree to her scheme. Their lives would never be the same.

He paused and traced his gaze down the entire length of her, from shoulder to slipper. "You look very—" Shifting his jaw, he flicked his eyes toward her breasts, tarrying there for a brief moment before veering back to her face. He said nothing more.

She pressed her lips together. It was awkward knowing he appeared to be at a loss for words because of her appearance. What was it about her breasts that fascinated him so?

He set both hands behind his back, straining the fine wool of his coat, and glanced around the receiving room.

Hoping to rattle a bit of a conversation out of him, she confided, "All of the gazettes and papers are ablaze about your story. I have never read so many versions of a man's life put to print."

"Neither have I."

"Is any of it true?"

"Pieces."

"Which pieces?"

"You and I don't have that long, tea cake."

No. She supposed they didn't. She smoothed her skirts, trying to think of something else to say. "Your parents must be incredibly elated having you back in their lives. I imagine you have been calling on them often, trying to embrace lost time, yes?"

His jaw tightened. "I don't have that sort of relationship with them. My father thinks me a farce and apparently so does my mother. I had my nephew deliver three missives into her hands this past week, asking she and I meet. I have yet to hear anything. And I'm beginning to wonder if I ever will. My father is probably controlling what she does and doesn't hear and what she does and doesn't think."

"Oh." How odd. Perhaps another subject was in order, for

she certainly didn't want to stifle what little conversation they were having. "I met Mr. Jackson. He came to supper last night. He seems very excited to train with you. Apparently, he hasn't had a student take the championship yet. He hopes you will change that."

He said nothing. Merely stared off over her shoulder.

This was not the same, quick-tongued man she'd met that first night or in the ballroom. It appeared she had a Samson on her hands. Off the hair went and so did he. "Is everything all right?"

His gaze jumped to hers. "Yes. Why do you ask?"

"You appear to be distracted."

"I am. Is there anything else you wanted to know?"

He seemed agitated. Maybe if she could get him to sit down, she could coax him into being more civil. She gestured toward the chair. "Please. Sit."

He eyed the chair. "It's too close to your chair."

She glanced toward it, her brows coming together in an effort to understand. Because both chairs were on opposite sides of the table and were not even near each other. "How far do you need them to be?"

He strode toward the cane chair, swung it up with a simple toss, strode past her and set it with a resounding thud in the middle of the room, several feet away from the tea table. "This is good."

She couldn't help but feel insulted, knowing he didn't even want to sit across the table from her. The man who had kissed her forehead, cheek and chin in her bedchamber and had also daringly waltzed with her before all of London now wouldn't even sit next to her in an empty room.

She heaved out a sigh. Perhaps a bit of poetry was in order. Poetry *always* put her in a good mood. Stepping toward the table, she slipped her poem off the table. Crossing to the middle of the room, where he stood, she held it out.

He stared. "What is it?"

"A poem I wrote for you."

His brows rose. "You write poetry?"

"One of my few talents. Though nothing worth publishing." She stuck it farther out.

He scratched at his chin, sidled closer and tugged the parchment loose from her fingers. He lowered his gaze to read it.

Bringing her hands together, she mentally sketched out the words he was reading and read them in her mind along with him.

Touch a finger to my heart.
Touch a finger to my soul.
Touch a finger to the reverence you alone control.
Take my hand, I beg of you, and lead us not astray.
I vow for a quarter of a million,
I will humbly respect you in each and every way.

A laugh rumbled out of him as he fingered the edges of the parchment it had been written on. He angled it more toward himself, as if he couldn't quite make sense of it. "This is…" His brows came together. He glanced up again. "Is there a point to this?"

She grinned. "I wanted to make you laugh."

His mouth quirked. "Well, you did."

"I'm genuinely hoping you and I could be friends. Is that at all possible?"

"Back to the friends, is it?" He muttered something, then folded and refolded her poem several times, until the parchment was a palm-size square. Without meeting her gaze, he tucked it deep into the inner pocket of his coat.

She blinked and couldn't tell if he had tucked it away because it was worth keeping or if he had tucked it away because it was that bad. It was probably because it was that bad. Her sense of humor wasn't always the best.

He puffed out a breath and scrubbed a hand through his hair. "Imogene. What you clearly don't recognize—for you have never seen me in the ring, and God forbid you ever do for I am a very different man when I swing—is that I'm equally brutal as the sport I play. By taking on the role of patron, you would be subjecting yourself to four months of me and my boxing morning, day and…night."

He said it as if night was a bad thing. "I know."

He captured her gaze. "I enjoy making people bleed merely to prove that I am stronger. Hardly a quality a lady such as yourself should be exposed to. It isn't normal. Nothing about me or my life is normal and that has been my life since I was forced to become a pawn at ten. Though I try to pretend I'm well beyond my past, and I sometimes have moments that I forget it exists, I haven't been the same since I was taken." He stared unblinkingly at her. "Nor will I ever be."

Her chest tightened at hearing him say it. She couldn't even imagine what he *wasn't* saying. After everything she had read and everything Henry had told her about his life, and the bizarre circumstances surrounding his disappearance, she sensed this man needed a friend. Not just an investor. She softened her voice. "What was done to you when you were taken? Were you…hurt?"

He glanced off to the side. "Not in the physical sense. No."

"Do you ever speak of it to anyone?"

"No. Not really. And now that I'm in London, I have to ensure I don't speak of it at all."

Imogene's brows came together. "Why not?"

"There is a reason why I was taken. There is also a reason why I didn't come back after I was set free." His ice-blue eyes became disturbingly hooded. "Do you have any idea what it's like to be burdened with a secret that isn't yours to keep? But if you don't keep it, everyone you love will suffer for it as equally as the person who deserves to suffer for it?"

Tears pricked her eyes at hearing the savage conviction in that husky voice. It was like meeting a version of herself at seven sitting in that chair, sobbing as the lye burned its way into far more than her tongue. It had burned her soul and every drop of trust in the one person who was supposed to oversee her care.

She swallowed. "Yes," she confided. "I do know what it is like to be burdened with a secret. I almost died as a child whilst trying to cradle one. But I know everything we endure makes us stronger and more willing to fight for what we do want."

He eyed her. "And what are you fighting for?"

The question was one she had never been asked aloud but one she had answered so many times in her head. "I am fighting for a chance to be my own person. To be independent. I am also fighting for my brother's happiness. A chance he never got because of me. I think it time I reverse the clock and give him back what he not only deserves but wants and needs. Everyone deserves a second chance at happiness." She hesitated and added, "Even you."

Nathaniel observed her. "Even me." Slowly closing the distance he'd been keeping, he paused before her and lingered. "What if I promise you I won't skip out?"

"I'm afraid I can't trust your word. I will require a commitment on your part and some knowledge that you will be bound to follow through."

He seemed to consider this. "So once the championship is over, which will be in four months' time, you and I will split all of my wins in half and we are done and free to go our separate ways. Is that right?"

Was he yielding? "Yes."

"And how we do we settle that, given we will be married?"

"Through divorce."

"And what grounds will we be able to provide to the church and Parliament after four months?"

"Henry mentioned an unconsummated marriage would best provide those grounds."

"Unconsummated?" He looked her over seductively. "No. I don't think so."

She swallowed. "No?"

"No." He edged toward her, his expression heated yet lethally controlled. "I have given this some thought before coming here. Lots of thought, actually. If I'm to submit to you, you will submit to me. It's not like you're wanting to take a husband after you and I are done. So here is the offer. In return for giving you complete control over my life and my boxing career, I expect you to bed me. And more than once, mind you. Which means...you and I will have to agree to a mutual separation. Agree to that and I'll sign the contract."

Their eyes locked.

Her pulse zinged from the intensity rippling between what little space slivered between them. There had to be worse things than submitting to a very attractive man who thought she was attractive, too.

Leaning in, he methodically grazed her cheek. "Do you need time to think about it?"

Her heartbeat throbbed in her ears.

His husky features tightened. "I'll ensure no babe comes of it."

"A babe?" she breathed out.

He traced her jaw more firmly, outlining it with a possessive intensity that made her tremble. Dragging his large hand into the curls of her bundled hair, he angled her face upward with a gentle tug. "Did no one ever tell you where babes come from?"

A fading breath escaped her. She had a feeling she was about to find out all the details respectable society had left out.

His other hand drifted toward the side of her hair and skimmed it. Watching his own fingers, he removed a hairpin and tossed it onto the carpet. Holding her gaze, he removed yet another pin, tossing it.

What was he doing?

His fingers indulgently pulled out another pin and another, until all of her blond curls fell around his hands and her shoulders in a curtain.

She raised her eyes to his, feeling naked.

He heatedly searched her face and wove his fingers through her hair, spreading it across her shoulders. "You look different with your hair down. Less prim. More willing."

She swallowed.

Tightening his hold on her hair, he raveled a section of its length around each hand, gripping it possessively as if he never meant to let go. "Can I kiss you?"

Her pulse thundered. "I...suppose." Her cheeks flamed in disbelief that she had just given him permission.

"You suppose?" His grip on her hair tightened. "I'll ensure next time, you're more enthusiastic." Dipping his head toward her, he captured her lips.

Her eyes fluttered closed. She swayed against him and his heat whilst his lips forcefully parted hers. The velvety, slick fire of a tongue that tasted of mint brandy slipped deep into her mouth.

Her heart pounded as it leisurely rolled against her tongue and teeth.

She thought a kiss was but a mere brush of the lips.

By goodness, was she ever wrong, wrong, wrong.

He tugged her hair harder with both fists. His mouth moved more forcefully against hers, until she could feel her very jaw aching. He was demanding she move her tongue.

So she did. She slid it against his.

A groan rumbled out from his lips against her own as he tugged on her hair again, stinging her scalp.

She didn't mind the tugging. It made her feel like a leaf dancing in the whipping wind, seeing the world from above. She slid her tongue against his less tentatively, giving in to his taste and touch.

He remolded his mouth against hers, rigidly rolling his tongue against hers with a pent-up explosion waiting to happen.

Her hands daringly roamed up that broad chest, her fingers skimming the smooth silk of his vest, which was so unlike the solid muscles beneath. In a glorious haze, her hands rounded those broad shoulders and clambered up and into his soft, thick hair. Her very fingertips tingled and curled like the rest of her.

His lips jumped away from her mouth and his hands unraveled from her hair. "No touching."

Her eyes flew open, confused.

"I do all the touching...you got that?" His hands jumped down to her wrists. His fingers dug into each wrist before he yanked them both behind her back, clamping them together. "Don't move."

She gasped and stumbled against him.

Still holding her hands behind her back, he leaned in and smeared his mouth down her exposed throat, his hot, wet tongue gliding down, down the curve. He nipped and sucked the delicate skin of her lower throat, causing her to shudder against him. His shaven chin grazed her. "I have this overwhelming feeling," he hoarsely said against her skin, "I'm going to enjoy our time together."

It was too much. She tried to steady herself but with her hands behind her back, she felt unable to.

"Keep your hands behind your back. And don't touch me." He instantly released her wrists.

She swallowed and did her best to obey, trying not to sway against him.

His palms now slowly veered down to her bodice. "Are you wet for me?"

She sucked in a breath when he slid his fingers up and down the satin material of her gown around both breasts, grinding himself into her with his hips and his—

It was hard.

He rolled his hips against her rhythmically, skimming fingers up to her throat and dragging them back down to her breasts.

The thump of a boot against the door frame made them both freeze against each other.

"A reminder that you are *not* alone," Henry called out from the open doorway, sounding incredibly riled. "When you two are done *negotiating,* find yourself in my study, Atwood. We have less than two hours before my wife comes home. So keep the goddamn clothes on. Gene? I'm astounded. I will say no more." Swinging away, his footfalls disappeared down the hall.

CHAPTER FOURTEEN

> With respect to the language that may have passed be-
> tween us, I admit that it may have not been the most
> chaste.
>
> —P. Egan, *Boxiana* (1823)

SHE HAD *NEVER* been more mortified.

Atwood tucked her head against the contours of his chest but said nothing.

She still clung to him, unable to move.

Pulling away from her, his large hands curved down the length of her arms with digging fingers until they dropped away completely. He eyed her. "I didn't force myself on you, did I?"

Her cheeks bloomed with heat. She brought a trembling hand to her hair, sweeping long sections of it away from the sides of her face. "No."

Swiping a hand over his mouth, he fisted that same hand and dug it against his teeth. After a long moment of silence, he grated out past that fist, "You are inevitable, you know that?"

Why was he biting his hand? "You don't appear to be in the least bit pleased by my inevitability."

He dropped his hand back to his side and gave her a side-long glance of disbelief. "No. I'm not. And I'll tell you why. Because I feel like I was put into a situation I knew I wasn't going to be able to get out of. For Christ's sake, the last thing I wanted was to be married again. And to you, no less. To you."

She stiffened, her womanly pride prickling. To her, no less? What did that mean? What was so wrong with her that he felt a need to emphasize it aloud with so much vile annoyance? And after he had indulged himself to the brim? She knew she was odd and couldn't speak well when it was needed most but did he really have to—

It stung. More than she wanted it to. "Leave," she choked out. "My brother will—" She wanted to add much, much more to the sentiment, but was too upset and her throat too tight with emotion. Her tongue was already feeling heavy and set to stutter.

He quirked a dark brow. "Your brother will what?"

She whipped a forefinger to the parlor entrance, knowing that if she spoke, it would only be in broken fragments that would make her look half-witted. And she was *not* going to be upstaged after that hip-grinding, breast-tweaking display her brother had to witness.

Nathaniel stared. "Why the devil are you so miffed?"

Oh, she would show him miffed, making her feel like a piece of fat he'd cut off the mutton when she was giving them all an opportunity of a lifetime. Just because she was naive to the ways of men didn't make her naive to the ways of being *demeaned*.

Shaking her finger rigidly at the direction of the parlor entrance, she hoped to God he would just go and spare her the humiliation of having to use words.

Lines of concentration etched his brow. He angled toward her. "Is this about your stutter?"

Her eyes widened. Oh, God. He knew. Her own brother had tattled about her stuttering as if she were some medical aberration in need of pity.

His countenance notably softened. "Imogene. I've been through far too much to judge. Believe me. I don't care what it sounds like. Say whatever you need to."

He felt sorry for her. Henry had no doubt even asked the man to play governess to her until the championship. It was... *humiliating*. Like she was being passed from one set of panicked hands to another.

Nathaniel eyed her. "One of the boys in New York had a stutter."

This just kept getting worse. She was now being compared to some American boy. Hardly a compliment.

Taking on a pensive look, he added, "I have an idea. Seeing we have four months of this ahead of us, why not deal with it now?" He lifted his shaven chin and undid his cravat, tossing it aside.

She scrambled back, her throat tightening all the more. What was he doing?

He casually undid the buttons on his waistcoat. "You and I are going to play Devil's Dare. It's a game men and women play in the Five Points. The idea is that I have to get you to take the Devil's Dare through verbal bribes before all of my clothes are removed and I'm forced to walk into the street naked. The Devil's Dare is this—you have to say something. So for each bribe I issue and each bribe you reject, a piece of my clothing is removed until I'm forced to walk into the streets in nothing but my goodwill. Now I know you like me well enough not to let me walk into the street naked. Or at least, I hope you do. Are you ready?"

She gaped. Was he being serious?

"Imogene, I will buy you a necklace made of rubies after I get my seven thousand."

She swallowed, trying to steady her breathing. What was he doing?

"Clearly, you reject." He shrugged off his coat from each muscled arm and let it fall to the floor. "Imogene, I'm not one for fawning, but I'll take you into a garden and pick flowers for you. Would you like that?"

Mother of heaven. Why was he—

"Clearly, you reject." Holding her gaze, he shrugged off his waistcoat. It rustled to his booted feet. "Imogene, I'll dance with you on the rooftop of whatever house we move into during our four-month marriage."

He didn't expect her to play along, did he?

"Clearly, you reject." He yanked out his linen shirt from his trousers, letting it fall past his hips. "Imogene, I will do something I have never done for a woman. I will take you shopping and hold all of your parcels."

She clamped a trembling hand over her mouth.

"Clearly, you reject. I'm also running out of clothing, so you better take up the next offer." He yanked off the linen shirt with a ripple of solid movements that exposed the menacingly well-sculpted muscles of a broad chest and arms that visibly shifted and tightened against scars that bespoke years of fighting. He tossed the shirt.

She gasped, her heart pounding in disbelief, and glanced toward the open doorway and back again at that bare chest, dreading Henry might come in and shoot them both.

"Imogene, I will always listen to whatever you have to say.

No matter how you say it or why you say it." Holding her gaze, he dragged his hands down toward the front flap of his trousers, planning on doing away with them next.

Oh, dear God. She had to save him *and* herself. "I accept!" she choked out.

His hands stilled at the flap of his trousers. His blue eyes intently held hers. "Good. Now tell me why the hell you're so miffed before the trousers come off and I walk out into the street naked. Don't think I won't."

She had no doubt the man *would*.

A savage need to get him back into all of his clothes before he really did walk out into the street naked created a wild burst of flurried emotions that allowed her to yell it all out. "*Insensitive!* That is what you are. *Insensitive!* T-t-to unravel my hair and kiss me and-and-and-and touch me like that in the most intimate of-of-of places, only t-t-to tell me I am unworthy of being wed, given the-the-the opportunity I am offering you, is-is-is insensitive! And I'm not going to even t-t-touch upon the fact that you are incredibly n-n-naked!"

She staggered and fisted her hands in disbelief, knowing she had not only said everything she needed to say, but had done it without even thinking or caring that he had heard her stutter. She had *never* spoken to anyone through a stutter since she was seven. Because it made her feel stupid. But for some reason, she didn't feel stupid. Not when he was the one standing before her half-naked.

It was the most liberating thing she had ever known.

He continued to intently observe her and half nodded, as if fully aware of what he had just contributed to.

"You need to learn not to care what people think. Most people revel in finding fault even in perfection. Don't kneel to that or them. Instead, ask yourself if the simplest of creatures would care. Those creatures whose only purpose in life is to survive. Would the birds and the roaches care? No. The birds will continue to fly and the roaches will continue to crawl whether you stutter or not. And if the birds and the roaches don't care, why the hell should you?"

Imogene swallowed, tears unexpectedly burning her eyes. She had never known anyone to have made *this* much of a genuine effort to help her. And it made her want to do more than agree to their contract. It made her want to love this man for the rest of her life.

He angled toward her. "I know full well I can be an insensitive asshole. I haven't had the easiest life. Though that is no excuse."

A complete calm veiled itself over her, knowing he was asking for forgiveness. She swallowed and nodded.

He strode toward her and veered in, leaning in so close the soap-scented heat of his half-naked body wavered. "You and I will have to learn to get along these next four months," he huskily offered. "We can do this. We're talking about a quarter of a million pounds. It's going to change all of our lives."

She met his gaze, trying not to lower her attention to that broad bare chest, and managed, "Can you put your clothes on?"

He sauntered back and pointed at her. "I'll try not to be offended." He swiped up the linen shirt he had earlier tossed and yanked it on. "There is one thing I will not tolerate over these next four months. 'Tis simple, really. I want no other men around while we're together. Save it for after we have gone our separate ways. It's less complicated."

His wife must have overindulged in men. "She broke your heart, didn't she?"

He paused. "Who?"

"Your former wife."

"I wouldn't say that."

She lowered her gaze to keep herself from watching the way his hands stuffed his linen shirt into his trousers. Everything about him exuded a casualness she didn't feel.

He gathered up more of his scattered clothes and pulled on his waistcoat.

She pressed her hands together. "How did you meet her? Was it romantic?"

"She and I didn't have that sort of relationship. I met her at the brothel I worked at back in New York in my younger years."

She gaped. "A brothel? You mean...?"

He hesitated in the midst of buttoning his waistcoat. "Yes. An establishment where women carouse naked with men for a set sum." He finished fastening the buttons.

She stared. She only knew of the word because she had heard her sister-in-law chide about it from time to time when ranting at Henry. The way Nathaniel was nonchalantly discussing this with her was somewhat disturbing. "And you worked at such a place?" she asked in disbelief. "Doing what? Being naked?"

With an amused tsk, he tied his cravat and smoothed it with both hands. "No. I was a servant for the establishment. A fully clothed one." He shrugged on his coat. "It paid well enough for a boy who had nothing."

"And your wife was one of these girls who...?"

A small smile tilted his lips as if he were fondly remembering what used to be. "Fancy story, that. Do you want to hear it?"

Did she? "Uh...yes?"

He still smiled. "I was sixteen when Jane, at almost seventeen herself, struts right in off the street, into the brothel and yells out at the top of her voice she's got virginity to sell. I never laughed so hard. That was what I loved about her. She knew how to make me laugh. She wasn't pretty, but she didn't have to be. She had this…*spark*. And the most amusing thing was…she really did have virginity to sell. She was doing it to help her mother with large debts. Madam Delora was ruffled and had quickly brought in a physician to prove her claim. It isn't every day virginity willingly walks into a brothel like that."

Imogene didn't know why, but it agitated her, knowing his former wife *still* put a smile on his face. "Why do you smile when you speak of her?"

He captured her gaze. "Why do you ask? Are you jealous?"

It was like he was taunting her. "'Tis merely a question."

"I have to smile. She was the first girl I…" He eyed her. "You know. Rolled around with in bed."

Her eyes widened. That was far more than she wanted to know.

He glanced away. "As it turned out, Jane wasn't as willing to barter herself as she had let on. She was scared witless once the auction had been set and men started bartering. I felt sorry for her and knew once she started down that path of prostitution, there would be no way out. So I gave her a way out. It was the right thing to do. She and I married before Madam Delora could hunt us down. Ended up we couldn't keep our hands off each other. That was also about the time I discovered the girl was overly fond of mixing laudanum with whiskey. Though I tried, I couldn't save her from that."

He sighed. "I liked her well enough," he muttered. "But what had started as helping a girl and having a bit of fun turned into a bloody mess. I had to change my name eleven times and move to eleven different places because she kept following me, trying to get money out of me. That's what happens when you help certain people out. They not only take advantage, they try to drown you. I quickly learned to avoid women like that." He was quiet for a moment.

Imogene's emotions sagged. There was genuine compassion hidden within that nonchalance. She softened her voice. "I'm sorry about what I said about you being insensitive. I can understand how life can make us such. I only hope you and I can learn to be friends throughout all of this. Real friends. Aside from Henry, I never had a friend. I wasn't very good at making any due to my illness. Other mamas would bring their daughters over to try to play with me, when I was younger, but I never wanted to speak lest I stutter. And then when I did play with them, I was usually fainting in the most awkward of times. I was hardly anything to play with. I'm still not much to play with." She hesitated, realizing that she had been rambling. "Forgive me. That had nothing to do with anything."

He stared, his blue eyes intently studying her face. "I usually know what a woman is going to say. Yet with you, I never do."

"Is that good or bad?"

"I've yet to decide. But I sure as hell know how I want to proceed." He continued to hold her gaze. "Here are the terms. You get everything you want from me, including complete control over my boxing career for four months, under the simple proviso that you physically submit to me—and nobody else—whenever I want you to."

She lowered her chin, her heart pounding. The pulsing intensity of that stare and those words made her think she was going to have to learn how to box herself. "Define *whenever*."

"As in whenever the mood takes me."

She swallowed and knew it wasn't going to be *that* much of a hardship being touched and kissed by him. Naughty though it was, she had rather enjoyed their interlude. It was incredibly...exciting. And it was not as if she was saving herself for another, *real* marriage. "If that is what will get you to agree...then...yes."

He gave her body a raking once-over. "Good. I'll go talk to Weston."

His once-over was a bit unnerving. "Yes. You should. He—" Dizziness suddenly overwhelmed her. She staggered toward the tea table she had spent most of the morning arranging and grabbed its edge, rattling the china.

Nathaniel jumped toward her and grabbed her shoulders to steady her. He quickly guided her down and into a chair. Leaning in, he searched her face. "Imogene." The concern in his voice almost made the dizziness worthwhile.

"I'm fine." She waited for the dizziness to pass. Thankfully, it did. She blinked rapidly, hating the way it always made her feel so helpless. "I'm fine."

He squinted. "How often do you have these fainting spells?"

She set a hand to her throat, trying to cool the pulsing heat overtaking her. "About once or twice a month. Though for some reason, as of late, it has become more frequent."

"Look at me." He nudged up her chin. "You're pale."

"Am I?" She met his gaze. Everything had ceased swimming and her limbs felt normal again.

"How do you feel?" he asked, still holding her gaze.

His concern was rather touching. It appeared so genuine. "The dizziness is gone." She tried to smile. "I'm fine."

"Are you certain?" he pressed, drawing away his hand.

"Yes." She eased out a breath and leaned back against the chair. "Thank you." She glanced toward the open doorway. "Henry is waiting."

He hesitated then straightened. "I'll be back." Inclining his head, he strode out.

She pressed a shaky hand to her cheek, a part of her relieved he was gone. How, oh, how was she going to survive these next four months?

CHAPTER FIFTEEN

His pitched battles are numerous.

—P. Egan, *Boxiana* (1823)

WITH A LIT cigar clamped between his teeth, Weston slid the double doors into each other and strode across the study toward Nathaniel. Taking a puff, Weston removed the cigar and rolled it between his fingers as white smoke floated out from his curled lips. "I can't help but feel I just sold my own sister for a quarter of a million to a man who plans on groping her for four months."

"I've never forced myself on a woman. So you needn't worry in that. Now put out that damn cigar, will you?" Nathaniel collapsed into the wingback chair just behind him and blew out a breath. There was no such thing as retiring from women, was there? "So what happens next? How do we make this legal?"

Weston dashed out the cigar in the ash pan on the side table, leaving it there. "I suggest we omit the banns. It takes too long. Your best way of going about this is to apply for a special license with the Archbishop tomorrow afternoon. It shouldn't take more than three days to approve, given record of your birth still exists in the county church over in Surrey. Obviously, there is no death certificate to go with that record of birth, so there won't be any objections. The Archbishop was rather intrigued by your story and is looking to support transitioning you into a respectable way of life. I spoke to him about the matter."

Of course Weston had.

"Once you have the license in hand, you and Gene can be wed by the end of this week. And with you being all over the papers, everyone will expect doves and violins. This is our chance to make the fighter everyone wants to see take on the role of the ultimate protector. It will elevate your name and sell more tickets."

Nathaniel tapped a fist to his thigh. "You have this all planned out, don't you?"

"Me? I'm merely ensuring it doesn't go wrong." Weston shook his head. "Did you know Gene already put in a bid to lease a fully furnished house you and she will be living in these next four months? She did it yesterday. I couldn't convince her to wait. It was like she knew you would agree to all of this."

The corner of Nathaniel's mouth twisted in exasperation. "Can I ask you something?"

"Yes. What?"

He thumbed toward the closed doorway. "She almost fainted again. I'm rather worried."

Weston sighed. "She has been suffering from it for years. Ever since the incident with the lye."

"I see. And the doctor knows about this?"

"Of course he does. He insists she is in good health and thinks it's related to her menses."

Menses. Now there was a topic he sure as hell didn't want

to go into. "Ah." Nathaniel cleared his throat. "So. What happens after the wedding?"

"I already spoke to Jackson and here is what he has planned. We all focus on your upcoming fight with Norley. We anticipate a good eight hundred pounds a side, with tickets going for a full guinea and a half, right here in London, Covent Garden, in four weeks. The bastard hasn't lost a fight since January and is making a march for the title. You beat him and we move on to Gill. You beat Gill and we move to Terry. You beat Terry, whose ego is bigger than his fist, and we are set to fight for the title of Champion that I *know* you will take."

Nathaniel half nodded, but his thoughts weren't with boxing anymore, but rather with a pair of hazel eyes and cascading blond hair he had been allowed to unravel. Sliding a hand into his waistcoat pocket, he touched the folded parchment Imogene had given him. Something about fingers and souls and reverence.

Weston paused. "Are you listening?"

Nathaniel's hand jumped out of his pocket. He glanced up. "What?"

Weston swiped a hand over his face, his ruby ring glinting against the remaining afternoon light that slashed through the windows. "Is Imogene going to be too much of a distraction for you?"

Nathaniel set both heavy hands onto the chair's armrests. "Not at all."

"Abstinence will make you a better fighter, you realize," Weston added in an awkward tone.

Nathaniel tried to squelch his amusement. "I take it you speak from experience?"

Weston cleared his throat. "No. I was just—"

"I told you I wouldn't force myself on her. I'm not that sort of man."

Weston raked a hand through his hair. "Good. I'm glad you won't— Because I'm having trouble with this."

"I can tell. And I understand."

Silence clung to the air.

Nathaniel shifted in his seat and tossed out, "Is there anything else you want or need to say?"

"Yes. We should discuss your schedule."

"What about it?"

"Jackson has it all set. Starting next week, you will be arriving at Jackson's Monday through Saturday at noon, spar until four and finish with weights at six. We have four weeks from tomorrow to get you ready for Norley. You're fit and more than able, but we need to get you ready and focused."

"And I take it Imogene still wants to be at all my training sessions and the fights?"

"Yes."

"I don't mind the training sessions, Weston, as it's a controlled environment, but I'm not too keen on having her at a real fight. A woman shouldn't be standing shoulder to shoulder with several hundred men whilst blood sprays."

"I plan on standing beside her. And believe me, it won't last. I once gashed myself with a dagger and to this day, I can still see her hands plastered to her face. If she doesn't have her hands plastered to her face, I'd be worried. It means she wants you dead."

"Good to know."

Leaning in, Weston said in a low tone of warning, "I expect you to treat her with the respect she deserves for however long this ruse lasts. Whatever you two do in the confines of that house and out of view is none of my goddamn business, given you and she will be legally wed, but I also don't want to be rolling up my sleeves and cleaning up a mess once the four months are done."

Nathaniel leaned back against the chair. "You needn't worry. She gets what she wants and I get what I want. I really don't see this going wrong."

"So says the devil." Straightening, Weston rummaged in his inner coat pocket. "I have something for you."

"What? Money?" Nathaniel chided. "Because I have a feeling, based upon my inability to say no to your sister, she is going to be incredibly expensive."

"You get your full seven thousand when we sign the contracts tomorrow morning." Weston pulled out a folded parchment and wagged it at him. "Here. This is all I will ask of you since she will be under your watch these next four months. See to it Dr. Filbert visits with her once a month and that she takes everything prescribed here."

"Of course." Nathaniel leaned forward and snagged it. Unfolding the parchment, he blinked. It was a long list of seventeen different ingredients for a prescribed tonic. None of which he had ever heard of, except for...*laudanum.*

Jane had died from laudanum. Having dealt with Jane and her dependence on the substance, Nathaniel knew all too well it caused dizziness. And God only knew what the rest of the ingredients did. He'd never heard of them.

Pulse drumming, Nathaniel rose from the chair and snapped his gaze to Weston. "You mean to say she consumes all of these ingredients on a weekly basis?"

"Weekly? Daily."

His breath caught. "Daily? What the hell for? Do you have any idea how dangerous laudanum can be?"

"'Tis for her throat."

"Are you telling me this doctor is trying to cure her stutter with this shite?"

"What is prescribed isn't for her stutter, *Dr. Atwood,* but the lye she was exposed to when she was seven. Her throat needed considerable healing and this is but a continued precaution."

Nathaniel grabbed Weston by his coat. "She has been consuming all of this on a daily basis since she was seven? Are you demented? Why would you submit to pouring filth down her throat? Have you ever considered that maybe this tonic she keeps taking is why the poor woman is staggering about?"

Weston used an arm to free himself and stared. "Dr. Filbert is the best doctor London has to offer and comes highly recommended by the Royal College of Physicians. It costs me thirty pounds every time he so much as tips his hat. Gene survived the incident because of him and these ingredients."

Nathaniel folded the parchment and shoved it into his pocket. "'Tis my duty, given she and I are partners in this goddamn boxing venture, to ensure she only takes what is necessary for the sake of her health. And in my opinion, swallowing things I can't even pronounce isn't fucking necessary. I'll call on this Dr. Filbert myself. Something tells me he won't be tipping his hat for that much longer."

Weston narrowed his gaze. "Don't overstep your bounds by thinking you have any right taking over her personal life. She was never interested in taking a husband. She wouldn't have even taken you. She just doesn't trust you to follow through and I don't readily blame her. Remember, Atwood, she wants the money. Not you. Money. You do know that, yes?"

So saith the man who was making a sizable profit off his own sister's scheme. Nathaniel leaned toward him. "Focus on your own life, Mister Divorce, and not mine. Because the moment she and I sign contracts, Imogene is no longer under your jurisdiction, but mine. And from here on out, I'll be sure to remind you both who is making that quarter of a million possible. Not you. Not her. *Me*."

Hitting a hard hand to Weston's chest to demonstrate who was really in charge, Nathaniel stalked out. No one was going to make him feel like he was a carriage step in need of folding. No one.

CHAPTER SIXTEEN

It was like a drowning man catching at a straw.
—P. Egan, *Boxiana* (1823)

A week later—early evening
18 Berkeley Square

IMOGENE LINGERED IN the middle of what was now *her* receiving room. It was so odd to think it was not only hers but that she had paid for it.

The heavy curtains around the French windows had been drawn, shutting out the night beyond, whilst several candles in sconces illuminated the length of the pale blue walls. Though the house was small and the furnishings simple, for it was all she could afford if they were to remain in a fashionable district, she was content knowing it was but a gate to a new life that was all but four months away.

Gathering her celadon skirts from around her slippered feet, she turned and made her way out of the receiving room and into the small foyer. Her "husband" of barely a few hours had already excused himself to lift weights he had carried upstairs.

Being wed to an aristocratic boxer or, rather, the celebrated "Missing Heir," which London was officially all ablaze about, wasn't quite what she thought it would be.

Their afternoon wedding, though incredibly exciting, had been a blurring mess. She couldn't even remember hearing herself say yes. Word had gotten out to every gazette and newspaper in London as to when and where the wedding was to take place. It resulted in complete chaos.

More than her sister-in-law, her brother and the Duke of Wentworth and Lord Yardley showed up—the entire boxing community did; Angelo's fencing community did; the cockfighting community did; the Master of Foxhounds did; lords and ladies of the aristocracy, though oddly, not Lord Sumner or his wife; a representative from the crown; and even Lord Banbury, Mary's not-so-secret lover, lingered in the back of the church.

It was awkward.

None of that even included all of the people gathered outside. Countless men and women waved and called out their congratulations, expecting her and Nathaniel to wave through the carriage window as if they were the King and Queen of England gracing everyone with their presence.

She actually thought it rather charming and kept telling Nathaniel to wave. But for some reason, he just sat against the carriage seat clenching his two fists, his eyes closed throughout their entire carriage ride. He also hadn't said a word to her, even when she had repeatedly tried to get him to talk. It was like the man was having excessive regrets. Though he exploded back into character and life once they had left the carriage and arrived "home."

Pinching her lips, Imogene lingered in the foyer. Between all that and the endless scowls her brother and Nathaniel had exchanged prior to, during and after the wedding, she felt mentally and physically roasted. It was as if Henry and Nathaniel appeared to have declared war on each other and neither of them was telling her why.

Men.

Pausing beside all of her trunks, which continued to sit untouched in the foyer, she set her hands on her hips. Honestly. She had told the housekeeper to hire footmen as soon as possible.

Stepping to the side, she peered past the narrow mahogany staircase, down the empty corridor leading to the back of the house. Every door was shut as if the servants had abandoned their posts.

This was well past awkward. There was no one around. And heaven only knew how long Nathaniel would be lifting his weights.

"Mrs. Langley? Are there any footmen available to tend to my trunks?" she called out to the corridor, her voice echoing. "I would like to retire to my room."

The ticking of the French hall clock was the only answer she received. Oh, bother. She supposed she could manage to drag one small trunk up the stairs. Fortunately, she had asked her lady's maid to follow her into married life these next four months but she wasn't about to ask the poor woman to come down and carry her trunks. Even at five feet and three inches, Imogene was still almost a head taller than the woman.

Imogene eyed the trunks and sidled toward the smallest one. This was one way of learning how to be self-sufficient. How difficult could it be? Footmen did it all day and all night. One trunk wasn't going to be her undoing. And it wasn't as if she had anything else to do.

She half squatted and winced as the whale boning from her

corset insisted she not bend. She grabbed the leather handle on the trunk closest to her feet and lifted.

It wouldn't budge.

She really shouldn't have packed so much.

"Oh, come now," she muttered under her breath, trying to convince her trunk to cooperate. "You aren't that big." She lifted again, this time using the strength within her legs.

The leather straps of the handle pinched her palms hard despite the protection of her gloves. She ignored the sting, gritted her teeth and focused harder on lifting the small trunk off the floor. Just as it was coming up, her grip gave out and the trunk fell with a resounding thud.

"Oh, go to the deuce anyway," she muttered, swatting a foot at it. "You, Mr. Trunk, are as about as useless as I am."

"Trunks can be quite stubborn, can't they?" a deep voice drawled from somewhere above.

Startled, Imogene popped back up to her full height and snapped her gaze up toward the top of the staircase.

Nathaniel leaned against the top rail of the banister, bare muscled arms crossed over his broad chest.

She almost choked.

Since she'd last seen him, he'd removed all respectable clothing and was scandalously down to only trousers and black leather boots. Those trousers were also slung incredibly low on his narrow hips. So low, they showed the dip of his well-muscled lower abdomen that veered toward his...*ehm*.

A small smile touched his lips as he observed her from above. "Enjoying the view?"

Her heart skipped. "Given you are obviously done lifting weights, you ought to put a shirt on."

"Get used to it. This is what I will look like not only in the ring but in your bed at night."

Lovely. He would remind her of that.

He lifted a dark brow. "Did you need me to oversee the trunks?"

The thought that he'd been watching her verbally scold her trunks was rather embarrassing. She rubbed her still-burning palms into the sides of her skirts. "Yes, please. I have a horrible tendency to overpack."

"So I've noticed." He unfolded his arms and descended the stairs, those piercing blue eyes never once leaving hers. "I'll carry everything up to your room later."

"I'm assuming there are still no footmen?"

He stopped on the last stair. "I'm afraid not. The housekeeper you hired apparently won't have us fully staffed until next week."

She rolled her eyes. "I knew I should have hired a different housekeeper. Mrs. Langley came a little too cheap."

"We will more than manage, I assure you."

"We will have to."

He intently held her gaze and lingered. "How are you? Good?"

A tingling heat unexpectedly rattled her body. Why did she feel as though he were suddenly trying to be...overly familiar?

She lowered her gaze and fumbled to strip her gloves from her hands to keep herself occupied. "Very well, thank you. Tomorrow we officially commence your training sessions with Jackson. I'm rather excited to be part of this venture. It makes me feel useful." She tightened her hold on her gloves, wondering if she should put them back on.

Nathaniel jumped over the trunk that separated them and landed at her side with a thud.

She almost jumped herself in startled astonishment.

Holding her gaze, he reached down and tugged both gloves from her hands and tossed them toward the stairwell. "Talk to me. Not the gloves."

"Oh. I..." She nodded and was now very much aware of him and that bare and incredibly well-sculpted, muscled chest. Why did she want to keep looking at it and him? And why did he continue to silently linger?

The pounding in her head matched the pounding of her heart, though she tried not to let on. "Is there something you wanted?"

He pressed himself closer, his trouser-clad thighs indenting her full skirts if he wasn't violating any key social rules. His hands skimmed her corseted waist. "Join me for supper. Before we retire for the night."

Imogene stood awkwardly frozen against the heat of those large hands which continued to penetrate the midsection of her stomacher. For some reason, *retire* didn't sound like *retire*.

His hands continued to skim her waist. "Am I making you uncomfortable?"

She glanced up at him, her cheeks heating. "If you have to ask, you most likely are. A shirt would help."

"Now, now, be nice." He edged back. "I will attempt to adhere to the conduct of a gentleman during supper. Though I can't promise as to what my conduct will be afterward." He extended a formal hand for her to take. "Is this how you aristos escort a lady to a table?"

"Uh...yes."

He nudged it closer. "Take it."

She inwardly winced at the awkwardness between them and placed her bare hand into his bare hand, feeling more than her arm trembling.

His large warmth curled possessively around hers and tightened. Tugging her around the trunks by the hand, he guided her down the empty corridor, past countless other rooms, until they approached a dimly lit room.

Her eyes widened when they entered what appeared to be a dining area. The sweeping walls that had been painted a soft gold seemed to glow like the inside of a chalice and lit white candles scattered the entire length of the room.

A white linen cloth covered a table that had been set for two, with polished silver, gleaming porcelain and crystal. Each set plate already had a more than generous amount of steaming roast beef and Yorkshire pudding. A decanter of red wine and two crystal glasses, which had already been filled, awaited in a celebratory manner.

Although it was a simple meal, it was astoundingly lovely. And charming. As if he had gathered what few servants they had to have a meal made just for her.

Releasing her hand, he strode toward one of the two chairs and pulled it out, his muscles shifting as he gestured toward it. Those blue eyes softly beckoned for her to take pleasure in the welcoming mood he had set.

Knowing she had better sit before her legs folded, she hurried toward him, smoothed out the backside of her skirts and sat. "Thank you."

He shifted her chair closer to the set table. Though he had already finished positioning her chair, he continued to hold the back of it with both hands. "Our first meal together as business partners."

She set her chin and stared before herself, trying to pretend his presence didn't wash over her completely. Even though it did. "Yes."

He drew away, rounding toward the other side of the table.

He sat in the chair directly across from hers and, leaning forward, took hold of his filled wineglass and lifted it toward her in a salute. "To the championship and my patron, who is making *everything* possible."

Wanting to distract herself from those haunting eyes and that bare chest, she retrieved her own glass, lifted it in a return salute, then brought it straight to her lips. She sipped at the tangy wine and wondered how she was going to keep up the charade of not being nervous.

"Whatever your needs may be," he said in a smooth voice that dripped of some sort of innuendo, "I'll see to it they are all met on my end. All you have to do is ask."

She set her wineglass next to her plate lest her sweaty hands cause it to slip. Trying not to be bested by a man who clearly knew more about what was going to happen to her than she did, she obliged, "I wouldn't offer up such generosity. I might take off to France with your full quarter million and marry Henry off to a French woman. I hear they know how to love a man. Which he needs."

A low rumble of a laugh floated toward her. "I'll be sure to keep you in view at all times and take everything I want from you now."

She wasn't even going to ask what a man who came to dinner without a shirt wanted from a woman. Plucking up her napkin, she spread it neatly and daintily onto her lap. Taking up her fork and knife, she lowered her eyes to her plate and ate. Slowly. Very, very slowly.

"Imogene."

She paused and finished chewing her food. She was beginning to wonder why she'd really been invited to dine with him. "Yes?"

He shifted in his chair and leaned toward the table. "I met with Dr. Filbert whilst I was waiting on our license and terminated all of his services. The man's only explanation as to why you needed to take your daily tonic was to ensure you didn't lose your voice. In his medical opinion, he thinks it possible after all the lye you had been exposed to. It made no sense to me, Imogene. None. And considering you suffer from unexplained fainting spells, I think it time we get you off his filth. I'm beyond riled knowing your brother, a seemingly intelligent fellow, had sold himself into this. Why did neither of you connect your condition to the tonic you were taking?"

Imogene's startled gaze flew to his. Whilst she was anything but fond of Dr. Filbert's quack juice, it had helped her survive the incident and had kept her in good health for years. "Is this why you and Henry aren't particularly fond of each other at the moment?"

He lowered his eyes, slid his long fingers around the base of his wineglass that sat on the table and swirled the red wine within. "Yes." Nathaniel stilled his glass. "As a boxer, I know a few things about tonics and their effects. I've learned to stay away from them. You need to trust me in this."

Imogene returned her eyes to her plate, irked knowing Nathaniel and her brother were quibbling over something *she* should be making a decision on.

She eyed him. "I am not at all pleased with you or my brother for mistreating each other based on something *I* should be deciding. I ask that you let me decide what will be done with Dr. Filbert."

He was quiet for a moment. "And what is your decision?"

"You told me all but a breath ago. You don't expect me to decide whilst chewing on my meal, do you?"

He shifted in his chair in what appeared to be agitation. "You will make a decision tomorrow. In the morning. Before we leave for Jackson's."

She blinked. "I will make a decision when I come to it. It may be tomorrow or it may be next year, but you will not treat me as my brother did. For you are not my brother. And lest you forget you are my husband *only* in name."

He shifted in his chair again, but otherwise said nothing.

She returned to eating her meal in awkward silence. Why did she feel like she had just slapped him? She sensed he was trying to help. She had honestly never connected her medicine to her fainting spells. She had been drinking it for far too long to have ever made such a connection. But what he said was possible.

She retrieved her wine, her gaze momentarily wandering across the table toward Nathaniel.

He wasn't even attempting to eat.

His full plate sat untouched.

With a half-empty wineglass still in hand, he leaned farther back against the chair, staring at her.

Her pulse jolted, realizing he'd been staring at her the whole time. She looked away and instead of grabbing her wineglass, which would only further blur her senses, she dabbed at the corners of her mouth with her napkin. "Are you not hungry?"

"No." He lifted his glass to his full lips, still watching her from above its rim. After a lingering taste, he lowered the glass again. "Are you done eating? Because I want you to be. So finish."

She fisted the napkin in her lap in disbelief. Did he really think he could command her to eat at whatever pace pleased him? When she was paying for their meal?

Swallowing the last of her food, she dragged the napkin from her lap and set it onto the table. "I will see you in the morning. I am retiring *alone* this evening. Good night." Pushing back her chair, she stiffly rose and left. Gathering her skirts, she hurried out of the dining room and back down the corridor toward the main foyer. The sooner she got into her room and locked the door, the better.

The jogging steps of Nathaniel behind her made her eyes widen. She skidded into the foyer, turning toward the stairs, ready to outrun him.

"Imogene," he called out. "For God's sake, if you have something to say, fucking say it. We're either partners in this or we're not. Which is it?"

She winced and stopped short of the staircase, where all of her trunks still sat. He was right. If they were going to survive these next four months and get him to be the best he could be to win that championship, they had to use words. Lots of them. And she cringed at the idea of all the stuttering ahead of her. Letting out a shaky breath, she turned and waited for him.

Nathaniel slowed his jog and drew close, blocking the expanse of the hallway. "What is it? What did I do now?"

"Commanding me about at the dinner table as to how fast I am to eat, when I am the one providing the meal, is humiliating."

He huffed. "Dealing with women isn't really a forte of mine, all right? I usually only bed them. I don't *befriend* them."

Imogene jerked her gaze up to his husky face. "Have you never had a female friend? Truly?"

He shifted closer, his gaze wandering from her eyes down to her nose until they paused on her lips. "No. I'm not interested in that."

A knot rose in her throat and the air between them grew hot and unbearable. It was obvious what he wanted.

And annoyingly, she wanted it, too.

CHAPTER SEVENTEEN

Where now are all my flattering dreams of joy?

—P. Egan, *Boxiana* (1823)

IMOGENE'S BREATH HITCHED as she waited for him to lean in and kiss her.

Instead, Nathaniel glanced away and appeared to be more interested in flexing his right hand.

She blinked. Why was it when she wanted him to do something, he didn't, and when she didn't want him to do something, he did? Without thinking about the consequences, she quietly asked, "Are you going to kiss me or not?"

His gaze snapped back to hers. "Do you want me to?"

Her shoulders fell. "Maybe not."

He yanked her against himself with an aggressive tug of her hips, causing her to gasp, and crushed the velvety, hard feel of his naked torso against her. "Let me." With the dip of his head, he captured her mouth, his hot, wet tongue overtaking hers.

She almost fainted. And she knew it had nothing to do with her condition.

He swung them toward the stairwell, causing her to choke

against his mouth. Still engaging her mouth with the rapid rotation of his hot tongue, he leisurely stretched himself out onto the stairs, lowering her onto his body as he positioned her legs to straddle his thighs.

It was heart-poundingly thrilling to lean over him and kiss him and touch him in the way *she* wanted.

He sucked on her tongue, slowly pulling it deep into his mouth. Releasing his hold, he circled his tongue on the inside of her mouth while his large hands roamed down her skirts.

Pressing his mouth harder against hers, he dug into the fabric of her gown with his fingers and he crushed her body even harder against his. The urgency within that tense, muscled body grew as he ground himself into her and rolled, ground and rolled.

As one of his hands held the back of her head, dominating her by keeping her in place, his other hand shoved up her skirts and slid beneath the muslin fabric, smoothing up her naked thigh.

She stiffened, but he only pressed his hand against her head harder, his tongue moving harder against hers. His other hand slipped between her thighs, which were ajar from straddling him. Her eyes popped open when his fingers slid between her wetness.

She tore away from his mouth and tried to shove down her skirts. His free hand jumped around her waist, locking her in place against his thighs, while the other still rubbed her wetness, causing her to gasp against sensations that had no right to be there.

He held her gaze, his chest heaving. "Trust me. I'm not going to hurt you."

Her cheeks flamed as his fingers, which were buried beneath her skirts, continued to flick and rub her, rippling stomach-twisting sensations up and down her entire body. She swayed and grabbed his shoulders hard, trying to steady herself against what he was doing.

She held his penetrating gaze as she rode his hand right there with him draped beneath her on the stairs. She rode harder, torn between wanting the sensations to increase or altogether end.

Curiosity and a mingled haze of everything she felt for him physically in that moment made her not only bold but stupid. She slid her hands down the smooth length of his hard chest, down, down and touched the rigid line pushing against the flap of his trousers right where his hand was savagely fingering her.

He hissed out a breath and slipped a forefinger fully into her wetness.

She froze from the violating aggression that pinched, but his thumb slid and rubbed, slid and rubbed against the nub that caused those incredible sensations, erasing the discomfort.

His finger quickened.

An unexpected torrent shook her body and she gasped against it as pleasure unlike anything she thought possible overtook her breath and her entire world. She collapsed against him.

He slipped his hand from beneath her skirt, his chest heaving, and dug his shaven chin into her hair.

The rush of cool air drifted against her lips, she realized he had long ceased kissing, and for a few passing moments, she couldn't even bring herself to open her eyes let alone move. All she could do was focus on their heavy breaths and how his large warm hands now firmly held on to her arms.

"We finish upstairs," he said in a low voice, slowly releasing her. "The way I want it."

She opened her eyes, shifted to sit up against his thighs and blinked down at him. "Finish? But I thought…" She thought they were done.

Still laid out on the stairs, he stared up at her with a set jaw that told her he was far from done. "What just happened wasn't even admission to ringside seats."

Her entire body blazed at the thought of her own hand going into his trousers. "You don't expect me to…to put my hand into your trousers, do you?"

He rolled his eyes and eased out from under her. "No," he muttered. "I don't force myself on women. But when you're feeling particularly generous, let me know, will you?"

Rising, he grabbed her waist and yanked her up off the stairs with a single turn. Without meeting her gaze, he adjusted his trousers against the rigid line of his erection still pressing against the flap. "We should settle your trunks into your room so your lady's maid can organize all of this for you."

Stepping around her, he leaned over and grabbed both sides of the trunk. Heaving it up with one sweep, he straightened and made his way up the stairs.

Imogene stared up after him as he disappeared to deliver it into her room. Lifting a trembling hand, she covered her still-swollen mouth, which burned from the heat of his lips. She could still feel the way his hips had ground and rolled against her and the way his fingers had penetrated her into oblivion.

No wonder people got married.

Nathaniel jogged back down the stairs toward her. "You

left the table because of me. Did you want to finish your meal?"

She dropped her hand down to her side, rather dazed at how casual he was in light of what they had just done. She shook her head. "No, thank you."

He yanked up another trunk and made his way up again.

She pressed her hands against the sides of her blazing cheeks and tried to catch her breath. She was probably going to have to make an effort and do for him what he had done for her. He had appeared disappointed when she insinuated she wasn't interested in returning the favor.

Atwood appeared again and jogged back down the stairs. He grabbed for her last trunk, toting it up with a toss, and went back up the stairs. Not once sparing her a glance.

Imogene followed him up, knowing she ought to oversee his...*needs.* Whatever that meant. Oh, God. She slowly headed down the corridor leading to their bedchambers.

Setting a nervous hand to her stomacher, she decidedly made her way toward the last door he had disappeared into.

Pausing in the doorway, she peered inside.

The large latticed window on the far side of the wall had been draped with verdant velvet curtains and gave a stunning moonlit view of the park laid out in the night beyond.

A large, four-poster bed loomed, taking up almost the entire expanse of the room. An abundance of crisp, white linens and honey-colored blankets and silk plush pillows complemented the soft, golden hues of the painted walls. For a man who claimed he had gathered whatever furniture he could for her, his taste was quite elegant and impeccable.

Atwood pushed the trunks up against the wall, next to the large, mahogany dresser and mirror that were already set with a fresh basin and pitcher of water.

She knew whatever lay ahead couldn't be any worse than the lye trauma of her childhood. And it might prove to be as pleasant as what had just occurred on the stairs. Setting her chin, she stepped into the bedchamber and closed the door behind herself.

He stood and turned, swiping his hands across the front of his trouser-clad thighs. His hands stilled as he glanced toward the door she had closed.

She smiled, albeit nervously, and made her way toward him, trying not to give away that her heart pounded so hard she thought it might pop out from her throat and hit the wall. "I'm...I'm feeling generous."

His fiery gaze met hers. "Are you?"

She nodded. "Yes. What do you want me to...do?"

He remained perfectly still, but that set, shaven jaw conveyed he was waiting. "Come here."

She moved in closer. Pausing before his tall muscled body, she suddenly felt light-headed. But in an insanely good way that had nothing to do with her illness.

She lifted her gaze to his.

He unbuttoned his trousers but otherwise said nothing.

She dared not look down.

Taking her hands into his own, he slowly drew them toward the flap of his trousers. "Push down the flap and the undergarment beneath." His voice was tense but equally patient and soft.

She swallowed and with trembling hands pushed down his flap and his undergarment beneath. She instinctively lowered her gaze to what she was doing. His thick erection fell heavily toward her, making her suck in a startled breath. Her hands stilled.

She had to touch...*that?*

His hands gathered hers again and set them firmly against its velvety, rigid length. He forced her hands to rub it.

It was surprisingly smooth and firm. She pinched her lips to keep herself from looking at it and glanced up, trying to remain calm.

His chest rose and fell in uneven takes. "Do you want me to do the rest?" he whispered.

She nodded.

He grabbed her waist hard and yanked her up and into his arms and carried her to the bed.

She clung to him in both dread and anticipation.

His mouth drifted close to her ear, the heat of his breath against her neck. "Do you trust me?"

She nodded. She hoped she did.

"I won't undress you or remove my trousers. That will make it less traumatic for you, given it's your first time. But I am going to tie your hands for a small while. Will you let me?"

She nodded, desperately trying to please him, even though she was frightened out of her wits.

Laying her out on the bed, he dragged up her skirts, exposing her lower half to him completely. Tossing off her slippers, he undid the garters, his fingers grazing her skin, and rolled down her silk stockings. "These are going on your wrists. That way the marks will be minimal."

Her breaths came in panicked takes. "Do you have to bind my hands?"

"Yes. But I'll take them off when we're done. I promise." He entwined his fingers with hers, her silk stockings separating their palms. His rugged face now hung inches above hers as he raised both arms up over her head, his hands tightening against her own. "Relax. Don't fight me or this."

Something about the way he was holding her hands against his, as if he were trying to mentally prepare her for what he was about to do, felt oddly guiding and loving.

His large, warm body kept her in place against the mattress..Releasing her hands, he quickly wrapped both stockings around her wrists and yanked them tightly into knots.

He wrapped them tighter and tighter, until her wrists were not only bound but immovable. "Keep your hands over your head," he urged heavily, making one last tight knot. "The rule is—I touch you. You don't touch me."

She blinked as the heat of his skin against hers penetrated her body and her senses. She sucked in a deep breath as his fingers trailed down her arms toward her breasts.

He leaned in and kissed her forehead, her nose, her cheek and then her lips. "Don't panic," he murmured. "I'm going to slip myself inside you and ride you."

Himself? In there? "With what?" she managed.

He positioned himself above her, his hand reaching between them and held his sizable erection toward her. "With this," he confided. "And it will hurt. But not for long."

Her fingers dug into the linens as he nudged her thighs apart and edged its tip into her opening.

"Imogene."

She swallowed, waiting, feeling incredibly vulnerable with her hands tied and knowing what he was about to do.

"Imogene, look at me."

Her gaze jumped up to his.

He continued to remain propped above her, his free hand smoothing her hair. "If you focus on the pain, it will be all you feel. So don't focus on the pain. It won't last. It is my intent to not only take pleasure but to give pleasure. Believe that." Those blue eyes intently held hers with the same measure of assurance he had given her when he had been asking her to speak through her stutter.

She relaxed, knowing everything would be all right. For he had said it would be.

Still holding her gaze, he tightened his jaw and with a quick solid thrust of his hips, he buried himself so deeply and thoroughly inside her womb, the pain seared her into gasping.

He stilled and held her tightly against himself. With a domineering hand, he buried her head against the curve of his shoulder, setting her face against it. "Bite your way through the pain. Go on. Bite."

She didn't even think twice. She pressed against him and clamped all of her upper teeth down onto his smooth shoulder to get through the pain.

He moved against her, jarring her. "Good. You can bite me harder. Because I'm about to ride you harder."

She bit down as hard as she could, bracing herself.

His hips rolled slow at first, those thrusts controlled and smooth. But it didn't last. "That's it. Take it." He pushed into her faster and harder, his broad frame tensing against her as he seethed out breaths.

Though each savage thrust stung against the tightness of her passage and grew in intensity, she managed to survive by keeping her teeth clamped on his shoulder.

He dipped his head toward her and sucked on the curve of her throat, making her melt and writhe in sudden blooming pleasure.

His bucking movements kept jarring her until she realized she wasn't in pain anymore. It was all pleasure. Sweet pleasure.

Unlatching her teeth from his shoulder, she threw back her head to better extend herself against her tied hands, and let his mouth roam and devour her throat. She felt those same stomach-tightening sensations overtaking her body. Again. Only it felt bigger. Fuller. Like it was about to rip her apart.

"Give in to it," he rasped against her. "Like you did on the stairs."

She gasped in overwhelmed bliss as he stroked and stroked into her. She jerked her wrists against the silk stockings, wanting so desperately to touch him and his broad back, but she couldn't. "Can I touch you?" she breathed out between each of his thrusts. "Let me...touch you."

"No." He pumped into her harder. His large hands slid up and into her hair. "Let me hear you." He rode and rode into her, harder and harder. "Come on. How does it feel?"

She moaned.

"That wasn't good enough. Louder. Like you want more."

She pushed out an even louder moan. For him. Only it felt like she was bringing her climax on by doing so. It was too much. "Oh!" She cried out and shook beneath him, giving in to the bursting pleasure his thrusts flung her to.

"Fuck, yes." Fisting her bundled hair hard with one hand and grabbing her tied wrists by the knot, he pumped into her again and again, banging into her until an anguished groan escaped him, too.

He stilled, burying himself deep inside of her and eventually paused. "Shite," he breathed out, still buried inside her. "I poured into you."

Her heart pounded as her eyes popped open. "What?"

He heaved out a breath. "Fuck."

Him and that word.

With a few swift tugs, he released her hands from her stockings and whipped them aside. Leaning in, he grazed her wrists with his fingers and gently rubbed them as if to take away what he had done.

She blinked at his shoulder buried above her, realizing she had indented visible, deep marks into the skin that was already covered with white scars. She slid a finger to it in concern. "Did I bite too hard?"

He rolled off to the side and collapsed onto his back. "I didn't feel a thing." His chest rose and fell as he stared up at the canopy above them. "I don't know what came over me. I couldn't even think. I just… I've never spilled into a woman like that before."

Shifting onto her side and toward him, she shyly pulled her skirts down around her legs, feeling a heavy, warm wetness between her thighs. "What do you mean you spilled into me?"

He glanced toward her, still on his back, and searched her face. "I poured my seed into you. Which means you can end up with a child."

Her stomach fluttered and crashed all at once, knowing a child might come of it. "And how will I know if…?"

"Your body will tell you." Shifting toward her, he propped himself on an elbow. "The most certain one is when your menses ceases. The moment it does, tell me. We'll ensure we address it and take it from there. Just be sure to tell me."

It was so odd. How was it that she felt like she had always talked to him like this? Even though she knew there were still so many caverns of his life she knew nothing of?

She had no words to describe it. She felt like she was living the life she was meant to live. A life where she didn't feel like she was being a burden to anyone. Nathaniel didn't make her feel like she was a burden. He made her feel like she was her own person and he was his.

Without even thinking, she placed a hand over her heart, then let it drift and placed it against the middle of his chest.

He lowered his gaze and fingered her hand.

Her heart squeezed. It was like his attempt at returning affection. It was so endearingly sweet. "How did we end up like this?"

He continued to finger her knuckles. "One delectable woman with a lot of money and one stupid man with none."

A giggle bubbled forth from her lips.

He smiled and continued to touch her hand as if every contour of her finger fascinated him. His features seemed at peace and at ease, as if he were content with this and them and what had happened.

Something whispered of a chance to get to know him. He wasn't guarded. Her heart fluttered as she sidled closer. "Tell me something."

"What?"

"What is it like being a boxer?"

He glanced up, his rugged face brightening. "It's the only time I feel like I can actually make the entire world bend against my hands. It's amazing."

She hesitated and tightened her hold on his hand. "I promise not to burden you over these next few months."

He eyed her. "You need to stop talking like that. I just took your virginity, and you're up and saying you're the burden?"

She swallowed. The beat of his heart against her fingers and the rising and falling of his chest became her world in that moment. She had never known anything like it. She felt so intimately connected to him. And yet…there was so much she had to know about him. What sort of secrets lay buried within him?

She shifted just enough to see his face better and eventually offered, "I imagine you were hurt knowing your own father and mother didn't come to our wedding. Especially when all of London did. Be our union superficial or not, they should have been there."

He slowly pushed away her hand and rolled onto his back. "I could care less." His tone indicated otherwise. "If my mother chooses to side with my father, what can I do? I'm done chasing this in my head. I can't keep sending her missives that just keep going unanswered. Nor am I about to hurt her in the same way my father hurt me."

His father? She blinked. "What do you mean? What did your father do?"

He vacantly stared up at the canopy of the bed. "I would rather not say."

She gently set a hand onto his chest. "Nathaniel. I...I am here to listen. Please know that."

He continued to vacantly stare up at the canopy of the bed. "I thought this was about a quarter of a million pounds. Not me."

She swallowed, that blunt response stinging more than her pride. It actually stung her heart. "Cease. I genuinely wish to know you."

"Why?"

"Because I like you. And because...I...I want to know which of the stories are true and which are not."

He pushed her hand off his chest. "I'm not giving that part of myself to you, Imogene. So don't ask me which stories or true or not. Because you'll never know."

Her brows came together. She tried not to let agitation bite into her. "How is it that you don't think me worthy enough of knowing things about you, and yet you feel entitled on dabbling in not only my body, but my world of stuttering and

Dr. Filbert and my medications? Let the dabbling be mutual if we are to play this game of who bends to whom."

"We are obviously done here." He sat up. "Good night. I'll retire into my own room." He adjusted his trousers around himself and his hips, buttoned the flap and pushed himself off the bed, landing on the wooden floor with an aggressive thud. He strode for the closed door.

She scrambled to sit up. "Nathaniel. Please don't be angry with me. I was merely conveying what I genuinely feel."

He opened the door. Abruptly turning toward her, his ice-blue eyes flared. "Discussing disturbing events of my life is no different than reliving them. And I'm not about to relive what I went through just so you can better understand what I already know."

By God. What had he endured?

Holding her gaze, he rigidly pointed. "And despite what you think, as your business partner, I have a right to ensure your health isn't being swindled by some balding quack. I've seen too many people shrivel and die in the Five Points consuming tonics for their 'health.' If I see you taking any of that medication, you had best be wearing a pair of leather boxing gloves. I won't say it again."

She scrambled up onto her knees, determined to prove to him that he wasn't in control of her life. She was. She pointed to herself. "*I* will decide what needs to be done when it comes to my medications. Not you. I."

"It's already taken care of and done. I talked to him. He knows that if he damn well comes anywhere near you, or attempts to administer any more of his tonics, I'll be putting a knuckle through his brain."

"But I wasn't there to listen in on the conversation and form an opinion."

"Yes, but I was."

"Since when did you become me?"

He stared. "Are you arguing with me? Because I don't like it. So I suggest you fucking stop."

She chanted to herself not to submit to a stutter, even though she felt it coming on from the riled angst that threatened to slap her *and* him. She focused on each and every word, ensuring it was precise, only it turned into a mess. "I think it-it-it is the-the-the principle of the matter and n-n-not whether I think you are right or-or-or wrong. I will drink that quack juice merely t-t-to demonstrate whose hand really holds the-the-the cup."

A muscle flicked angrily in his jaw. "I dare you."

She set her chin. "T-t-tomorrow afternoon at four. In the-the-the parlor. Be there."

After a long pulsing moment of silence, he shifted toward her and grated out, "You and I will be at Jackson's. I've got training all day tomorrow. Or did you forget?"

She stared, swallowing a sense of calm she desperately wanted to feel.

"There is no reason for you to take that damn tonic, Imogene," he bit out. "There is absolutely nothing physically wrong with you. Or don't you know that?"

She squeezed her eyes shut and set her hands on her ears, not wanting to listen to him anymore. She stuttered. That was what was wrong with her. And she wished upon all wishes that stupid tonic would fix it. Only it never did. And she hated knowing it. She hated, hated, hated knowing that she would forever be at the mercy of looking stupid.

The bed suddenly shifted and a hand grazed her wrist. "Imogene."

Startled, she opened her eyes and glanced up to find Nathaniel leaning in.

His blue eyes intently held her. "Did you need me to sleep with you tonight? I can."

Astounded by his concern, she blinked rapidly and slowly shook her head. "I… No."

He sighed. "I can't have you riled to the point of stuttering. It isn't right. How about you and I come to an agreement with regard to your medication?"

She swallowed. "What sort of…agreement?"

"Go for two months without your tonic and see how you feel. If you decide you still need it after those two months are over, we'll call in another doctor. Not Dr. Filbert, mind you, but someone else who isn't biased. Can you agree to that much?"

Rather dazed at the unexpected bend of his nature, she half nodded. "I… Yes. I can…I can stop taking it tomorrow. I can give it two months and…decide then."

"I'm glad to hear it." He pushed off the bed. "If you need me, just knock on my door." Holding her gaze for a pulsing moment, he turned and strode to the open door.

Stepping out, he closed it with a soft thud.

As always, she never knew what to expect from the man. He was so stubbornly hard and yet so…endearingly soft at the times she needed him to be. She lowered herself slowly to the bed and nestled her cheek against the cool, smooth linens. It was quite possible she was already beyond enchanted with this boxer.

This could complicate things.

CHAPTER EIGHTEEN

Sir, my friends think that had the weather on last Tuesday, the day upon which I contended with you, not been so unfavourable, I should have won the battle; I therefore challenge you to a second meeting, at any time.

—P. Egan, *Boxiana* (1823)

The following morning

NATHANIEL WAS GOING to straight punch someone, knowing there was already a group of chroniclers lingering outside the house with pencils and writing books in hand. Since when did his life become not his own?

Since Imogene, is when. Since Imogene. Damn her.

Stopping at the bottom of the main staircase, Nathaniel thumped at the middle wall with the side of his fisted hand until it burned. *"The carriage and I have been waiting fifteen minutes!"* he called out loud enough for her to hear. "Are we going to Jackson's or not?"

He stepped back and checked the hall clock set against the far wall. He rolled his eyes. "There is a clock upstairs, too, you know!" he yelled out. "I checked last night!"

"There is no need to yell like the boxing savage that you are," Imogene chided from atop the stairwell. "We are on time and will get there in barely twenty minutes if we avoid Park Lane."

He glanced up at her. "A woman's time and a man's time are obviously—" His brows went up.

Imogene regally descended the stairs, draped in a stunning lilac and lace gown that more than complimented her figure. It personified it. The lavish skirts swayed rhythmically against her elegant movements. The woman even wore an oval bonnet, which had been trimmed with white silk flowers and lilac satin ribbons.

How the hell was he or anyone else at Jackson's going to fight with all that satin and lace in the way?

Landing pertly before him, she set her chin and smiled. "Do I meet your approval?"

"Approval is one thing. Being practical is quite another. You're overdressed."

She lowered her chin. "Overdressed?"

"Isn't that what I just said? You're overdressed."

She glanced down at herself. "But I thought it pretty."

A character is what she was. One he wished he didn't like so goddamn much. "It is pretty. But that isn't what I'm trying to say."

She glanced up. "What are you trying to say?"

"That you're overdressed. If you had any more lace on you, we would probably be able to open a dress shop."

She sighed. "What am I supposed to wear?"

"I don't know…maybe something with a little less—" he rigidly gestured toward her ribbons and silk flowers "—*female* paraphernalia."

"But everything I own is female. I *am* a female."

He stared. "Imogene. Men are going to be spraying sweat across the room. Or didn't you know that?"

"Of course I know that." She plucked out a lace napkin from her reticule and wagged it at him. "That is why I brought this."

Oh, God. "*That* will barely clean up my middle finger."

She pursed her lips. "Your middle finger isn't *that* large."

He snatched it from her and shoved it into his trousers. "If you need it, you know where to find it."

She leaned away. "You can keep it."

"I will. I would tell you to change but we don't have time." He thumbed toward the door. "Now move. Before we're late."

Adjusting her carriage shawl about her shoulders, she leaned in, her hazel eyes now sparkling with an unusual amount of mischief. "I hear—and from a most reliable source, mind you—that your wife intends to turn you into a boxing champion. So whatever you do, don't disappoint her by tripping on the lace napkin stuffed in your trousers." With the flip of the ribbons on her bonnet, she brushed past toward the entrance door. "Now come along. You, sir, are late."

Everything about her made him want to grab and squeeze. Hard. He rotated toward her and jogged toward the door, setting himself against it. "Before we go. There are chroniclers waiting outside. They will be asking questions about me and the upcoming fight, most of which I'll not be responding to. We only pause long enough to appear sociable, I answer four questions and we leave. All right?"

She eyed him. "I don't have to talk to them, do I?"

Pushing away from the door, he grabbed her hand. "No. In fact, I prefer you not say anything. Chroniclers have a tendency to be aggressive. So don't give them any opportunity to engage you."

She nodded, now looking a touch panicked.

"Imogene." He shook her hand. "I won't let anything happen to you. I'm a boxer. Remember?"

She paused, her features relaxing. "Right."

"Now come along." Opening the door, he hooked her arm around his and guided them out into a bright, sunlit day, closing the door behind them.

"Lord Atwood!" Several men in topcoats and beaver hats, who had been lingering by the iron railing dividing the house from the cobbled street, hurried toward them. "Lord Weston assured us you would be available to answer questions."

He was beginning to hate Weston. "I'm certain he did." His arm tightened against Imogene's, silently imploring her to remain calm, as they descended to join the group of men. "Regrettably, I only have time for four questions, gentlemen. My wife and I have an appointment."

The mustached gent closest to him leaned in and quickly asked, "Norley publicly announced last night over at Cardinal's that, with your wife being your investor, you won't last past a few rounds. He says you look like a kept man and that your marriage is a farce. What have you to say to that?"

Nathaniel smirked, knowing Norley was desperate to be making public comments. "Norley should be spending more time training and less time talking. If I look like a kept man, I'm damn proud of it. Next question?"

Another man pushed closer. "There are those who claim you are parading as the missing Sumner heir merely for publicity purposes. Is that true?"

Nathaniel stared the man down. "I wish publicity meant that much to me. Next question?"

"Since when does an aristocrat go into the realm of professional boxing?" someone tersely tossed out.

Nathaniel shifted toward the man. "I don't really consider myself an aristocrat, gentlemen. I certainly didn't grow up as one. I lived on the streets and barely had enough to pay for clothes and food. Boxing is what kept me alive. And that is why I keep doing it. Next and last question?"

A stockier, round-faced man called out, "Rumor has it, you have been associating with Harriet Wilson during unconventional hours. Are you her latest protector and what does your wife of one day have to say to that?"

Imogene stiffened against his arm hold, her startled gaze flying up to his.

He hated chroniclers. But what he hated even more than chroniclers was knowing Imogene now thought he was cavorting with other women. A jealous woman was not a happy one and he had an upcoming fight with Norley to focus on.

Releasing Imogene's arm, Nathaniel strode up to the chronicler who had asked the question, snatched hold of the man by the lapels of his topcoat and with a violent thrust, flung both the man and his beaver hat in full reverse toward the pavement. "Does that answer your question?" he bit out. "Whatever woman I am with, for whatever the reason, she always gets my full attention. Call it a rule of mine. Respect it."

Turning back to Imogene, he grabbed her by the waist hard and pushed her toward the direction of the waiting carriage. "Any more questions like that, gents," he called out over his shoulder, "and I'll ensure more than your pencils break. Keep it to boxing. Not my goddamn life."

Hurried booted steps and more questions filled the air, trying to catch up with him. "Will your father be watching any of the fights?"

Nathaniel almost whipped around and launched himself at the man who asked the question but knew if he did, he'd probably end up at Scotland Yard for it. He had spent his entire life shoving aside his life and now his life was intent on shoving back. And whilst he had tried to do right by his mother and his sister by not implicating his father—or killing him—the reality was that, in an attempt to better his life, he was throwing open all doors to secret sniffing chroniclers and all of London. Regardless of whatever his path to the championship brought, he knew he was done bowing to the past. It was time that the past bowed to him. And it would.

Hoisting Imogene up and into the open door of the waiting carriage, he climbed in, slamming the door behind himself, and threw himself into the upholstered seat across from her. He hit the ceiling of the carriage with a fist to signal the driver to go.

When the jogging faces of the chroniclers disappeared, he fell against the seat. This was but the beginning. He hadn't even taken his first fight yet.

He paused. His chest tightened at realizing he was sitting in the carriage. God, it was always something. He detested how it made his skin crawl. There were times he was capable of focusing and pretending small spaces didn't bother him and there were other times—like now—that it not only bothered him but made him nauseous.

Shite. He dug his fist against his mouth and tried to focus on something. Anything.

Imogene intently observed him. "What is it?"

He swallowed past the knot in his throat and did everything he could to keep himself from rocking. "Nothing. I'm fine."

"You don't look fine."

He tried to look out the window, reminding himself he had the means to get out. "I just don't care for small spaces.

Once we get out, I'll be fine. Just leave me alone. Leave me to focus."

She quickly rose, settled herself beside him and leaned in close. "I remember when we were in the carriage the last time. You sat with your eyes closed the whole while and wouldn't even speak to me. I thought it was me."

"Yes, well, it isn't."

She hesitated. "Tell me how I can help."

He lifted his eyes to hers and held that soft gaze. An odd sense of peace overcame him knowing that she was genuinely concerned for him. Him. Not the quarter of a million. *Him.* And why the hell did he care?

She smiled and took hold of his hands. "You look better already."

He nodded but said nothing.

She playfully lifted a brow. "So who is Harriet Wilson?"

He snorted at the unexpected but welcome topic and leaned toward her. "If I knew that, I would have answered the question. Chroniclers are known for trying to make their own stories more exciting. Get used to it."

She nodded, gently swaying the ribbons of her bonnet, and continued to attentively hold his gaze.

He tried to stay focused on her and only her. "Distract me from the fact that I'm still in this goddamn carriage. What are you thinking about?"

She smoothed a hand across the coat on his forearm. "You. What is it about the carriage that makes you so uncomfortable?"

He shifted against the seat and knew there were some things he wasn't going to be able to keep from her. "I was kept in a cellar during my captivity. And sometimes, I still feel like I'm...in it."

Her startled gaze flew to his. "A cellar? Nathaniel, why were you kept in a cellar?"

He stiffened. "Imogene. There are some things I just don't want to talk about. And this is one of them. Especially now."

She nodded, her hand gently rubbing his coat and arm. "Forgive me. I understand."

God. He wanted to touch her again, as he did last night, but knew, damn her, he'd never be able to again. Not after what he'd done to her, tying her up and seizing her virginity as if it were his to seize.

He dug his gloved hands into the seat to keep him from thinking about what he'd done. "Stop touching me. For God's sake, *stop.*"

Her hand edged away. "I'm sorry."

He adjusted his coat, annoyed with himself for still wanting her so much. He had stupidly misled himself into thinking he could fuck her and think nothing of it. The problem was, something happened the moment he'd claimed her. Something that had never happened to him before. He had started wanting her in more than that way.

He wanted her in every way.

This was becoming far more than mere attraction or a wink at a business contract. He liked her a bit too much. Which was a problem. Because she was rattling the cage of something he swore to avoid for the rest of his life: passion. He knew what it did to people. It made them rip everything apart.

He had to avoid getting any more attached. He was used to detaching himself from people. He'd done it all his life. What was one more person?

Rising from his seat, he strategically placed himself across from her, feeling as if now *she* were choking him, not the carriage. He was morbidly relieved when they rolled to a stop and Jackson's appeared outside the glass window.

IMOGENE REMOVED HER bonnet, folding the satin ribbons, and set it quietly onto the bench beside her, feeling quite over-dressed. From the other side of the room, Nathaniel and nine other men, including Mr. Jackson, stripped down to shirts and waistcoats.

She pinched her lips, feeling awkward about seeing so many men strip at once. It made her stomach churn and her throat burn.

Some of the young men were smirking as if aware of her discomfort and purposefully positioned themselves in a way that best displayed their dressed-down muscled bodies.

Men were so annoying.

One moment they were human. The next they were not.

Nathaniel being an example of that.

The man hadn't tossed so much as a word or glance at her since they had left the carriage. It was like she had ceased to exist now that they had stepped into *his* realm. Boxing.

Jackson called out to the men, "Mr. P. Egan will be making the rounds this week, given the upcoming championship. Impress him, gents, and the glory of his remarks and the popularity it will bring are yours."

Imogene's brows went up. Mr. P. Egan? Why, she knew that name. She had been reading the man's boxing scribbles from Henry's study in an effort to better understand what she was investing in. She pertly sat up, feeling unusually pleased with herself for knowing *something* about boxing.

"And on we go," Jackson called out. Jackson turned to Nathaniel and pointed. "We will be focusing on the Norley fight. Norley always goes for the head. The temple in particular, though he is most known for breaking the jaw. So let me play his game."

Jackson thrust a large leather glove onto each of Nathaniel's hands and, using the leather strings, wrapped, tied and knotted them into place. Every man in the room followed suit, the leather gloves that had been strung from the hooks on the wall now on every hand in the room.

Nathaniel angled himself across from Jackson, bringing both leather-clad fists up. All of the other men found their sparring partners, as well. With a sounding call from Jackson of *"Set to!"* every man started swinging.

Every time they all hit each other with those large leather gloves, Imogene flinched as if she were getting hit. When did men crawl into the idea that beating the blood out of another man was acceptable?

A quarter of a million, she chanted to herself. *A quarter of a million.* She needed to remind herself why she was watching men maim each other into oblivion.

She stared, unable to believe how ruthless they all were. *Especially* Nathaniel. With his black hair scattered and growing damp, eyes fiercely narrowed and focused, and his large, muscled body hunched and tensed, there was not an ounce of humanity left in him.

He wasn't the same man.

He darted in, his face intent on gashing, and savagely delivered a quick blow to Jackson's side, making Imogene wince. Jackson darted in equally fast, yelling out a command, and returned a hooking blow that snapped Nathaniel's head aside.

She choked back a startled yelp as Jackson hit him in the head again. Her hands jumped up and covered both eyes, her heart pounding in disbelief at having seen Atwood get hit so brutally.

Oh, God. This wasn't even the actual fights or the championship.

This was mere training.

Grunts and rapid thuds echoed around her in a whirling blur. That was when she realized something.

Nathaniel could get hurt. Badly.

CHAPTER NINETEEN

It required something more than fortitude, to act thus in opposition to nature, as well as considerable Ingenuity in husbanding his strength, that he might be enabled to reduce his opponent to his own level.

—P. Egan, *Boxiana* (1823)

Evening

IMOGENE VEERED TOWARD her closed bedchamber door and leaned against it, intently listening to Nathaniel's footsteps disappear down the corridor to his room. She splayed her fingers across the cool, smooth wood and swallowed against the tightness throbbing within her throat.

After a short supper, and barely a few words exchanged about nothing in particular, he insisted on retiring early into his own room. It was like he had lost all interest in her as a woman. He didn't even try to touch her. Not once.

Was it because she had been unable to watch him fight and had stupidly sat with her hands plastered against her face even though she was the one investing in every hit? Some patron she had turned out to be. What had started out as a mere agreement had morphed into her realizing dreams were never quite the same once they became reality.

A knock to the door made her jump. She scrambled to open it. Yanking open the door, she was disappointed to find it was only her lady's maid come to assist her into her nightgown. Not Nathaniel.

A half hour later, after her lady's maid had uncorseted her for the night and gathered all of her clothing, leaving Imogene to herself in the comfort of a nightdress, Imogene pushed away from the closed door.

It was rather obvious Nathaniel was not coming to visit her. Drifting toward her dressing table, she sat in a half daze and leaned over the porcelain basin of water. Dipping her hands into its coolness, and using a sliver of soap, she washed and rubbed her face and throat clean. Using the folded cloth set by the basin, she dried her skin.

She bit back a shiver against the chill the cold water brought and sprinted across the room, crawling onto the bed. Grabbing for the linens, she wrapped them around her body and stared at the wavering light and shadows the candlelight created across the high ceilings.

She was still very dazed. The training session had jarred her into a reality she hadn't even thought about.

Nathaniel could get hurt badly.

She squeezed her eyes shut and blew out a slow breath. Her mind was going to eat her alive. She needed to talk to him. Or she wouldn't be able to sleep.

Opening her eyes, she dragged all the linen from off the bed with her and wrapped it up tighter around her shoulders and body, pinning it closed with her arms around her nightdress. Padding across the room, she pulled open the door and leaned out.

A faint light peered from under his door at the end of the corridor. She bit her lip and shuffled her way toward it until she reached his bedchamber door. She raised her linen-buried hand to knock but then paused and drew it back.

In some way, she feared admitting that she already genuinely cared for him. Mostly because she knew her affection would never be returned. There were far too many scars covering that soul and that life.

With heart-pounding certainty that she would somehow find the right words to say to him, she raised her hand and knocked. There was a pause and then steps crossed the floor toward the door. She tightened her hold on the linens and felt an uncertain lurch of excitement and dread take over, knowing she was about to see him again.

The door opened and light flooded the corridor.

She blinked up at him.

His tousled black hair hung in his eyes and though his cashmere robe was tied firmly at the waist, the collar still hung slightly open, exposing his throat and a V-shaped section of his bare, muscled chest. And his face. His poor jaw and cheekbone covered with welts and bruises from the training he had done with Jackson.

She swallowed. Was it so wrong to want him for more than what they had originally agreed upon?

His blue eyes raked the length of her as dark brows came together. "Is something wrong?"

How could he pretend that his face and his body didn't hurt? "Might I come in?"

He draped an arm across the doorway, leaning toward her and lowered his chin. "No. I'm not interested in engaging you like that anymore. We're done."

The way he said it made her pulse lurch. What did that mean? "I wasn't looking to…" She couldn't say it.

His expression remained stoic. "What were you looking to do then?"

He wasn't going to make this easy, was he? "I need to talk to you."

He cocked his head. "Then talk."

"Is there a way for you to take less fights?"

He eyed her. "Not if we're talking about the championship."

She held her linen tighter against herself. "I'm worried," she admitted.

"About what?"

"About you."

His brows rose. "Why?"

"The more I think about you getting hurt in a boxing match, the more I panic. I don't care for it."

He shifted against the door frame. "I suggest you not worry and that you go to your room. I've had a long day."

She threw him an exasperated look. "Do you think me incapable of genuine concern after what I saw today? Mr. Jackson was irresponsibly *vicious* toward you. *Vicious.* Banging your head around like…like…you were some…some…ball on the croquet lawn. It's supposed to be training. Not an introduction to Roman Empire Crucifixion."

A gruff laugh escaped him as the edges of his eyes crinkled. "The point of training is to be prepared. Real fights, tea cake, *are* a form of crucifixion. Men die in the ring all the time and I'm trying to ensure I don't die myself."

He wasn't helping. Her misgivings only seemed to increase. "I don't like it. I don't like any of this."

He tipped his entire body forward, appearing more and

more agitated. "Might I ask what you thought boxing entailed prior to watching it today?"

"Well, I…"

"What? Two pillows and a rooster?"

"No. I knew what boxing entailed. I will have you know that I've read the entire volume of Mr. P. Egan's book on the matter. And more than four times."

"Have you?"

"Yes. I just…"

"You just what? We married to ensure you can watch me do this, morning, day and night. Everything we're doing morning, day and night is because of you and a chance at a quarter of a million pounds. And suddenly you have a problem with it?"

She fidgeted beneath the intensity of that gaze. "It isn't that I have a problem, I just… When I saw you getting hit like that, I… It…it became too real. All of this is becoming far too real."

He dragged his arm down the door frame. "So what are you telling me?" His voice and his features darkened. "That we're done? That you're pulling your goddamn investment? Is that what you're telling me?"

"No, I…" She glanced down the corridor and back at him. "If we do this, you have to promise me you won't get hurt."

He searched her face. "Imogene. It's boxing. I'm going to get hurt. So I can't promise you otherwise."

Hearing him say it made her want to sob. Henry had made him sound inhuman when it came to boxing, as if nothing could ever touch him. Only she had spent the entire afternoon watching him getting not only touched but brutally knocked around. "Nathaniel, I—" She grabbed his waist hard and frantically tugged him close, burying herself against his warmth. She shook him, trying to make him understand. "Henry claimed you were untouchable, so I didn't even think that— If you get hurt, the money will be nothing more than a curse. And I've been cursed enough in my life. I don't want any more regrets. I don't."

He stilled. After a few breaths, his large hands slowly skimmed across her braid and down her back. "You needn't worry about me," he murmured. "I'll be fine."

"How do you do it?" she asked against him.

"Do what?"

"How do you take hits and pretend it doesn't hurt?"

His fingers dragged up into her hair. "I've spent my whole life doing it. I'm used to the pain."

She dug her head into him, those words stabbing her. Despite his never saying it, this man had suffered like this his whole life. It was heartbreaking. For at least she knew she had many, many glorious and happy moments with her papa and mama and Henry. Without pain. Without strife. It hadn't always been bad. It felt like it, but it hadn't been.

He drew away, unlatching her arms from his waist. "Go back to your room. All right? Because I really don't need this right now." He stepped back but didn't meet her gaze.

A crazy little voice told her that he not only wanted her but needed her, despite his telling her to go. And wild though it was, she was determined to listen to that voice, because she had to stop putting herself before this man. It wasn't right that he was physically endangering himself merely because she had asked him to. Merely because there was a lot of money involved.

She squeezed past him and into his bedchamber. "I'm sleeping with you tonight. And every night until the championship."

"No. I have to focus on my fighting."

She swallowed. "I'm not asking you to bed me."

"Then what are you asking for?"

"I simply want to sleep with you. That way, neither of us will be alone. Is that so wrong?"

"I'm more than fine with being alone."

"I don't believe you. As such, I'm staying. And you can't make me leave."

He glanced toward her and hesitated. Huffing out a breath, he eventually half nodded and swung the door shut with a thud.

Biting her lip, she glanced toward the open wardrobe where all of his clothes hung and paused. At the bottom of that wardrobe, peering out on an angle, beyond the open doors, was a small leather-bound book that had been strung closed by a red velvet sash. It looked more of a female origin. Not something that would have belonged to him.

It appeared he had tried to stash it from sight, only to have failed. He had probably been perusing it when she had knocked.

He crossed toward the wardrobe, as if fully aware of where her attention now lay and leaned down, tucking it out of sight. He closed the lacquered doors into each other and faced her, meeting her gaze in a distant manner that indicated she say nothing.

How could she not say anything? "Who is she?" She tried to hide the ache within her voice but it was no use.

He stared. "Who?"

She gestured to the wardrobe he had just shut. "I saw the book with the sash. Don't pretend I didn't see it."

He shifted his jaw, a lethal look surfacing beneath that

distant facade. He angled toward her. "If I didn't know any better, I'd say you were jealous."

She wasn't one to lie. "Maybe I am. Maybe I am jealous toward a man I gave my virginity to." Unable to hold it in, she confessed, "I haven't been the same since last night. I think about it with almost every breath I take. In many ways, I have become yours without meaning to. In many ways, you have made me yours."

He was quiet for a moment, as if startled by her admission. "I didn't mean to complicate things between us."

"But you did."

"I know. I did." He raked back his hair and then muttered, "It's my sister's diary."

His sister. The one who had been wed to the ever-good-natured Duke of Wentworth. The one who had died. Now she felt insensitive and half-baked. "I'm ever so sorry. I didn't— Were you reading it?"

He glanced away. "I haven't been able to. I'm not much of a brother."

She stepped toward him, anguish overwhelming her. "I can help you read it, if you want. I know how difficult it is. I was never even able to set flowers on my mama's or my papa's crypt. I always had Henry do it for me. I finally did it myself a few years ago, and though it was overwhelming, it made me feel like I was visiting with them. You should read her words. It would be like visiting with her, too."

He turned away and, setting both hands wide against the wardrobe, he leaned heavily against it. "What do you want from me, Imogene? Why do you keep trying to dig into me and my life? What do you think you're going to find?"

Her stomach churned. It was obvious he wasn't used to

people caring. "Are you not used to someone genuinely wanting to partake in your life?"

He pushed away from the wardrobe and swung toward her, a muscle flicking in his welted jaw. "No. Not really. In my opinion, when your own father can turn against you, anyone can. I've learned to keep things simple and at a distance. It's best that way. More important, it's best for me."

She inwardly shriveled at hearing those words. She had been blessed to have always known the support of her family. Even though now all she had left of that family was Henry. "I won't turn against you. You and I are friends."

His expression remained cool. "I don't know what we are."

"I know we are friends. We have shared enough to be that much. Have we not?"

He set his shoulders but said nothing.

She swallowed hard and knew this man needed to understand that she genuinely cared for him. Because she did. And it was obvious it was something he had never heard enough of in his life. "I would be fooling myself into saying everything I have done thus far, including giving you my virginity, was done for a quarter of a million. This afternoon, whilst I was watching you get hit, what I felt in that moment was something money cannot buy. That emotion of genuine concern was there for you. It really was. It still is. I want you to know that. I like you. Very much. And I care for you. Very much. More than I should probably be admitting to."

His harsh features notably softened as did those ice-blue eyes that held her gaze. "Get into bed. It's late."

She clutched the linens around her, trying to balance not only herself but her whirling thoughts. She nodded and drew in deep, calming breaths, then let them out. She knew the moment she got into his bed, she would be doing far more than submitting her body to him. She would be submitting her heart to a man who clearly needed one.

NATHANIEL KNEW THAT letting Imogene stay in his room and in his bed was a mistake. As if her confession hadn't riled the last of him, she looked like a dream, bundled up from shoulder to toe in ivory linens, her nightdress peering out from beneath. Her beautiful face glowed with the rising flush her words had brought and that blond, braided, rumpled hair only seemed to add to his wanting to savor what little time he had with her. Because their four months was going to pass with but a breath and he didn't want to get any more attached. Especially knowing that no one had *ever* gifted him with the amount of patience and understanding and respect that she had. Be it for a quarter of a million or not. "Get into bed," he said again.

She nodded and, using the post, assisted herself up into the bed. He made his way toward her and the bed, counting each and every step to keep himself from altogether lunging. Sex was not a good idea. Not when all of the lines between pleasure, need, escape, yearning and sentiment were already blurring in his head like a dream he couldn't get out of. He drew back the linens, sliding in beside her. Blowing out a breath to steady his mind, he settled back against the mattress and into the softness of the pillows, trying to get his sore and exhausted body to relax after a long day of hell.

He didn't snuff out the candles. He never did. He always let them burn out on their own as he had never been one for sleeping in the dark.

Imogene's hand and then the entire length of her bare arm slipped out from beneath the linens and wrapped itself around his waist. She nestled in close.

That touch and the way she nestled against him, as if he were hers to nestle with, sent a searing heat right through the core of everything he was. It was as if she needed him and wanted him. His cock hardened when he remembered exactly what she was capable of doing to his body. "Imogene," he whispered, fighting his need, fighting his want. He couldn't afford to lose control as being with her begged him to. "I won't be able to sleep if you touch me like this."

She nestled against him even more, bringing with her the faint scent of perfume, and inquisitively lifted her hazel eyes to his. "You can take hits all day, but not a mere touch at night?"

He couldn't pretend he didn't want her. Because he did. And he was about to damn well burst knowing it. "Sit up."

She paused. "I thought we were going to sleep."

"I'm not interested in sleeping anymore."

She paused again. "But I am."

"If you want to sleep, tea cake, leave the room."

She eyed him. "But I don't want to leave the room."

The no-good imp. "Then sit up."

An arched blond brow went up. "And what if I don't?"

"Then I will be forced to sleep on the floor."

She eyed him again and slowly, slowly sat up. "I'm sitting. Now what?"

Though his muscles still burned and were annoyingly sore from his training, he grabbed hold of her thighs. Yanking her up and onto his hips, he positioned her on top of him, forcing her to straddle him. He settled back against the pillows again and shrugged off the top part of the linen from around her. "Let me look at you."

Her flushed features gave way to prim awkwardness. "You are looking at me."

He held her gaze. "Not in the way I want to. Lean down toward me."

Biting her lower lip, she leaned forward against his hips. Her long blond braid fell over her slim shoulder and swayed toward him.

Reaching up, he undid the lacing of her nightdress as calmly as he could, even though he wanted to rip it in half.

She quietly submitted.

Like he wanted her to.

Tightening his jaw, he dragged her nightdress down her arms and tugged it to her waist, exposing creamy, white shoulders and incredible, full breasts and pink nipples he hadn't had the pleasure of seeing when he'd taken her the first time.

He let his gaze and his hands unwittingly trail across all that smooth, exposed, flawless skin. Everything about her made him want to believe life could be perfect. Heat raced beneath his skin, throttling the voice of reason in his head, which warned that he needed to be gentle. Not rough.

His eyes trailed over those breasts and paused at noticing that her nipples had hardened. His breath hitched in his throat and reason altogether flitted.

His arousal pressed against his robe and the nightdress that separated them. Sitting up, he gritted teeth against sore muscles, undid the belt and tugged his robe off his body, whipping everything to the floor except the belt.

He now lay completely naked beneath her. "Put your hands behind your back."

She hesitated. "And what if I want to touch you?"

"I'm not one to hand over that kind of control. Not during sex. Now put your hands behind your back."

She quietly set them behind her back, holding his gaze. "I'm only doing this because you want me to."

He loved the way she submitted to him so graciously and yet she still remained her own. "I know." He leaned toward her, pressing her naked softness against his hard chest, and wrapped his linen belt around her wrists, knotting it tight to ensure she couldn't free herself.

He leaned back against the pillows.

Leaving her nightdress bundled around her waist, he possessively cupped her bare, full breast, dragging that hard nipple against his open palm. He raveled a part of the linen that still clung to her body around his other hand, fisted a thick handful of the cool linen, then ripped it down and away from the rest of her body. It spilled off the bed and onto the floor.

She stiffened but otherwise didn't move, even when his hand left her breast and circled under her arm toward her back. Her chest rose and fell as if she were having trouble breathing.

Which he sure as hell knew he was.

He gripped her waist, digging the tips of his fingers into her warmth. "Put me inside you."

She hesitated, her cheeks blazing, and tugged at the belt behind her back. "I...I can't."

"I'll position it to make it easier. Lift yourself up a bit."

Lowering her gaze, she lifted herself just enough to expose his thick shaft from beneath the nightdress it was buried under.

He held the tip of his cock toward her opening and rasped, "Now go down on it."

Though she hesitated, she slowly slid herself down onto it.

A low hiss escaped him as her tight wetness surrounded his rigid length. Pleasure pooled through his entire body, tightening his core as he grabbed her waist and guided her up and down against his cock. The friction brought a shiver of heart-pounding awareness of the climax ahead.

She closed her eyes and tipped her head slightly back, exposing the entire length of her neck to him and pushing out her swaying breasts, as her arms remained tied behind her back.

He'd never seen anything so erotic. His fingers trailed up and slid down the length of her smooth, endless, glorious skin. He gripped her waist again and bucked into her, unable to remain calm or gentle.

She fell toward him but he caught her and pushed her back up. Her panicked gaze captured his from above. "I didn't hurt you, did I?" she whispered.

God, but she was stealing away pieces of his heart. A heart he didn't know he had to give. Here she was bound because he willed it and she was asking him if *he* was hurt. "No. You didn't hurt me." Tightening his jaw, he pushed up and up into her wetness, unable to believe she was actually letting him do this to her.

The shyness he had earlier seen in her hazel eyes flourished into a womanly pride as she moved against him. It fired his soul to know that he was the only one to have done this to her. "Kiss me. With your tongue."

She edged down onto him in between the rolling of her hips and pressed her mouth against his, slowly tonguing him.

He closed his eyes and groaned. Gently, playfully, he forced his tongue against hers, tracing every stroke.

As he thrust against her again and again, he forced his finger between them and slid toward her small nub. With each hard thrust, he rubbed his finger between her wet folds to ensure she felt *everything*.

She moaned against his mouth, her thighs quivering in response, and tongued him harder, her body digging into his in an effort to balance herself against her tied arms.

He could feel that delicious yearning building within her as her hips rolled faster against his own with an urgency that made him want to bite.

Her mouth broke away from his as she quaked. She cried out, stiffening, and then moaned.

Knowing she was climaxing, he rode up into her faster.

Feeling his world was about to explode from the rippling effects of the ultimate pleasure he couldn't wait to touch, he quickly lifted her in an effort to pull out.

To his astonishment, she ground down onto him hard. Her passage gripped his cock so firmly and fully, he gasped out in spiraling ecstasy and spurted his seed into her. Once it erupted, he no longer gave a damn but gave in to it. He viciously dug deeper into that passage, trying to stretch the walls of her womb with his length. The feel of that tightness tossed him into a delirious state that shattered the last of his rational mind. "Jesus Christ."

He fell back against the pillows in disbelief. Keeping himself still inside her, he reached up, cupping her throat, and drew her face down to his. Pressing his forehead to hers, he rasped in a scolding tone, "If we keep at this, a babe is inevitable." Setting her against his chest, he reached around and untied her hands. He massaged those soft wrists, trying to melt away whatever discomfort the belt had caused her skin.

She quickly wrapped her arms around him and nestled against him. "I wonder what it would be like to hold a child of my own," she murmured. "Do you ever wonder what it would be like? To have your own child?"

It was as if she wanted a babe. He tried not to think about

what a babe would do to this. Whatever *this* was. "Children make me nervous."

She peered up at him. "How so?"

He was quiet for a moment. "They're too vulnerable."

She smiled. "I think you would make for a very good father. Strong, yet yielding. You have a depth of compassion within you that reveals itself at the right time every time. 'Tis what I admire about you most. Your compassion."

No woman had ever told him that or noticed that.

She tightened her hold on him.

It was the first time he ever felt like he was truly being held. Not for the purpose of seduction but for the purpose of companionship. Real companionship.

It was so bizarre. All of this. Not only the way she held him, but even the fact that they had been discussing children. It was a part of him he had never allowed himself to submit to. Not given what happened to him as a child. "Imogene," he whispered.

"Hmm?"

"What are we doing? What is this?"

The room grew quiet and all he could hear was her breath and his.

"I don't know," she whispered back. "But I feel like I belong to you. I feel like I belong in your arms."

God. He smoothed her hair, knowing she was giving him the same answer he was giving himself. "We really need to talk."

"About what?"

"About us. I can't have you thinking…"

She slid a finger down his chest and whispered, "I take it you don't want us to be involved like this?"

Why did it stab him hearing her say it? "I'm not…I'm not

ready for something like this." He closed his eyes. "I'm not ready to submit myself completely."

Her finger continued to trace his chest. "Maybe all you need is time. I have that to give. Tell me the moment anything changes and I will be here waiting."

The blind faith in her voice made him tighten his hold on her. It was like she was hoping he would give in to more. A part of him wanted to kneel to that, but he honestly didn't know if he'd be kneeling in honor or if it would be an obligation or...more. He couldn't dig into what he was really feeling. Or rather, wanting to let himself feel. "If anything ever changes," he murmured, "you will know."

She nodded against him.

He let out a breath, knowing he also had to talk to her about their day at Jackson's. "I don't mind having you at the training sessions, Imogene," he confessed, "but I can't have you at the fights. I kept missing shots and taking hits I normally don't take because I kept seeing you. I hated the way you kept covering your face, because I knew I was making you do it. And I can't have that. If we mean to win the championship, we have to focus on what will and won't work. And having you at the fights, and me worrying about you, whilst you worry about me, won't work. Do you understand?"

She said nothing.

"I will do everything to win. I won't let you down."

She half nodded, her hand tracing up his neck and into his hair. "If I promise not to attend your fights, you must promise to take fewer hits during those fights."

"I will do my best."

"Nathaniel?"

"Yes? What?"

"I stopped taking my medication today."

Why did he feel like she was telling him because she wanted him to be proud? He pressed her harder against himself. "I'm glad to hear it. Hopefully your fainting spells will cease."

"Yes. Hopefully." She paused again. "Nathaniel?"

"Yes?"

"Tomorrow night, after training, and your bath and supper, will you take me up on the roof of our town house and dance with me? Like you said in the Devil's Dare you would? Because I would like that."

How had she remembered the things he'd said? Even the things he didn't want her to remember? "Is that what you want?"

"Yes."

"Then the rooftop it is."

She nestled into him again but said nothing more.

Though he wanted to believe that there would be far more nights like this, he wasn't the sort of man who had grown up believing in anything but punches. Strangely, though, he was learning to believe in one other thing. Her.

CHAPTER TWENTY

It was a tremendous task—a most daring attempt—and superlative *science*, and *that* ALONE produced the victory to Power.

—P. Egan, *Boxiana* (1823)

The following evening—11:15 p.m.
The rooftop of 18 Berkeley Square

As IMOGENE DREAMILY stared up at Nathaniel—his shadowed face mere inches above hers—and they silently rocked from side to side, not really dancing as much as swaying beneath the star-ridden sky, a strange flutter of anticipation took hold of her. One she had never felt in all her life.

The soap-scented heat rising from his hard, muscled body, and the way the breeze scattered his still-damp hair, awoke a burning and a yearning within her. The sort of yearning she dared not question but only submit to.

Wordlessly, his large hand left hers. That firm arm encircled her corseted waist and dragged her closer against him. The force of his smoldering gaze held her in place as steadily as did his arm.

The way he looked at her, as if he truly believed her to be beautiful, made her revel in being a woman.

The breeze shifted strands of her hair from her chignon across her cheek. He lifted his other hand and brushed it aside. His eyes held hers as his fingers slid down the side of her neck.

Her heart pounded relentlessly, knowing this was what loving a man felt like. Being blissfully happy by simply looking at him. "You took fewer hits today from Jackson," she whispered. "He barely touched you."

His warm fingers moved to trace her chin. "I tried," he said softly.

She smiled.

A muscle quivered in his tight jaw. Slowly, he leaned down, his eyes half-closed as they focused on her lips.

She tilted her lips upward, waiting.

The night sky above them seemed to sway.

His mouth feathered hers, seemingly hot against her lips. His wet tongue slowly slid its way around the contours of her mouth, tracing her lower lip and then her upper lip in measured detail.

She swayed against him, eyes closed, enjoying the feel of that tongue as it playfully traced its way down to her chin.

He edged them toward the brick chimney and gently set her against its rough surface. He released her, settling himself beside her against the chimney. "What were you like as a girl?"

Her eyes fluttered open as she leaned heavily against the chimney he had brought her to. She glanced toward him, noting the way he had set his dark head against the rough brick and stared up at the sky.

It was like he was trying to connect to her soul by gazing at those stars.

"Odd," she replied. "I always separated all my food on my plate, to keep everything from touching. The moment anything touched, I wouldn't eat it. It agitated more than the chef, I assure you. I always kept my books in alphabetical order and despised having any of the pages bent or creased. I kept all of my dolls organized by hair color and always played alone. So in answer to your question, I was a very odd child. I'm still odd, I find."

He smirked and leaned toward her. "At least you don't have a fetish of wanting to tie women up."

Feeling her cheeks burn at the thought of how he needed to tie her every time he wanted her, she asked, "Do all men do that?"

He leaned back against the chimney and stared up again at the night sky. "No."

"Why do you do it?"

"I enjoy it."

"Why?"

He shrugged. "I enjoy being in control."

She hesitated. "Do I not give you enough control?"

A gruff laugh escaped him. "More than you should."

"Then why do you still feel the need to bind me?"

His amusement faded and he eyed her. "You don't enjoy it, do you?"

She shrugged. "It isn't that. I would like to be able to touch you, is all."

He shifted against the chimney. "I've never engaged a woman without binding her hands. I've been doing it ever since I was sixteen."

She stared. "You have? And is that…normal?"

"No," he muttered. "I just feel more comfortable when I know I'm in control. That way, I know nothing can go wrong."

"And what do you expect to go wrong?"

He shrugged. "I can't readily explain it. It's more of a feeling. Not that anything will, but that it could. The assurance of bindings allows me to not think about anything. It allows me to let go."

She chewed her lower lip for a moment and eventually confided, "I don't mind knowing it pleases you. I would let you do anything to me knowing it pleases you."

Another gruff laugh escaped him. "Now, now, we really need to teach you to be a little less submissive or we'll be moving into whips and chains and God knows what else."

She elbowed him. "I have a little more self-respect for myself than that. I only submit to you because *I* want to. And only sexually."

He clicked his tongue. "That isn't completely true. You submit even when you don't want to. I've seen it. You let me take complete control. Complete."

"That isn't true."

"It is. If I wanted to strip you naked here on the roof, I know you would let me."

She stared. "I would not."

He pushed away from the chimney and, turning toward her, set both hands against the side of her head. "No?" Leaning in close, he held her gaze, reached down with his other hand and dragged up her gown to her knee. Still holding her gaze, he slid his hand up her thigh.

She couldn't breathe, her chest was so tight.

Still holding her gaze, his fingers trailed to the inside of her thighs and without warning his finger slipped deep inside of her. "You see. You would. You allow yourself to become too overwhelmed. You hand over control to me every time."

She choked, her hands pressing against the scraping brick. Her entire body pulsed right down to her scraped palms and her limbs quaked in an effort to stay upright. "You aren't being fair."

A breath escaped him. "Life isn't always fair." Removing his finger and hand, he slid away from her skirts, letting them drop.

To her astonishment, he turned her around and, taking her hands from her sides, propped them both high against the brick she now faced. "Keep them there. And don't move."

His hands skimmed and drifted toward her back as he commenced unhooking her gown from shoulder to waist.

Between disbelieving, hazy breaths, she glanced back at him. "What are you doing?"

"Undressing you. Isn't that obvious?" He finished unhooking her gown and, removing her hands from the brick wall, pushed the sleeves down her arms, exposing her corset and chemise beneath. With a quick tug, he yanked down her skirts from around her hips, causing them to pool around her slippered feet.

She gasped, glancing across the shadowed rooftops and countless candlelit windows below and within sight. She tried to scramble to gather her gown back up. "This is not a way to go about proving your point!"

His booted foot held down the bundled mass of her gown against the ground, keeping her from being able to pull it back on. "The real world doesn't grant favors, Imogene."

Damn him for making her realize just how little control she had. "You've made your point. Can I have my dress back?"

He leaned toward her. "Show me you don't like what I'm doing. Don't tell me you don't like it. Fight to get your dress back. Come on. Hit me. Do whatever you need to do to get it back."

She pulled in her chin, her heart pounding. "I'm not about to hit you. Even if I do want my dress back."

"Is that so? And what if I do this?" His boot swiveled against her gown, grinding into it.

She snapped a finger toward it in disbelief. "You're ruining the silk! That is my favorite gown."

"You think I care?" He held her gaze but didn't remove his boot. "What are you going to do about it?" He set his other boot on it.

The entire world was probably watching all of this. Whilst she stood in her chemise. Shoving at him hard with exasperation so he would let go of her gown, she muscled her entire body into making him move.

Only he didn't.

Which only riled her more. Of all the— Gritting her teeth, she reared back an elbow and connected to his stomach. A bit harder than she had intended to. She froze.

He edged back and softly clapped. "Bravo. You delivered your first hit. How did that feel?"

"Wrong." She bustled back toward her heap of a gown, oddly pleased with herself for having won it back. Jumping into it, she yanked it up and into place. "So I'm a little submissive. What of it?"

"What of it? I'm going to teach you how to put your fists up when you need to. Because there are times to be submissive and then there are times you can't be. Admit it. You enjoyed winning your gown back, didn't you?"

"A little." Perhaps even more than a little. She appreciated the sense of control at getting her gown back. She was so accustomed to having to rely on others—knowing she could rely on herself was affirming. And Nathaniel had given her that.

Though she wasn't sure about physically fighting. It did not feel natural. Or respectable.

"Don't I get a thank-you?" he asked.

"For what?"

"For helping you deliver your first punch."

"That is hardly something I should be thankful for."

"I see." Swiveling on his heel, he walked to the ledge of the rooftop and laid himself right where it sloped off and down onto the cobbled street forty feet below.

Her heart popped. "Don't do that! What are you doing?"

His head jumped up to look at her, but he stubbornly remained on the ledge. "Say thank you," he chided with a lopsided grin, now hanging an arm off the edge.

The man was insane. "You—" With her gown hanging open in the back and her trying to keep it from slipping off her body, she scrambled toward him. "Come away from there! This isn't funny anymore. You are frightening me!"

He sighed and rolled toward her. "We clearly have a lot of work ahead of us."

Falling onto her knees, she grabbed him, her fingers digging into his wool coat, and squeezed him tightly against herself. Her heart still pounded in disbelief. She shook him. "Don't ever do anything like that again! Be it to prove a point or not! Are you daft?"

A gargled laugh escaped him. "At least I know you like me well enough not to push."

Almost two weeks later—6:15 p.m.
Jackson's

NATHANIEL STRIPPED HIS leather gloves from his hands and paused. Mad though it was, he was beginning to believe in something called serendipity. He couldn't explain it, but it was as though everything that had happened in his life thus far had happened to lead him to one thing: Imogene.

The woman with those bright, eager eyes sitting on the bench against the wall. The woman who had gone—albeit slowly—from holding her hands against her eyes the first week to forgetting herself now and making full swings from her place as she watched him and the other men, the satin and lace sleeves of her gown flying. She would even occasionally yell out, *"Harder!"* startling some of the men into missing swings.

It was adorable.

And he had to do something about it.

Knowing there was no one else in the club but him, her and Jackson, he turned to Jackson, who was hanging up gloves from the group that had left and said to the man in a low voice, "Give Imogene a pair of gloves. She and I are going to spar."

Turning toward him from the rack of gloves, Jackson's brows went up to his grey hairline. He glanced back at Imogene, who sat in her pink satin and lace gown beside a book and bonnet. Jackson snorted. "If anyone passing the windows were to see a woman boxing in *my* club, I would never be allowed to own a business again."

Nathaniel pointed toward the shutters outside the windows. "Close the shutters, give me the key and I will ensure I lock everything up so you can retire. I'll drop the key off on my way back home. Our day is done anyway."

"Yes, but—"

"Have you seen the way she was swinging all week? Give her a chance to let it out. She is making all of this possible. For all of us."

Jackson stared at him for a long moment, then tossed him a pair of leather gloves by the strings. "Don't put them on her until the shutters are closed."

Nathaniel caught the gloves. "Yes, sir."

Jackson shook his head, withdrew a key from his waistcoat pocket and held it out. "Drop it off the moment you lock up."

Nathaniel took the key and shoved it into his waistcoat. "Yes, sir."

Jackson shook his head again and strode toward the entrance door. Closing the door behind him, he folded the shutters over the windows and latched them into place, darkening the training room. Fortunately, all the lanterns had already been lit.

Jogging over to the door, Nathaniel bolted it shut and then walked toward Imogene. He theatrically held up the gloves by their strings and strode toward her. "Meet your new friends. Left glove and right glove."

She lowered her chin but didn't move from the bench. "Those aren't my friends. They are *your* friends."

He grinned and halted before her, wagged a finger toward her hands. "I've been watching you all week. Your very face brightens when the men string up their gloves. It's you and I now. So hold up those hands and let's do this."

She slid her hands behind her back, burying them in the folds of her gown. "I shouldn't."

Kneeling before her, Nathaniel tapped her knee with his free hand and held her gaze. "I know you want to. Come on." He held up the boxing gloves by the strings, causing them to swing before her.

She bit her lip and eyed the leather gloves. "Am I allowed to? Even though I'm a woman?"

He knew she'd been eyeing the gloves. "Yes, you're allowed to. Jackson closed up the shutters and the door is officially locked. Just make sure you don't get Jackson into trouble and start telling your female friends about this."

"I don't have female friends. So we really don't have to worry, do we?" She giggled and grabbed for the gloves, setting them onto her lap. "Now what?"

He laughed. "You put them on, is what."

"I know, but how? Does it matter which hand goes into which?"

He flicked the right glove and pointed to her right hand. "That goes on that one. And the other on the other one. Once you get them on, I'll string you up."

She nodded and quickly tugged on each glove. She held them up before herself awkwardly, the lace of her sleeves falling to her elbows. "Aren't they a bit heavy?"

"They are meant to do more than protect the hands during sparring. Their weight also builds mass in the arms during training." Leaning toward her, he wrapped the strings and tied them firmly and tightly into place, until the strings indented the leather. He genuinely enjoyed strapping her hands. Even binding her into gloves was incredibly erotic.

She met his gaze, her mouth quirking. "Do I get to hit you? Hard?"

A laugh escaped him as he pushed down her now-bound strings. "Yes. As hard as you like."

She lifted a hand and tapped at his shoulder with the rounding part of the glove. "Go get those gloves on right quick, lest you lose the championship to me."

Another laugh escaped him. As of late, it was as if all he did was laugh. She brought it out in him more and more, damn her. "Walk over to the floor."

"Yes, sir!" She popped up off the bench and bustled toward the boxing floor, holding both gloves up high over her head of bundled curls.

He called after her, "You don't need to hold them that high, you know. The idea is to protect your face, not your hair."

"Oh. Right." She turned and lowered the two leather gloves, setting them against her chin. "Like this. Like you do."

Something about the way she said it made him draw in a slow breath. It made him realize how much she really had been watching him.

He loved knowing it. Because his boxing was an extension of everything he was and would always be and to have her acknowledge that part of him, despite its savageness, was more than endearing. It was downright soul rendering.

Casually crossing toward her, he rounded the floor and paused before her. This was going to be fun. He snapped up both bare fists. "Are you ready to take me on?"

Though she held up her gloved hands at her chin, she glanced toward his hands. "What about your gloves?"

He kept his fists up. "What? You don't trust me without them?"

She hit her gloves against each other, thudding them. "The real question is, do you trust *me?*"

"Ooooo. That sounds like a challenge I'm looking to lick." He rounded her. "Come on. Come at me, tea cake."

She pursed her lips. "At least try to pretend I'm one of the boys. You wouldn't call them *tea cake* whilst sparring them, would you?"

He lifted a brow. "If they looked like you, I would."

"Now *that* deserves retribution, my lord." Her features tightened with genuine focus and she darted forward, swinging out a fist.

He skidded aside, impressed she could move so quickly. He let out a low whistle. "Very good. Do it again."

By the end of the hour, the woman had worked them both into a dripping state of sweat. He couldn't help but be in awe. She not only stayed with him throughout every swing but hadn't asked to rest once. In what felt like a breath, she had become a little boxer. His little boxer.

"Last hit," he called out. "This time let it land. That way, you know how it really feels to follow through with a swing." He moved in close. Much closer than he normally would with an opponent.

"Are you certain you want me to actually hit you?"

"Quite. Come on. Come at me."

"What if I hit you too hard?"

He wanted to kiss her. "Don't be ridiculous. If I can't take a hit from you, I shouldn't be boxing."

She gasped. "Was that a jab at my being a woman?"

Now he *really* wanted to kiss her. "Will it make you swing at my head?"

"As a matter of fact, yes. Because women can hit just as hard as men if given the chance."

"I see. Then yes. It's a jab. Women can't hit."

"Oh, now, that deserves a hit. Watch this." She turned toward him, her flushed features still focused, and swung at his head with her right hooking toward it.

He purposefully didn't move and let it bounce off his head. Though it hit him impressively hard given her light weight, he added in an exaggerated "Ooof!" and threw himself onto the ground, enjoying the rest.

"Nathaniel?" she echoed, scrambling toward him and kneeling beside him, gloves jabbing into his sides. "Did I really hit you that hard? Or did you fall on purpose?"

He bit back wanting to laugh and rolled onto his back, throwing his arms out beside him on the floor. "Both."

Reaching for her, he grabbed her hard by her corseted waist and yanked her down onto himself, forcing her to hang above him. "You win the bout, given I can't get back up. Now name your prize. I'll give you anything you want. And I do mean anything. So think good and well on this. I'm in a rather vulnerable position. Rare for me, you know."

She grinned down at him, long curls falling out from her pinned hair. "I get whatever I want? Can I hold you to that?"

He nodded, tracing his gaze adoringly from those bright hazel eyes to her unraveling blond hair. "Anything. Because I'm more than impressed. What do you want?"

She leaned down, touching her nose to his nose and whispered, "You. Can I keep you? Forever, my lord?"

He stilled beneath her, searching her face. It was as if she meant it. His hands jumped to her face and held her possessively in place, right where she was, her nose touching his nose. "And what would you do with me if I let you keep me forever?" he asked in a low tone.

She hovered above him. "I would spend every moment adoring you. In the way you deserve."

It was as if she was admitting to loving him. As if he deserved to be loved.

Tightening his hold on her face, he covered her mouth with his and savagely kissed her, not only *wanting* to give in to the idea of her, but *needing* to give in to the idea of her. It was obvious he was done for. He'd never seen that coming.

CHAPTER TWENTY-ONE

Act well your part—THERE all the honour lies!

—P. Egan, *Boxiana* (1823)

The Wentworth House
Two weeks later—evening

EXCUSING HERSELF FROM an old gentleman whose words slurred from one too many cognacs, Imogene scanned elegantly dressed guests quietly conversing at the small gathering. The Duke of Wentworth—being the endearingly supportive brother-in-law that he was—had decided to host an intimate party for a select few the night before Nathaniel's first fight toward the title of Champion. Whilst the duke hadn't been all that pleased with Nathaniel taking on the role of an aristocratic boxer, the man still genuinely supported Nathaniel in his decision and tried to openly acknowledge it.

Oddly, she hadn't seen Nathaniel in some time. He had disappeared somewhere within the small crowd. Sashaying into a pause, she found him and his nephew propped against the farthest wall in the room intently discussing something.

Garbed in black evening attire, an embroidered waistcoat

and a silk cravat with his black hair suavely swept back with tonic, Nathaniel looked as debonair as ever. And the way he had casually set his broad shoulder against the wall with his head slightly cocked in conversation made him appear even more so.

It was astounding to see him look so at ease in a social setting he had initially resisted attending. He was worried the duke and his nephew wouldn't be as accepting of his boxing aspirations, but they had proved him wrong.

The duke and his nephew supported him completely.

She smiled, still watching him. He seemed so different from the man she had first met. More at ease with himself and the world. She sometimes liked to think that she had brought about that change.

Nathaniel glanced toward her in midconversation. With the quirk of his full mouth and the perusal of her chartreuse gown, he inclined his head, acknowledging her from across the room.

Her stomach fluttered and that incredible feeling of being acknowledged by a man like him in *that* way, and in public, was something she knew was going to stay with her all her life.

There were times she wondered what was happening between them. They were partners in everything and yet...they were not. She was still achingly waiting for him to verbally acknowledge that he adored her as much as she adored him.

Shifting against the wall, Nathaniel returned his gaze to Yardley and said something seemingly more involved to which Yardley shook his head, half-amused.

Knowing she ought to give Nathaniel time alone with his nephew, she let out a breath and rounded the room, trying to find someone else to talk to. With only two dozen people present, as opposed to the ten dozen or more that usually attended gatherings or balls, she felt more at ease.

She had never been all that fond of crowds.

A pretty redhead dressed in an elegant primrose lace and satin gown, sidestepped toward her, startling Imogene into a quick halt.

The woman playfully smiled and confided in a conspiring, American-Irish accent, "The name is Miss Tormey. We're going to be relatives, you and I."

Imogene pulled in her chin. "I beg your pardon?"

Trying to flick open a fan with a sweep of her gloved hand, Miss Tormey rolled her eyes, realizing the fan hadn't opened. She manually pried it open and grouched, "It never opens right. No wonder men don't bother with these. I only use it because Lady Burton kept telling me it keeps people from reading lips. Which you Brits like to do all the time." Setting the now-open fan strategically beside her face, Miss Tormey leaned in. "Robinson and I will be announcing our engagement tonight. In about an hour. I wanted you to know, seeing you and I are about to be family."

Imogene blinked. "Uh…congratulations." Realizing she had no idea who the woman was even talking about, she asked, "Who is Robinson?"

Miss Tormey grinned, her green eyes brightening. "That would be Lord Yardley. Robinson is his nickname. You know, like Robinson Crusoe. The character from that book." Her grin faded and she took on a more pensive look. "I actually read the book for the first time last week. It wasn't even good. Cannibals and pirates don't make for what I call a good story. There wasn't even a romance in it. In my opinion, men ought to stop writing books. They are wasting not only their time but ours. Though mostly ours."

Imogene stifled a giggle. She rather liked this Miss Tormey. "So you and Lord Yardley are set to wed?"

Miss Tormey nodded, sending her gathered strawberry ringlets swaying about her face. "Yes. He and I would have been married weeks ago, but you aristos are all about formality and ba ba ba."

Ba ba ba? Another laugh escaped Imogene. "Well, congratulations. With you marrying Yardley, that would indeed make us family. Nathaniel is incredibly fond of his nephew. He always tries to find time for not only him but the duke between all his training. 'Tis endearing to know how well they all get on."

"Let us hope it lasts, yes? Or you and I will be at a loss." Miss Tormey leaned in again, still holding up the fan to their faces. "Is it possible for you and I to get to know each other? I need more than just male company."

Imogene gently grabbed the woman's arm. "I would very much like that. Shall we take tea in the next few weeks?"

Miss Tormey lifted a rusty brow. "How about whiskey instead? I'm going to need it, knowing that I'm staying in London for the rest of my life."

Imogene stifled another laugh. "I have never had whiskey, but I'm certain if you can sip whiskey, so can I."

"Oh, you don't sip whiskey, lady friend. You guzzle it. I'll show you how." Miss Tormey tilted her head toward the other end of the room. "I never thought that heathen would ever take a wife. Is he treating you good?"

Imogene's heart skipped at seeing Nathaniel striding toward them. "Incredibly good," she managed.

"I'm glad to hear it." Miss Tormey flicked her fan shut. "I should paddle away. I doubt the man is coming over to see me. We'll do whiskey sometime. After I'm officially engaged, that is. I hear society grants a little more lenience to a woman then. Thank God. Because I can't keep at this." Miss Tormey swept past and made her way toward Lord Yardley, who was mouthing something to her from across the room. Miss Tormey set her fan to the side of her mouth and returned the silent mode of conversation.

Imogene bit back a smile. They were adorable.

Nathaniel sauntered up close and lingered before her, setting both hands behind his back. "I see you met Georgia."

Imogene glanced up at him. "Georgia?" She blinked. "I take it you know her well enough to call her by her given name?"

Nathaniel rolled his tongue on the inside of his mouth before blurting, "You can say that. She lived in the same ward I did back in New York. Apparently, she and Yardley are announcing their engagement tonight. The poor boy. He is beyond saving."

"I think he did quite well for himself. She appears to be incredibly witty and genuine. I like her."

He smirked. "Hopefully not too much. It's bad enough Yardley is getting married to her. I don't need to lose you to her antics, too."

A smile touched her lips. "Lose me to her antics?" she taunted. "And who says you have me to lose? It isn't as if you have committed yourself to me. I'm still waiting."

Nathaniel shifted his jaw and observed her heatedly for a long moment. "You and I need to resolve that."

Her lips parted and for a moment she was too astounded to respond. "Do you mean it?"

He leaned in close and rumbled out in a low tone, "Meet me upstairs. I'll be waiting." He strode past and after exchanging a few words with some guests in passing, he veered out of the receiving room, disappearing into the candlelit corridor.

She glanced around, her heart pounding. What on earth did he have in mind? Surely not…*that*. She puffed out an exasperated breath and brought her gloved hands together, unable to keep from fidgeting. No one seemed to have noticed Nathaniel had left the room.

Tarrying for a few minutes more, she edged her way closer and closer to the open double doors, trying to look interested in a painting on the wall, until she was out of the room and in the corridor.

Gathering her skirts, she bustled her way up the main staircase and paused on the landing. "Nathaniel?" she whispered into the unnerving darkness that fingered its way toward her.

A large hand caught her arm from around the corner of the landing, making her yelp. A tug and a spin yanked her entire backside firmly against the contours of a tall, muscled body.

Her heart skipped. It was Nathaniel's body.

"Good evening, *wife*," his gruff voice hoarsely said into her ear as he pulled them into a dimly lit room just off the stairwell.

A tremor overtook her ability to think. He never referred to her as wife. "Good evening…*husband*."

He locked the door with one hand, as his other hand pressed her backside harder against a very notable erection she could feel through her skirts. "I missed you." He pushed her against the door.

She caught herself against the door, her breaths uneven.

He jerked up her skirts to her waist. "Keep your hands where they are. I don't have anything to bind you with."

She stared at the panel door in disbelief as his warm hands rounded and rubbed her exposed bum.

He moved his hands toward her bare thighs. "Now this is my idea of a real party."

Unable to breathe all that well, she choked out, "We really shouldn't be doing this, you know. People will notice we are gone."

"Let them," he murmured, sliding a tongue down the side of her neck. "We're married. Or did you forget?"

Her eyes fluttered closed against the thrilling sensation of his tongue. She felt his hands unbuttoning his trousers. It was a bit overwhelming to know he wanted her enough to do it just up the stairs from a respectable gathering. "You can't wait until we get home?"

"No." Nudging her legs apart with his knee, he set the tip of his erection against her opening. "Ask me why we're doing this."

She swallowed, feeling faint against her need for him. "Why are we doing this?"

He thrust deep into her wetness from behind.

She gasped, rattling the door with her hands, which were planted heavily against it.

Leaning toward her ear, he rasped, "The moment you climax, I'll tell you why we're doing this." Holding on to her hips, he slowly slid in and out of her.

She heavily breathed in and out, trying to regain control of herself, her pulse throbbing in her throat and her heart threatening to burst as he jerked into her.

She felt her core tightening against his aggressive, slick thrusts. She swayed against the door as he moved against her harder. Her hands slid against the wood as she tried to stay upright and he pushed them back into place. She instinctively pressed back against him, wanting and needing more of his erection.

His seething breaths mingled with hers in the silence of the room. Each thrust he dug deep into her, making them both gasp.

Her world tipped and her climax overwhelmed her. She bit out a moan, quaking against those violent thrusts that banged her into the door.

After several more ruthless presses, he stilled deep inside of her womb, flattening them both against the door, and groaned loudly, letting his seed pour into her. After a few heavy breaths he bent his head and nipped the inside curve of her throat from behind. "Will you be mine?"

Her eyes popped open. She swallowed, and with her cheek still against the door, whispered, "As in forever?"

He slowly pulled out and let her skirts drop back down around her legs. He gently smoothed them around her and kissed her neck before stepping back. "As in forever."

Astounded, she turned toward him as he buttoned the flap of his trousers back into place.

She stared up at him, the idea of them being together for the rest of their lives making her heart squeeze in unexpected yearning. "What brought this on?" She wanted to hear him say it. She wanted to hear him say that he was as madly fond of her as she was of him.

"Watching you tonight made me realize something."

"It did? What?"

"That I hated whenever you left the room. That I hated when you weren't looking at me. That I hated not being able to touch you in public." He finished buttoning his trousers and adjusted his coat. "I think it time I announce I'm thoroughly smitten."

She bit back a lopsided grin. "You are?"

"I am." He grabbed her hand and unlocked the door with

his other hand, throwing it open. "I'm talking smitten enough to have children."

She excitedly trotted after him as he hurried them out into the corridor. She lowered her voice. "How many children do you want?"

"As many as you are willing to give," he tossed back, swinging her toward the staircase. He leaned down and kissed her cheek. "Now head downstairs. I'll join you in few minutes so we're not too obvious."

She turned toward him and captured his gaze in the dim, candlelit corridor. "I adore you."

Stepping toward her, he grabbed her waist hard and jerked her toward himself, startling her. He bent his head and set his forehead against hers. "And I adore you, too."

She almost melted in his arms. "You do?"

"I do." He traced his lips against her forehead. "I adore the way you make me feel."

Marvelously content, she nuzzled herself against his chest for a moment, then unlatched his arms and thumbed toward the stairs. "I should probably go. Heaven only knows what the entire room is thinking."

He set a hand to the back of his neck and eyed her. "My asking you to make this permanent isn't going to change anything between us, is it?"

She smiled. "I won't let it."

He dropped his hand. "Good."

Sashaying toward the staircase, she purposefully swayed her hips as best she could for him and tossed over her shoulder, "All that said, don't think you can buy out this investor by tossing words of adoration. You still have a title to win."

CHAPTER TWENTY-TWO

Tremble!

—P. Egan, *Boxiana* (1823)

Nine weeks later—Late afternoon
18 Berkeley Square

NATHANIEL'S POPULARITY in the boxing community had reached an unprecedented crescendo that had sold out every last ticket in Covent Garden at a guinea and a half apiece for the Terry-Atwood fight. Nathaniel, bless his fists, had already beat Norley, Gill and Hatchet. All that was left was to beat Terry and then the next fight was for the title itself.

Sitting in her receiving room at an hour when every man in London, including her own brother, who was acting as Nathaniel's second in the match, was gathering to watch the Terry-Atwood fight, unnerved Imogene.

Nathaniel had asked her to stay home, as he did whenever it came to every real fight. Even though she didn't want to, she did because he had asked her to. Everything she did as of late, she did for him and because of him.

And he knew it.

He had changed her life in so many glorious ways. She never felt alone anymore. And though they never really once said the word *love* to each other, she knew he loved her as much as she loved him.

Since she had ceased taking her medication, she no longer felt dizzy and hadn't fainted once. Not once. It was unbelievable.

She felt...incredible.

That is, until she had commenced vomiting due to overwhelming nausea whenever she ate anything. She thought it odd until she noted her menses had also ceased and spoke to her lady's maid about it. It was rather obvious she was pregnant. Though her belly had yet to show, she knew she was set to have Nathaniel's babe. It was as exciting as it was unsettling. She decided it was best to announce it after his fight tonight. So he wasn't so distracted with the news.

She couldn't deny she was exceedingly fond of her life with Nathaniel. Overly fond. Every night, after his training and a bath and a supper the cook would always have waiting, he would nestle them into bed and tell her all about his progress and how much he was learning from Jackson. His voice was always so husky and eager to share. Sometimes they fell asleep talking, while still in each other's arms, and sometimes they stayed up, rolling around until all the clothes came off and words were no longer a necessity or an option.

It was glorious.

He was glorious.

And yes, she was madly in love with the man.

During the day, when she wasn't at Jackson's watching Nathaniel train, she would call on the quirky but fabulous Miss Tormey or her brother, Henry, who was already laying out all divorce plans and had hired a solicitor. Imogene also busied herself with accepting or rejecting endless invitations to dinners and gatherings, all whilst going through newspapers and gazettes, reading through anything she could find pertaining to Nathaniel.

She made it a priority to ensure nothing was being printed that might damage his growing popularity.

Imogene burrowed into a chair beside the window for better light and angled the latest sporting chronicle toward her. She perused the *Remarks* section, wondering if there was anything that had been written about Nathaniel, and sat up.

There was one.

And it was a remark written by none other than Mr. P. Egan himself. Her eyes widened. Mr. P. Egan. It was something Nathaniel and Mr. Jackson had been ardently waiting for. A remark from the man.

She only hoped it was good.

Bringing the paper closer, she read aloud:

"The Honourable Lord Atwood, known as the 'Missing Heir' to the sporting world, has far exceeded the anticipation of this pugilistic observer who has been keenly watching him through every fight. What has been noted repeatedly is a man not only of gigantic strength, but one possessing a degree of scientific knowledge and impressive self-possession. He stands well on his legs, goes fearlessly against his opponent, and uses both hands with equal quickness, hitting well out from his shoulder, and throwing all his energies into the force of his blows. At present, I regard him as a 'rara avis in terris.' For those unfamiliar with Latin, and for shame on those of you who are, allow me to translate: 'A rare bird on earth.' If there is any remarkable man capable of taking the title of Champion of England, it is our missing heir. Let it be known, that, as always, I was the first to scribe it."

Imogene jumped from her chair with a bursting squeal, shaking and shaking the paper. If Mr. P. Egan thought Nathaniel was taking the title, it was not only possible, but it was going to happen.

It was going to happen!

A blurred movement from the street made Imogene turn to the window. She froze as a lacquered, black carriage pulled by enormous, midnight-colored stallions rolled up to the town house.

A footman opened the door of the carriage, unfolded the stairs and dutifully guided the hand of a veiled, petite female draped in lavish, verdant morning attire.

As the stallions restlessly pawed the ground, the woman, whose face was eerily hidden beneath a black lace veil, turned her head toward Imogene. Though Imogene couldn't see any eyes or a face, she felt the woman's gaze penetrate her straight through the window.

It was like death making a personal call.

The newspaper floated with a rustle from her hands to the floor. A knot formed in her stomach that had nothing to do with the babe as the woman gathered her skirts and made her way up the entrance stairs.

The calling bell rang.

In panicked dread, Imogene glanced toward the open doorway of the receiving room as the butler passed.

Her throat closed up and though she wanted to call out to the butler not to even open the door, she couldn't move or think or get her tongue to cooperate.

Within moments, the butler returned with a silver tray and presented her the card.

Imogene hesitated and leaned over the tray, not wanting to touch it. The ivory calling card read:

Lady Sumner

She glanced up in startled astonishment. Dearest heaven. It was Nathaniel's mother.

"Are you at home, my lady?" the butler inquired.

She swallowed against the tightness in her throat and nodded. "I… Yes. I'm at home. Show her in at once."

"Yes, my lady." The butler departed.

Imogene lingered in the middle of the receiving room, her heartbeat as erratic as her thoughts. After snubbing the wedding and repeated letters and invitations she had sent to the Sumners despite Nathaniel's grudging mutters about her letting the matter go, what would make his mother break her silence now?

The veiled figure Imogene had seen through the window appeared in the doorway and lingered.

"Is he here?" the woman asked in an eerily quiet but regal tone from within the veil.

Imogene pressed her hands together in an effort to remain calm and crossed the room toward her. "No, my lady. He is not and won't be until after midnight. He usually joins my brother and the boxing community at Cardinal's after a fight."

Lady Sumner gathered the veil with gloved hands and, with a trembling sweep, folded it back onto her bonnet, exposing beautifully assembled grey hair. An aged face with startling blue eyes that reminded her of Nathaniel's held her gaze.

Imogene drew in a breath, not at all expecting what she saw.

The entire left side of the poor woman's aged face, including her eye and the corner of her mouth drooped from what appeared to be an ailment. "I apologize for the state of my face," Lady Sumner said matter-of-factly.

Imogene shook her head. "Please don't...don't apologize, my lady. 'Tis an honor to be in your presence. I was hoping you would eventually call. Nathaniel is incredibly proud and refused to make the call himself after he had already sent several missives, which all went unanswered by you. Though he never admitted to it, I know he was incredibly hurt by your silence."

Lady Sumner averted her gaze and dug her gloved fingers into the side of her face, indenting that disfigured flesh with every tip.

Imogene swallowed, sensing something wasn't quite right with this woman. "Are you unwell, my lady?"

Lady Sumner's hand fell away and instead now dug into her arm. "I didn't want to hope." Her voice sounded eerie, almost faint. "I doubted it. Sumner made me doubt it, too. He said it wasn't possible. Until I saw a sketch of him in a sporting chronicle this morning that Wilkinson insisted I see. The moment I saw it I...I knew. This overwhelming, inexplicable feeling that I was looking at a grown version of my son seized me. It was as if—" A sob escaped her. She set a hand to her ruined face, those shoulders quaking against emotion.

Imogene hurried to the woman, tears blurring her vision. She gathered the woman into her arms and tugged her close. "I'm so sorry."

The woman sobbed against her. "I need it to be him."

Imogene cradled the woman, rocking her through tears. "It is indeed him. Have no doubt in that."

The woman drew away from Imogene, using the veil to dab her eyes, though her hand prevented her from doing it properly. "I have yet to accept any of this as true." She sniffed several times and buried herself within the veil. "Have him call on me tomorrow morning. The earlier the better. Tell him I will be ardently waiting." The woman nodded through the veil and grabbed Imogene's hand again. "Forgive me for not having attended the wedding. Are you and he happy?"

Imogene smiled. "Yes. We are. Very."

"Good." Lady Sumner shook her hand and kept shaking it. "What is he like? What has he grown into? A good man? The sort I can be proud of?"

Imogene's heart squeezed. "Indeed. He is that and more, my lady. Though I will say he is haunted by whatever happened. He doesn't tolerate small spaces and sometimes falls into silence when certain topics of conversation are introduced. Despite that, he manages to rise above it. I think his boxing helps him with that."

Those fingers now dug savagely into Imogene's hand, almost startling her. "He shouldn't be boxing," she rasped. "Lest he get hurt. Tell him to cease. Tell him I will not tolerate it."

Imogene stared, wanting those digging fingers to let her go. She understood Lady Sumner's concern, but something didn't feel right. "I ask you ease your grip upon my hand."

Lady Sumner's digging fingers eased. "Does he mention my husband at all? Does he blame him for anything?"

Imogene's throat tightened. Even though Nathaniel had alluded to it many times, it was not her place to say it. "I know nothing, my lady, for he does not wish to speak of it. All I know is that your son has suffered greatly."

"My daughter believed he was alive up until the very last breath she took. She believed in a way I did not." Lady Sumner released Imogene's hand and sobbed. "What a wretched mother I am to have ceased believing in my own son."

"Shhhh. No. Do not say such things. You have endured far too much to—"

"I betrayed him by not believing." Lady Sumner leaned in, swaying the veil against her face. "Tell him to call on me in the morning. Tell him I must see him and hold him. *Tell him.*"

Imogene tried not to cry, sensing that this poor woman was almost too broken. It was so sad. "I will tell him."

Lady Sumner reached out and blindly patted Imogene's cheek with a gloved hand, those fingers skimming Imogene's cheek on an angle. "You have such a pretty face," she murmured. "I used to be pretty, too. When I was younger." Lady Sumner grew quiet. "I have nothing now. Not the love of my husband and not even a face."

The poor, poor woman. "You have the love of your son. And I promise he will come to you tomorrow morning."

"Yes. Do. Tell him I will have crumpets and strawberry preserves waiting for him. They used to be his favorite." Lady Sumner nodded. "My husband didn't believe it was our son. But I will make him believe. You tell Nathaniel that." Stepping back, the woman slowly turned away and drifted down the corridor without so much as bidding a farewell.

Tears blinded Imogene as she rubbed a hand against her belly in disbelief and stood in the silence of the receiving room. Lady Sumner seemed anything but grounded.

Whatever Nathaniel had endured, and whatever his father had done, was about to make itself known. Imogene only prayed it didn't break him *or* her.

CHAPTER TWENTY-THREE

His pugilistic talents, perhaps, might have been forever
obscured from the world, and himself content to drag on
a life of rustic insipidity, had not the smiles of the fair sex
awakened his brave heart and brought them to action.

—P. Egan, *Boxiana* (1823)

Covent Garden

IT WAS LIKE the man was made of iron.

A determined roar ripped from Nathaniel's throat, which
was instantly swallowed into the echo of the shouting crowds.
Terry barely stumbled against the savage hit Nathaniel had
squarely delivered to the side of the man's head.

Jumping forward again, Nathaniel straight punched and
felt his fist finally penetrate through those upheld hands.
Smashing Terry's nose with a masticating crunch he could
feel against his knuckles and arm, Nathaniel felt blood spray
across his chest and slather his hand.

He had him.

Nathaniel hit the man again and again, from jaw to temple,
determined to finish him.

Terry staggered back, his gashed features distorted from the fight that had lasted well past sixty rounds. Terry suddenly collapsed onto the wooden boards, limp.

"To the line!" the umpire shouted at Nathaniel as the crowd boomed with riled shouts and cheers that muted the words. "Thirty seconds! And I count!"

Jogging over to the chalked box, Nathaniel waited with both fists still up as the umpire counted out the time. The pulsing of Nathaniel's battered flesh seemed to swell against the afternoon sun, and though he felt his mind wanting to leave his body, he knew he had to stay focused.

Terry's second jumped out from the corner post and yelled down at Terry to get up, shaking him repeatedly. "To the line, Terry! *Terry!* For blood's sake, to the line! Don't let the bastard take this from us!"

Rolling onto his back, Terry momentarily stared up into the afternoon sky, his chest pumping hard.

"Stay down," Nathaniel chanted against his own fists that hovered before his face. "Stay down, you son of a bitch. I need this more than you do."

"Thirty!" the umpire boomed as he pointed a finger at Nathaniel. "And this here ends the fight! I proclaim Atwood to be the lead for the next and last fight of Champion to be set by any contender!"

Nathaniel dropped his hands heavily to his sides and closed his eyes as cheers drummed against his head and his soul. He had done it. A part of him couldn't believe it. He'd taken down a man who hadn't gone down against anyone. And the title of Champion was next.

It was as though the world was finally kneeling to him. *Finally.*

Reopening his eyes, he swung toward the crowd. Weston

picked up a bucket of water from the corner post and tossed it at him with a celebratory whoop. "To the upcoming Champion of England! It's yours! I damn well know it is!"

The cold water drenched Nathaniel's face and body like the heavenly blessing that it was. The heat of his throbbing body flickered away into a soothing, cooling bliss. Swiping his face, he let out a laugh he couldn't even hear and scanned the bobbing crowds of well over several hundred men.

It was astounding to know *he* had brought them here.

He paused at glimpsing the duke and Yardley both grinning up at him from the masses pressing in against the wooden posts that roped off the crowd from the fight.

They came. Like they always did.

Nathaniel grinned past the biting pain and held up a fist toward them, shaking it in the air in their honor.

Yardley and the duke held up their fists in turn and also shook them, sending out mutual support.

In that moment, as Nathaniel threw out both arms and walked about the wood stage, welcoming the attention of the crowd that chanted, *"Atwood! Atwood! Atwood!"* he believed anything was possible.

Though he had a long night ahead of him, including debriefing with Weston and Jackson and cavorting with the entire boxing company from Jackson's club, he couldn't wait to go home and announce his win to the woman who had made all of this possible. To the woman who made his life worth living and was his, all his.

Biting back an exasperated grin, he leaned over the side of the posts and shook countless hands that were repeatedly being thrust his way.

Life didn't get any better than this.

CHAPTER TWENTY-FOUR

However painful it is to state, it becomes
our duty not to withhold the truth.

—P. Egan, *Boxiana* (1823)

2:34 a.m.

AFTER THE VALET had poured several more steaming basins of narcissus-infused water over his bruised shoulders and back, Nathaniel carefully arranged a wet towel on his head to soothe his now-scabbing face and settled in the copper tub. It was like lounging in paradise. "You can retire," Nathaniel breathed out to the valet. "Thank you for staying up so late and tending to me."

"But of course, my lord. 'Tis an honor. Congratulations again and good night." The valet gathered everything, except for Nathaniel's robe and a dry towel, which he left on a chair beside the tub, and dutifully departed, closing the bathing chamber door behind himself.

Nathaniel leaned farther back against the tub, wincing against soreness and welts, and closed his eyes, savoring the silence and the sensation of ultimate rest. It was the best part of the fight. That delicious sense of having conquered all and being able to glory in it in the privacy of his own bath and home.

He didn't miss New York. Not one fucking bit.

The door creaked open. Slippered feet quietly entered the room and the door creaked closed again. "Nathaniel?"

A smile touched his lips at hearing Imogene's soft voice. He didn't even bother to open his eyes or remove the towel from his head. That beautiful voice was enough to glory in. "I should warn you, tea cake, I'm naked. The only thing covering me right now is the towel on my head."

"I know." Her voice was still soft.

He smirked but still didn't open his eyes or move. "Try not to take advantage of me. I'm feeling rather helpless right now. I wouldn't be able to fight you off."

Her steps drew closer. "Judging by your marvelously cheeky mood, you won."

He sensed she now lingered beside the tub.

"I most certainly did," he drawled up at her through the towel. He purposefully stretched out, letting her see whatever she wanted to. "Start thinking about what we're going to do with all that money when I take the title in three weeks. I'm thinking of sending several thousand banknotes to Matthew out in New York. I haven't heard a damn thing from the man, which probably means he needs money. After we take care of him, I say we do some traveling. I'd love to go to Spain for a few months. I hear men there challenge bulls in a public arena. *That* would be well worth seeing. What would you like to do? Where would you like to go? Any ideas?"

Oddly, she said nothing. Not a word.

He paused. It wasn't like her. Usually when the woman crept into his bathing chamber to sit beside him as he soaked after a fight, he couldn't get her to cease squealing and talking about the fight and money ahead.

Opening his eyes, he lifted the front of the towel from his head, draping it back, and glanced toward her.

Dressed in a simple white nightgown, with a long braid pushed back over a slim shoulder, she knelt beside the tub, her chin tucked against the copper rim, both hands holding her in place against it. She winced as her gaze drifted across all the scabs covering his temple, cheekbone and nose. "I never get used to seeing you hurt."

He leaned toward her, lingering on how pretty she looked. It reminded him of the first time they had met. Her in a simple braid and a nightdress. "Ah, you know me. I heal quick." He reached out and dabbed the softness of her cheek with a wet finger. "Are you all right? You seem a bit quiet."

She half nodded and held his gaze, her hazel eyes glistening with tears. Her full lips trembled. A choked sob suddenly escaped her, tears now streaming down her face. "I...I waited all night f-f-for you."

He sat up, astounded. His heart pounded, for he had never seen her cry. And she was stuttering. It had been so long since she had. "What is it?"

She swiped at her face with shaky fingers. "Your mother called on me t-t-today. While you were at-at-at...the fight."

His lips parted. After months of silence, and missives left unanswered, his mother had finally emerged to acknowledge him. But what did that mean? And why now? "What did she say? And why are you crying? Was she disrespectful toward you?"

She shook her head and swiped more tears away. "No. But it was overwhelming." Her features twisted as she captured his gaze. "She didn't seem mentally sound, Nathaniel.

What is more, she was asking me if your father was in any way to…to blame for your disappearance. It was as if she knew something."

He closed his eyes and leaned back against the tub. It was all unraveling.

Imogene was quiet for a long moment. "What happened to you, Nathaniel? Don't you think it time I know?"

Jesus Christ. He was not in the mood for this. Reopening his eyes, he stared at her. "I'm trying to recover from a fight here. I'm trying to rest."

Her tear-streaked features morphed into a more stubborn gaze. "Your mother insists we call on her tomorrow morning, and in truth, the thought scares me. You intend to send me into a quagmire I know nothing of? Is that your intention?"

Annoyed, he pointed at her. "You aren't coming with me. Let me be clear in that."

"No. I have every intention of supporting you through whatever it is that is happening."

"You are overstepping your goddamn bounds. You'll stay here at the house where you belong."

"I'm not—"

"When I tell you to do something, Imogene, you do it. You got that? You do it."

Her startled face gave way to hurt. "Do not speak to me like that."

Seeing her crumpled face was like slitting his own throat. But he also knew he couldn't expose her to the darkest recesses of his life. "I'm sorry. I shouldn't have said that. 'Tis simply my quagmire to conquer, Imogene, not yours."

Her hazel eyes flared. "'Tis not yours alone anymore when it causes me agony. Or don't you understand that? Don't you understand what I feel for you? Or are you so fully absorbed in your boxing that you haven't noticed that I am well past adoring you?"

He swallowed, lowering his gaze. He had noticed. The way she looked at him was different. The way she physically submitted to him was different. And he was different because of it, too. "Are you in love with me?"

She said nothing.

He searched her flushed face, his chest tightening. "I know you are. And I want you to say it. Because I'm ready to say it, too. I'm in love with you. And I've known it for some time."

She eyed him but said nothing in return.

His jaw tightened. "I just told you I'm in love with you."

She stared.

He stared back, his pulse thundering. "You have nothing to say?"

She closed her eyes. "What am I to say to a man who claims to love me but refuses to trust me?"

"What the devil are you talking about? I do trust you. There isn't a person I trust more."

She shook her head and reopened her eyes. "No. You don't. If you did, you would be able to confide in me what happened to you."

He shifted toward her, sending the water rocking back and forth against the tub and around him. "If I reveal that part of myself to you, Imogene, it will change the way you look at me. And I don't want that. I don't need that. I have crawled my whole life to get to where I am. I am done crawling. I'm done."

Her features softened. "I won't let you crawl." She set her chin against the rim of the tub again, tilting her head, and met his gaze. "I am here to uphold you in the same way you always uphold me. Love is not a moment, Nathaniel. It is every moment. Including the ones you fear."

He held her gaze, his breath barely lodged in his throat. A part of him roared within from all the unspoken words he himself had yet to share. Like how beautiful she was in mind and in soul. How her smile made him smile every time. And how he would never hurt her in the way he had been hurt by so many throughout his pathetic life.

In thinking all of these things, he knew there was no disguising what had happened to him. This was well beyond mere love. This was true love.

Something he thought he'd never touch.

He looked away, drew in a ragged breath and let it out. If he didn't tell her the truth, she would pull away from him. And if he told her the truth, she could still pull away from him. Either way, he was damned.

Leaning back against the tub, he draped the wet towel floating in the tub onto his head so he didn't have to look at her and muttered, "Ask me whatever you want."

She hesitated. "Do you mean that?"

"Since when do you know me to say something I don't mean?"

Her fingers delicately grazed his shoulder, avoiding any welts. "My brother mentioned that it wasn't a group of American Loyalists."

He tried to keep his tone emotionless. "No. At the time when it happened, it was a seventeen-year-old Venetian aristocrat. He was barely seven years older than me."

Her fingers stilled against his skin. "Who was he?"

"A close friend of my father's. And though young, Casacalenda was an incredibly old soul. At fifteen, though he had tried to stop it, his sister was murdered by his own

father, who went into a rage at discovering she was pregnant outside of wedlock by a servant. His father was hanged
for it by the Venetian counsel, which in turn, made Casacalenda the wealthiest ward of the state with his father's title
to boot. Casacalenda sought to escape all the attention and
the trauma by leaving Venice and went to New York, where
he decided to stay until he came of age. He went wild trying to find himself."

"Why did he take you? What did he do to you?"

"It may be difficult for you to believe, but I was actually
treated exceptionally well. He and I even became friends and
were bonded by a shared disaster—my father."

She shifted against the side of the tub, leaning closer toward him. "If you were bonded, why did he keep you in a
cellar?"

Nathaniel rearranged the towel on his head in agitation,
trying to disconnect himself from what he was about to say.
"Casacalenda was afraid I'd leave. The man had no family
and no friends. I became his hope and his confidant. Morbid though it was, I was all he had. So he kept me in a cellar for five years."

A gasp escaped her. "For five years he kept you to himself and in a cellar? Why would he do such a thing? I don't
understand."

Nathaniel was quiet for a long moment before saying in
a low tone, "What I am about to say stays between us. Do
you understand? No one, and especially not my mother, must
ever know of this."

"I won't tell a soul. I vow and I swear."

He sat up and shifted in the water, thankful he had the
towel to keep him from looking at Imogene. "Casacalenda
and my father randomly met at a high-end brothel when my

father first arrived in New York. My father was drawn to forbidden lifestyles. Wherever there were disreputable women, there he always was. The two men became exceptionally good friends and soon took to sharing everything. Women, opium, gambling binges, everything. They were their own two-person version of the Hellfire Club."

She was quiet.

Still in disbelief that he was actually telling her, he blurted, "Then one night, my father, having had too much opium, seized Casacalenda and commenced forcibly kissing him and stripping him. My father knew Casacalenda dabbled with men and gave in to what he had always wanted himself but had never been able to admit—his preference for men. It resulted in their coupling by the end of the night and turned into a very passionate relationship that lasted well beyond two months. My father, who had spent his entire life suppressing his true nature, given his name and status, panicked at realizing he was in love with a man. He therefore tried to leave New York and the relationship behind. Casacalenda refused to let him go and stood outside our house almost every night, waiting to be acknowledged. As a boy of ten, I only saw one side of the coin. Given my father was despondent, and my mother and sister were as equally disturbed as I was by seeing a man we didn't know lingering outside our window, I decided on a scare tactic with a pistol to get the man to leave my family alone. It didn't go as planned. I was ten and stupid. Casacalenda shoved me into a carriage when my pistol misfired and decided to use me as a bargaining chip to get my father to see him."

Nathaniel shook his head, bitterness biting into him. "He delivered a missive to my father days later, saying he would only return me in exchange for one of two things—admitting to the world that he was in love with a man or leaving his wife so they could be together. I'd never seen someone so absorbed with wanting another person to the point of delusion. Casacalenda demanded my father's decision even be delivered in person. So I sat with my hands bound beside Casacalenda in a carriage off Broadway, waiting for my father to show and fighting the terror of being kept by a man whose final moves I couldn't predict. I knew my father would give in to whatever Casacalenda wanted. I was his heir. His pride. His only son."

Nathaniel swallowed and threw back his head, sending the towel swaying against his shoulders. "But my father never showed," he choked out. "It was as equally crushing to Casacalenda as it was for me. I couldn't believe it. And neither could Casacalenda. My father abandoned us both to protect his name and didn't even inform the authorities of the missive lest it be discovered he was a sodomite. Casacalenda was so overwhelmed and distraught, he locked me in a cellar and told me he needed time to think about what would happen next. That time turned into five fucking years because he knew I was all he would ever have of my father. He also knew that if he let me go back, my father could hurt me, given what I knew about them and their relationship. So in the end, a complete stranger cared more for me than my own father. In the end—" Tears overwhelmed him. He squeezed his eyes shut and couldn't say anything more, lest his voice crack.

One foot then another splashed into the water outside each of his naked thighs in the tub, startling him into opening his eyes as Imogene climbed in and lifted the front of the towel from his face, forcing him to look up at her. She lowered herself into the water, her nightdress floating up to her waist as if nothing mattered in that moment but him. She gently cradled his face with soft hands, fresh tears streaming down her cheeks. "Why did you not return to your family?" she whispered brokenly. "Even after you were grown and able to protect yourself?"

"If I had returned," he whispered back, "I would have cast a shadow on everyone and everything. Sodomy is a hanging offence and society would have brutally ostracized my sister and my mother if so much as a whisper of it touched the ears of anyone. I also genuinely feared I would kill my father, given all the anger I had toward him. I had it in me to do it. Which is why I…stayed away. I thought it best."

She searched his face, still cradling his face in her hands. "I love you. I love you even more knowing that you put your family before yourself. You give me strength and pride to be your wife. Do you know that?"

Nathaniel's breath burned in his throat as he grabbed her face and tugged her down against his nakedness, biting past the pain throbbing in his bruised body. He savagely held her against himself, feeling as if the greatest weight had been lifted not from his shoulders but his life. "Say it again," he whispered. "I need you to say that you love me again."

She pressed her cheek against his chest. "I love you. Endlessly. Hopelessly. And I will say it every moment of my life in any way I can."

Unable to restrain all the pent-up emotions within him, and feeling as though he would burst if he didn't show her just how savagely in love with her he was, he lifted her head and kissed her hard on the mouth. Parting her lips with his own, he made love to her mouth with his tongue, giving in to everything she was. His cock grew heavy and thick as it pressed against her wet thighs and nightdress.

She slid a hand between them and, shifting his length toward herself, she slid down firmly to the hilt of his cock. He gasped against her mouth in disbelief as she rode him hard, sending the warm water around them swaying.

All he could do was take it.

She was in complete control.

She broke away from their kiss and held on to the sides of the tub, working against him faster, her nightdress soaked and sheer. "You trust me now. My hands will remain unbound from this moment on. Do you understand?"

Gone was the shy soul he had first met.

Imogene, his Imogene, was all woman now.

And she was his.

"I understand. Completely." He did, and he was astounded as to how little her unbound hands affected him. Grabbing her waist, he let her ride his length, the pleasure surpassing whatever pain his tortured body had endured during the fight. Gritting his teeth, he focused on not letting go of his pleasure until she had found hers.

Between ragged breaths and hip thrusts, he urged her on, sensations heightening and coiling within him as she moved against him faster. Water lifted and sprayed out of the tub, leaving less and less water around them.

She threw back her head and cried out, trying to keep herself upright as she clamped down against him.

His seed spurted inside her warmth as he spiraled into oblivion. It was so blindingly intense he couldn't even groan past the pulsing of his pleasure that erased every last bruise, scrape, gash and welt on his body. He sank down into the water, letting it dip against his chin, and closed his eyes, reveling in the ultimate bliss of knowing she loved him.

She slowly bent down toward him. Her wet lips kissed his forehead several times.

He smiled but didn't move or open his eyes. Everything was perfect in that moment. Nothing existed but her and him and perfection.

"Nathaniel?" she said in between soft kisses.

"Mmm?" He still didn't move or open his eyes.

"You are going to be a father."

His eyes flew open and his heart popped right along with the rest of him. He scrambled to sit up, sending more water splashing everywhere, and winced at overextending his muscles. He grabbed her waist to balance her and frantically searched her flushed face and bright hazel eyes. "Me? A father?"

She bit her lip and nodded. "I have known a small while."

An astounded half laugh escaped him, knowing he was going to have a family of his own. "Jesus Christ. I don't know what to say. I—" He grabbed her face and kissed her not once, not twice, but five times. He released her and lifted her nightdress, setting a hand to her bare stomach, which barely showed there was a babe nestling within. He glanced up at her, still holding his hand against her belly. "You should be resting. No more walking. No more sex. No more anything for you. You will damn well stay in bed until the baby comes."

She rolled her eyes and stood, letting her soaked nightdress flop to her thighs. "Let us not overreact." She carefully climbed out of the tub, casually stripped her nightdress from her body and wrapped a towel around herself. "We need to sleep and call on your mother in the morning. 'Tis fairly obvious she needs to see you."

Nathaniel watched as she pattered toward the door, opened it and disappeared into the adjoining bedchamber.

Staring after her, a shaky breath escaped him. He was

going to be a father. A man who was going to hold a child he helped create and guide through every breath and life. Regardless of what tomorrow brought, nothing was ever going to take this moment away from him. He would ensure he became *everything* to that babe. And everything to Imogene, his sweet Imogene who carried their child.

CHAPTER TWENTY-FIVE

The Earl, from his great propensity to *larking,* kicked up innumerable rows (among which, the coffin scene will long be remembered).

—P. Egan, *Boxiana* (1823)

Sumner House
Late morning

"ARE YOU CERTAIN she wanted us to call?" Nathaniel insisted.

Imogene glanced toward him, adjusting her reticule from one gloved hand to the other. "Yes."

"How odd." After twisting the calling bell for the fifth time and lingering beside Imogene outside the entrance, the door suddenly swung open with a frantic shout, startling them both.

Wilkinson stumbled toward them, his livery and aged face smeared with copious amounts of blood.

Nathaniel's eyes widened as he sucked in a breath and jumped before Imogene, trying to shield her from seeing any of it. "Holy fuck!" he roared. "What in God's name is—"

"Lady Sumner!" Wilkinson choked out, his gaze darting

back toward the stairwell, where a group of panicked servants lingered. "She sliced his lordship's throat whilst he was
still sleeping this morning. The authorities are coming and
none of us are able to get her to leave the room or the body."

Dearest God. Nathaniel shoved past Wilkinson and darted
into the house. "Where is she?" he yelled.

"Up the stairs to the right!" Wilkinson yelled back. "The
last door!"

Nathaniel sprinted up the stairs. Jumping onto the landing, he dashed in a blurring pump of limbs until he skidded
to a halt before the last door.

"Nathaniel!" Imogene shouted after him, surprisingly already on the landing, hurrying after him.

The door leading into his father's bedchamber was half-
open. A woman wailed from within, though no other sound
came.

His mother was in there.

With his dead father.

"Nathaniel!" Imogene called out, running toward him.

He snapped out a hand. *"Stay there!* Don't you dare come
any closer!"

She jerked to a halt and froze, her eyes wide.

Nathaniel pushed the door farther open and almost staggered as the heavy, acrid smell of blood filled his nostrils.

His limbs grew numb as his eyes darted to the four-poster
bed. His father lay sprawled against the twisted, blood-soaked
linens, staring lifelessly up at the ceiling, the flesh of his
throat jaggedly hanging wide-open.

A bloodied razor was still in his mother's hand as she lay in
a crumpled heap beside the bed with her face pressed against
the wooden floor. She wailed, rocking against the floor.

Oh, God. Oh, God. Rushing toward her, Nathaniel's booted

feet slid. He caught himself and looked down, his heart thundering within his ears as he stared at the floor around him in disbelief. Thick, dark pools of blood smeared parts of the wooden floor.

Nausea gripped him and the room momentarily blurred and swayed. He scrambled down to the floor toward his mother and loosened the razor from her shaky fingers. Flinging it across the room, he gripped her shoulders and lifted her slowly toward himself and off the floor.

"It is you," she wailed, her ruined face, which Imogene had warned him about, twisting in agony. "I knew it was you." Her blood-smeared hands jumped and touched his face, tugging him close. "He told me last night. Knowing you were coming, and that I meant to embrace you, he...he told me. He told me how he never truly loved me and only ever loved that...that...*man!* How he—" She sobbed and shook Nathaniel roughly. *"Say that he deserved to die for all that he did. Say it!"* she screamed.

His breath froze in his throat and his chest tightened. He savagely held his mother against himself, burying his face into her grey hair. Hair that had been completely blond when he had last seen it. His poor, poor mother. "Shhhhhh. Shhhhhh." It was all he could manage.

How could he blame her? He'd wanted to do it himself so many goddamn times. He would have done it, too, had it not been for his nephew, who had made him see that it wouldn't change anything. He only prayed she didn't hang for this. God, how he prayed. For he'd already lost Auggie and wasn't about to lose his mother.

LADY SUMNER HAD succumbed to a form of apoplexy and quietly passed long before the King's Bench could even announce a verdict pertaining to the murder of Lord Sumner.

No one, not even Nathaniel, had expected Lady Sumner to live due to her frail physical state and her equally frail mind. And though it was not the ending Nathaniel had hoped for, he felt genuinely blessed that he had been able to spend every last moment, up until her last breath was taken, at his mother's side.

Nathaniel and Imogene set aside training for the championship, which was beginning to loom, and silently rode out to the church to visit the family crypt, where his mother, his father and his sister had all been buried with generations of Sumners past.

Having to bury his entire family all at once was more than Nathaniel was ready to swallow. It was also the first time he had come face-to-face with his sister's crypt.

Below her full name were words that had been scribed by the duke himself, who'd had them carefully etched into the smooth stone. It read:

This lovely bud so beautiful, so fair, called hence by unjust doom, came to show how sweet a flower in paradise could bloom.

Setting both hands against the name of his sister, Nathaniel stumbled down to his knees and choked on the tears he could no longer hide or hold. "Auggie," he choked out. "Ensure Mother is loved in the way she never was by our father. Ensure it."

A gloved hand gently smoothed his head. Imogene tilted him lovingly toward herself, cradling him against her corseted waist.

Nathaniel embraced Imogene by the waist, whilst still kneeling on the stone slab of the church. Knowing he was free to be himself, and that it was only him and Imogene and their babe that she carried within her womb, he cried. He cried for the years he had lost with his sister. He cried for the years he had lost with his mother. He cried at not having the chance to have shared in their lives the way he would have wanted to. But most of all, he cried knowing he would never be able to be with either of them again. They were gone. Forever.

Whilst Imogene rocked him against herself in the silence of the church, where candles flickered in glass sconces against marble walls, a renewed sense of hope seized him. He couldn't ever get Auggie or his mother back, but he could make them proud. He could create the family they had never had.

Releasing Imogene, Nathaniel swiped at his face with trembling hands and staggered up to booted feet. He stared at his sister's name. "I will read everything you wrote," he choked out. "You will be remembered. Always."

A bird interrupted his words, startling him as it landed perfectly atop the crypt within the church. It peered down at him, shifting its grey head from side to side.

He stared up at it, astounded that a bird had found its way into the confines of the church whose doors had all been closed. He felt as if that bird had been sent by Auggie herself.

"It's her," Imogene whispered, as if sensing it, too. Imogene gently slipped her fingers into his hand.

He swallowed, tightening his hold on her hand.

The bird lingered, chirping softly down at him. With the quick spread of its grey-feathered wings it darted past and swooped up toward the vast arches of the church where the stained glass filtered in the afternoon sun.

A shaky breath escaped him as he watched it fly off.

Imogene lifted his hand to her lips and kissed it gently, her tears smearing against his hand.

He'd never felt so loved.

EVERY WEEK THEREAFTER, in between training sessions that brought him closer to the set date of the championship fight, Nathaniel and Imogene would linger before his mother's and his sister's crypt. He would pull out his sister's diary and read from it aloud, determined to unveil the sister he had never had the honor of knowing the way he had wanted to.

He found himself surprisingly stronger after all that had come to pass and was actually able to read his sister's words aloud without breaking down. With a voice he was able to keep steady and calm, he read endless passages dedicated to him and life and love, whilst Imogene reassuringly held his hand and lingered beside him in silence before the crypt. There were times he felt as if Augustine were there with him, holding his other hand.

His sister had been a person of wit, humor, compassion and intelligence. Though there were touches of bitterness that sliced their way through her perfection.

It was like being able to listen to his sister speak when he read passages. By far, his favorite of Augustine's words were the ones Imogene had squeezed his hand upon first hearing. "There are no guarantees. Only...*possibilities.* And that, I will admit, is more than enough for me."

It was a motto he vowed to live by in honor of his sister and in honor of his Imogene, who now carried his child. His Imogene, who had tenderly held him and his hand through the best of times and the worst of times, whilst proving to him that love, sweet love, was not a mere moment but... every moment.

CHAPTER TWENTY-SIX

No men are subject more to the caprice or changes of
fortune than the pugilists; victory brings them fame,
riches and patrons; their bruises are not heeded in the
smiles of success; and, basking in the sunshine of pros-
perity, their lives pass on pleasantly.

—P. Egan, *Boxiana* (1823)

The Championship
Friday, 7:45 p.m.

A WOMAN HAD to do what a woman had to do. Be she pregnant or not. Besides, the evening coat Imogene wore perfectly
hid everything. In fact, she rather liked male clothing. It was
surprisingly comfortable.

Yardley, the duke and her brother, Henry, all dubiously
stared her down from the other side of the darkened carriage
where they sat shoulder to shoulder.

"The man is going to kill us," Henry insisted as the carriage pulled up alongside the torch-lit courtyard leading to
the crowded male masses beyond.

"It's dark enough to mask my face. He won't see me in the

crowds." Imogene gestured toward her evening coat, waist-coat and the trousers she'd had specifically tailored for her well before the event. "I'll also have you know, I look incredibly convincing. I paid the tailor well beyond what he usually gets paid."

Yardley jabbed a thumb toward Imogene's top hat. "And what if someone knocks off your top hat and exposes all that hair?"

"Then I have all of you to protect me from whatever chaos will ensue." Imogene adjusted the heavy top hat on her head, hiding her knotted hair under it, and smoothed her high collar, making sure it wasn't crooked. "At worst, we get booted and the ton talks about it for years."

The duke shifted in the seat with a grunt. "I'm surrounded by rebels. First Georgia, now you."

The horses whinnied as the carriage came to a complete halt well outside the sprawling field lit with countless torches. In the distance, an illuminated elevated wooden stage was roped off with posts.

Nathaniel stood against the corner of one of those posts as several men gathered on each side of the stage.

The ring.

Just outside the carriage window loomed endless pushing crowds of men heading toward that elevated stage.

Imogene's pulse hitched as she leaned toward the window. "That there is a lot of men."

Henry pulled the cloak around himself. "Stay at our side at all times. At worst, you have my walking stick. Use it." Leaning toward her, her brother chided, "And if you so much as start sauntering about the field like a woman, you're on your own."

She rolled her eyes. "I won't saunter. I promise."

The carriage shook, announcing all of the footmen were stepping down. Imogene drew in a deep breath and pushed it back out. Lifting her chin to keep the starched tips of her high collar from pinching her skin, she gripped the head of the walking stick tightly. This was it.

The carriage door swung open and the driver swept out a hand for them to step out toward the pavement dimly lit by surrounding lampposts.

One by one, the duke, Yardley and Henry stooped to keep their top hats from hitting the narrow doorway as they stepped out of the carriage.

Imogene stood and was about to ask her brother to assist her down, when she realized that tonight, she wasn't restrained by the rules of a woman. Or to a corset for that matter. A very strange yet liberating feeling. Even if she was being choked by a collar and cravat.

Bowing her head slightly, to keep her top hat from being knocked off, she hopped down onto the gravel walk, omitting the last step the way her brother always did. She straightened and consciously widened her legs in case hopping down like a man wasn't convincing enough.

Henry, Yardley and the duke wordlessly squared around her, fencing her in with their bodies, and together they made their way in through the crowds.

The rumbling noise of endless conversations drifting into the night air infused her with a sense of pride, knowing she and Nathaniel had made it to the championship.

The duke, Yardley and Henry eventually paused from their moving stride to place their tickets into a bucket.

Noting that the young ticket collector was staring at her as he held out the bucket, she offered a formal nod as men often did to each other.

The man blinked at her in the hazy, yellow light of the torches filtering toward them. It was as if he was trying to decipher what it was about her that didn't sit well with him. He uncertainly gave a curt nod and swung the bucket toward another group of men.

Henry pointed toward the elevated stage. "That way. There is an area beside the stage reserved for us. And be sure you don't let Atwood see your face until *after* the fight."

She wasn't about to argue with Henry on that. Nathaniel most likely would stop the championship altogether if he knew she had muscled her way into seeing the fight.

Walking through the pushing crowds, the strong, tangy smell of endless cigars permeated the air.

"Bets!" someone called out. "Is anyone making bets? Here, here! Place any and all! Last call! Last call!"

Her eyes darted over to a balding man dressed in a well-tailored black buttoned coat as he held up his hand toward others coming in.

Sensing various men were watching her from under bushy brows, Imogene inwardly cringed and stayed as close to her band of protectors as she could.

When they all finally made it toward the stage, she bit back her relief, knowing she was officially in. The duke, Yardley and Henry fenced her in again with their frames, keeping anyone from pushing in too close.

Shouts resounded through the fields.

Eventually, the milling of the crowds settled as everyone waited for the fight to begin.

She could see Nathaniel stripping his linen shirt and tossing it toward his assigned second. From between Henry's and Yardley's shoulders, where she was tucked, she watched her husband roll his head from side to side and bounce in muscle preparation.

Her heart thundered in her ears, realizing at that moment that he was hers. Hers. Always.

On the side of the stage a very large, well-muscled man with piercing black eyes and thick side whiskers stood solidly unmoving as he stared Nathaniel down with a calm that exuded lethality. It was Benjamin Enfield. And much like Nathaniel, the man hadn't lost a single fight. According to her brother, the man was also known for breaking jaws. Every single jaw the man had ever hit had been fractured from the skull. And though most of the men had survived said broken jaws, one hadn't.

She could feel the skin beneath her collar beading with sweat. Her hold tightened on the cane she held.

The umpire eventually pointed to the visibly chalked square in the middle of the wooden stage that was illuminated by the nearby torches impaled into the ground. Still pointing, the umpire yelled out, "Take your place on the chalk, gentlemen! The bout for the title is about to begin!"

Cheers roared, pulsing against the night air.

Nathaniel casually strode toward his side of the chalked square and snapped up both fists, the muscles on his chest and broad back tensing.

Enfield did the same, still staring Nathaniel down.

This was it. She lowered the cane to her side and felt a numbing flutter overtake her, knowing that no matter what happened she was here to support Nathaniel. He had come this far and had been through so much, he deserved this win and more. And above all, she wanted him safe.

Shouts amongst the masses grew steadily louder. Cheers and laughter rumbled out every now and then.

Tucking herself closer against the side of her brother's arm, she watched the umpire's arm swing down between both men and heard him boom, "Set to!"

Enfield jumped forward with unprecedented speed and smashed a hit against the side of Nathaniel's head.

Imogene winced as Nathaniel also jumped in and swung out a quick hook, viciously hitting Enfield's exposed side.

Imogene flinched as the men brutalized each other over and over, punching flesh and skull and anything within reach. Blood now sprayed and it took a moment for Imogene to realize it was Nathaniel's. His nose had officially been christened by the blows. Trails of glistening red liquid beaded across his sweat-sleeked skin as he hammered out more swings that made his opponent stagger.

The surrounding shouts seemed to blur and all that remained was the pulse of her heart and the pulse of each movement Nathaniel made.

Rounds were called out and new ones commenced as both Nathaniel and Enfield took falls on the stage, bringing rounds to an end over and over again. An hour later, she was beginning to see that not only Enfield was exhausted—Nathaniel was, as well. Nathaniel staggered about the stage, and his features, though taut and determined, were bloodied, swollen and looked more and more dazed.

Tears stung her eyes as she sensed he was having trouble standing. She inwardly chanted that he remain upright.

Nathaniel, whose lacerated features had been disfigured by the unrelenting blows of what was now thirty rounds, attempted to stagger up off his knees, bloodstained trousers barely clinging to narrow hips. Another bare-knuckled fist bounced off his sweat-soaked head as more blood splattered from his nose and mouth. Nathaniel collapsed onto the wood boards and stilled.

The umpire counted out.

Nathaniel's second jogged out and shook him. Nathaniel didn't move.

A silent scream seized her as she shoved against her brother. "Dearest God!" she choked out, trying to move past his solid frame. "Henry, let me pass. I must go to him! I must!"

Henry, Yardley and the duke each grabbed her and held her firmly in place to keep her from going to the stage.

"Quiet," Henry ordered down at her. "He will rise. You needn't worry in that. He always uses every second of a fall to rest."

A sob escaped her as the umpire counted out the last fifteen seconds. She stared past tears, praying and hoping. To her astonishment, Nathaniel suddenly rolled onto his side and shoved himself up onto booted feet. He staggered back to the chalked line as the last two seconds were counted.

Her lips parted as she glanced up at her brother.

Henry grinned, leaned in and drawled, "I told you. The man is fighting for my right to a divorce and a quarter of a million. Forget about you. He won't let *me* down."

She shoved her brother in exasperation and fixed her gaze back on the stage where Enfield and Nathaniel were already back to thudding fists into each other's flesh.

It was relentless.

They both were.

It was as if they were equally matched.

What if—

Nathaniel and Enfield suddenly thwacked each other in

the head at the same time. Both reeled back in unison and instantly collapsed onto the wooden stage.

She gaped.

Neither moved.

Both had knocked each other out.

Stunned silence pierced the night air as the umpire hesitated. "Both men down! Unprecedented! They have thirty seconds to rise and stand at the chalked line!" The umpire snapped up a hand and dutifully commenced counting out, "One! Two! Three! Four! Five! Six! Seven! Eight! Nine! Ten! Eleven!"

What now? Imogene frantically grabbed Henry's arm and shook it, trying to understand what was happening. "What happens now?" she rasped. "If they are both out, what happens?"

Henry stared out at the stage in what appeared to be complete disbelief. "I have never seen a double hit like that. By God, it could damn well be a draw. The very first in the title's history."

She shook his arm again. "A draw? And what does that mean?"

"They would have to meet and fight again."

Her gaze darted back to the stage, dread seizing her. She didn't want Nathaniel going up against Enfield again. It would only double his chances of getting hurt. And he was hurt enough.

She leaned against her brother and focused on Nathaniel's body, which still lay on the stage opposite Enfield's. "Get up," she whispered, placing a hand against her belly buried beneath her coat. "This is yours, Nathaniel. Get up. End this. Do it for Auggie. Do it for your mother. Do it for our babe. Do it for everything you ever wanted to fight for. Just do it."

Men roared, drowning out her words.

As if hearing her, Nathaniel suddenly staggered to sit up, calling out to his second. His second darted forward and helped him rise, guiding him to the chalked line as the rules allowed. Nathaniel waved the man away and slowly held up his blood-slathered hands and waited, swaying slightly.

Enfield's own second desperately tried to do the same, only Enfield couldn't even sit up.

"Thirty!" the umpire boomed as he pointed a finger at Nathaniel. "And this ends this incredible fight! I proclaim Atwood to be winner of *the* title of Champion of England! May all of England bless this here man for representing our nation so well!"

Nathaniel dropped his hands to his sides and closed his eyes.

Imogene screamed in disbelief as the endless cheers and shouts of a field full of men drummed against her head and soul. He did it! He did it!

Henry whipped toward her, eyes wide, and grabbed her, jumping up and down as if he were a rabbit on fire. *"Gene!"* he roared, still jumping up and down. "Jesus Christ, he—" Henry spun away and punched the air around him as if he had taken the title himself. "Take *that,* Banbury! You and Mary are going down! I'm taking that money and— *Yes!"*

It was obvious London was going to be swept by scandal. A choked laugh escaped her as the duke and Yardley joined in on punching the air as if that was the only way men knew how to celebrate.

Biting back a grin, she wedged herself between her brother and Yardley and announced, "Whilst you all punch the air, I'm going to congratulate my man."

Henry froze and grabbed her. "Oh, no. Oh, no, no. You're

going home. Do you have any idea the scandal this would bring if anyone knew a woman had come to a fight? And dressed as you are!"

She pointed up at him with the reprimanding head of her cane. "I'm not the one getting a divorce. *That* is going to create a scandal. Not me coming to a fight. Now excuse me." Darting past, she pushed her way through toward the stairs leading to the stage and scrambled up past the ropes toward Nathaniel, thankful her belly wasn't large enough for anyone to notice.

A large bucket of water was poured over Nathaniel by his second, drenching his black hair and sloughing blood off his face and bare chest. Nathaniel let out a laugh and took to shaking the hands of men now surrounding him.

"Ey!" a man yelled, popping out both arms and stepping in front of her. "Where do you think you're going? This stage is reserved for chroniclers, the opponents and the committee, sir."

Sir? How nice that she looked that convincing. "I'm actually here to see my husband. Lord Atwood. I'm his wife and his investor. And therefore part of the committee."

The man gaped, stepping back.

Stripping off her top hat, which released her bundled hair and sent it cascading down and onto her shoulders, she flung it toward Nathaniel to get his attention. "Nathaniel!"

Nathaniel paused in between handshakes from the men that surrounded him and stared, his wet, swollen features appearing about as stunned as swollen features could be. *"Imogene?"* he yelled out, shoving his way frantically through the men toward her. He scanned her appearance as he shoved his way closer. "What are you doing here? And what the devil are you wearing?"

She grinned and rushed toward him. "I couldn't miss it. You were amazing!"

Nathaniel seized her by the arms and scanned her again, shaking her. "Jesus. You shouldn't be here. Not in your condition."

Still grinning, she grabbed his waist, to ensure she didn't touch anything that might hurt, and shook him in turn. "You, my lord, just took the title for the Champion of England whilst your wife proudly watched. What now? Are you taking on those bulls in Spain like you promised me we would?"

Nathaniel let out a riled laugh. "Hell, we buy all of Spain! Imogene! We did it!" Grabbing her face, he leaned in and kissed her lips soundly. Then winced. "We kiss later," he rasped down at her. "Once I have regained my ability to."

"Regain it fast, my lord," she teased. "Patience is supposedly a virtue, but I don't think I have it."

He searched her eyes, still cradling her face and whispered, "I can't believe you are actually here. I can't believe you are actually standing here with me. Breathing in this moment with me."

She smiled and whispered back, "Know that I am here to breathe in every moment with you, Nathaniel."

He searched her face. "Forever and always?"

She leaned up and gently kissed his chin. "Forever and always."

EPILOGUE

Few, if any, can boast of such patronage as our hero—
who, if reports speak true, may now smile.

—P. Egan, *Boxiana* (1823)

Ten years later
Christmas evening at the Wentworth House

"AGAIN! *SHOW US AGAIN!*" they all piped in resounding unison, bobbing up and down whilst sending short trousers and above-ankle skirts and little polished boots and slippers shuffling and swaying within the large receiving room.

Those a little less able to focus on the excitement merely crawled around said trousers, skirts and boots in the opposite direction, babbling their way toward the candlelit Christmas tree where scattered, ransacked boxes, dolls, wooden horses, balls, books and other countless toys layered the floor.

Nathaniel lifted a debonair dark brow toward the large group of young spectators. "Dare I?" he challenged.

"Yes, yes! Again, again! *Again!*" A riled group of nineteen children—four of which were Imogene's and Nathaniel's, three of which were Henry's and his French wife Orphée's,

five of which were Robinson's and Georgia's, and seven of
which were Matthew's and Bernadette's—herded past crawling tots and skidded toward the evergreen-draped hearth.

Nathaniel remained steadfast before the hearth on one
trouser-clad knee theatrically demonstrating how he had
single-handedly won the title of Champion of England ten
years earlier.

With both hands behind his back.

And one eye closed.

Imogene tsked and called out from where she lingered beside Georgia, Bernadette and Orphée, "Years are fading that
memory of yours fast, Nathaniel dear. Do you want me to
take over and tell them how it really happened?"

"You weren't there, tea cake!" he called back with a quirk
of his mouth.

"Wasn't I?" Imogene called back.

Nathaniel smirked and angled himself toward his captive
audience. "Can't a man glory in what little remains of his
fighting years?"

She tsked again. "Once a boxer, always a boxer. He may
have retired from putting up those fists but he didn't retire
from thinking about it."

Georgia leaned toward Imogene. "At least yours remembers how you two first met." Georgia puckered her lips and
thumbed toward Yardley, who sat cross-legged on the floor
with his youngest in his lap. "He remembers everything but
that."

Imogene burst into laughter. "I suppose I shouldn't com-
plain then, should I?"

Yardley glanced up, adjusting his son onto his other knee,
and hollered across the room, "Ey! I heard that."

"Leave us upstanding gents alone for one breathing moment. It's Christmas!" With green eyes dancing, Henry snatched up a ball and playfully whipped it toward their direction.

Orphée, Bernadette, Georgia and Imogene darted out of the way, giggling.

Augustine, Imogene's oldest child at almost ten, darted toward the tree, blond braids swaying, and swiped up another ball, whipping it toward Henry. "A ball for a ball!" she taunted, bouncing it off his leg.

Ballad Jane, Georgia's oldest, also darted in and whipped another ball. "And here is another ball for a ball!"

Bernadette quickly pointed at Matthew and the duke before sweeping a finger toward Henry. "Gentlemen, throw this ruffian out. Before he gives the children any more ideas. This game of a ball for a ball sounds like a fire waiting to happen. Do you have any idea how many candles are on that tree? Queen Victoria ought to be scolded for introducing such a hazard into every household."

"You needn't worry," Matthew called out to his wife. "I'll throw the real ruffian out into the snow!" With a charging gruff roar, Matthew darted toward nine-year-old Augustine and tossed her up into his arms, sending her half-screaming and giggling.

Candles, bouncing balls and screaming children aside, it was another *very* Merry Christmas. Imogene grinned, knowing it had been yet another glorious year with not only the man she loved but the children she loved and the friends and family she loved. She couldn't ask for more.

She paused. Well, no…she could ask for one more thing— her husband in their bed by the end of the night. A woman had to unwrap *something* on Christmas.

* * * * *

AUTHOR'S NOTE

Historical bare-knuckle boxing is a creature that took me quite a bit of time to understand. It isn't even a breath near the boxing of today. The rules were very different and the men were very different. Chaos and the fist ruled without restraint. Mr. P. Egan's *Boxiana or the Sketches of Ancient and Modern Pugilism,* was a huge starting point as it was printed in the era which I was writing in. But it also only raised more questions I needed answered. I didn't understand the terminology or the slang and had to learn everything from scratch.

Prior to 1743, there weren't any set rules and men died even trying to box. It was a brutal sport that went back to the days of the Romans and Greeks and beyond. Rules were tacked here and there in the name of the sport itself, but none were officially adhered to or followed until a certain British gentleman by the man of Broughton came along and changed boxing history.

On August 10, 1743, Broughton introduced a set of rules meant to regulate the wild world of pugilism and its men. Although there were only seven rules written and set up by Broughton, it was an introduction to fair play which many felt the world of boxing was missing.

One of the most important rules of the seven was actually number seven itself, which read: "That no person is to hit his adversary when he is down, or seize him by the ham, the breeches or any part below the waist; a man on his knees to be reckoned down." It's obvious by the rule itself that prior to Broughton's rules, men hit anything they could get their hands on. Even after the rules were set, holding on to your opponent's hair was still considered legal because it was located above the waist.

These seven rules set by Broughton were adhered to until another change in boxing history occurred when the Marquess of Queensbury endorsed a boxing code drafted and written by Mr. Chambers in London in the 1860s. Rounds were set up to prevent exhaustion, no wrestling was allowed and gloves became standard.

In the era prior to the Queensbury rules, in New York City itself and the United States, bare-knuckle boxing was illegal due to its savageness. Fights were held in secret locations—usually near wharves—that were usually announced at the last minute. The rounds were determined not by time, but the moment one of the fighters hit the ground. The match didn't end until someone couldn't get up after a thirty-second period of time after hitting the ground or if one of the fighters called out, "Enough." To say "Enough" before a boxing crowd, however, was like saying "I'm not good enough to fight, boys." So it was rarely ever used by bare-knuckle boxers. In fact, I haven't come across a single recorded fight prior to the 1860s that had a man call out "Enough." Which says something about the men who were fighting. They didn't kneel for anyone unless dead. And unlike the few rounds of today, men in the 1830s could fight well over seventy rounds, usually lasting as many as two or three hours, depending on how much fight there was in a man.

What fascinated me the most, however, was how the men of the 1830s had to train their hands to take hits without breaking them. Men strategically built calluses on their knuckles by training on trees. Yes. Trees. Trees were everywhere and they cost a man nothing. Think of a tree being used like a punching bag. Men would actually knock the bark off with their knuckles in order to pad their hands well with scars and calluses alike. Other men used axes to strengthen their swing and their muscles. Either way you look at it, these men were badass. They defined the hero I saw in my head.

Reading about boxing in the 1830s, I knew I had to throw my hero into being a boxer and mold him around it. I hope you enjoyed glimpsing the historical boxing world. I genuinely loved researching it. In fact, I hope to one day return to it, because there are still so many facets of historical boxing I have yet to explore and touch.

DELILAH MARVELLE

All of Marvelle's scandalous and graceful ladies are available in eBook!

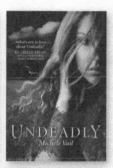

HARLEQUIN®

Find out more about our
latest releases, authors
and competitions.

 Like us on facebook.com/harlequinaustralia

 Follow us on twitter.com/harlequinaus

 Find us at harlequinbooks.com.au